# Some Dark Force

## A VICTORIAN THRILLER

### CHRISTINA BOUFIS
### VICTORIA OLSEN

PENNY DREADFUL MEDIA

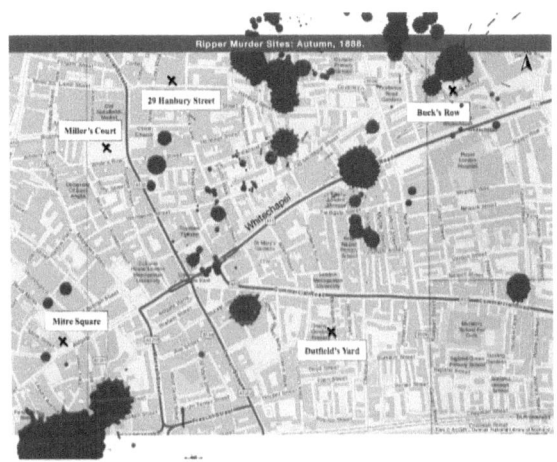

*Whitechapel, 1888. Map source: National Library of Scotland*

*News from Abroad*

THE COLONIAL ENGLISHMAN
April 1, 1888

## MINE SHAFT COLLAPSES IN SOUTH AFRICAN DIAMOND FIELD

A recent tragedy at the Bloedberg Mine outside Kimberley revealed the limits of modern scientific approaches to diamond mining. Mineralogists have long posited that shafts could be extended into the shale layer beneath the hard pack soil surrounding the Orange River, providing access to the rich fields of diamonds formed there at the dawn of time.

The management of the Bloedberg Mine was the first to put that supposition to a practical test. Despite warnings from local engineers and the resistance of Tswana miners, Mr. Jacob Randall excavated the deepest shaft ever documented—to an astonishing 620 meters below the surface of the earth. The shaft was built in record time at the extraordinary cost of one million pounds sterling. It is accessed by way of a winding gravel road through the sprawling Diablo camp, where 200 migrant workers live and toil.

The new shaft, called Diablo, opened in March and was soon yielding substantial finds like a rough stone measured at 80 carats and significant veins of ore. Shifts were doubled this month after accidents depleted the workforce. "It's hell down there," said one worker who refused to give our correspondent his name. "You hear unnatural sounds. You see things no one should see. I ain't going back." These rumours reflect local unease with the history of this site, which translates to Blood Mountain in English. Fifty years ago, a small party of Voortrekkers was attacked and massacred here by British mercenaries on leave from Port Natal.

This extraordinary triumph of man over nature came to a sudden end last week when the shaft collapsed with a crashing reverberation that was felt miles away. Forty workers were pinned below and several rescuers said they observed a glowing yellow stream of sulphurous vapour escaping from the deepest section of the mine, along with a howling noise. An investigation will be held in May. Lord Rutherford, owner of the mine, has removed Randall from his post and plans to oversee the investigation himself.

# *Prologue*

*"LUCY. COME. COME TO ME NOW."*

It is her mother calling. She must obey the summons.

Lucy does not think. Instead, she rises quickly from her bed, pushes back the curtains, and unlatches the window. Rain pelts her face, runs down her neck, and wets the bodice of her nightclothes. She feels none of it.

Lucy closes her eyes. She knows what she must do. She will be reunited with the woman who gave birth to her. Finally. She has been waiting for this moment her entire life, to be with her mother and see herself reflected in the love of her mother's eyes.

Lucy throws her arms wide. She feels as if she can fly into the night. And yet, what is that sound? There's a scurrying underneath the window. She senses something scaling the wall beneath her.

A flash of lightning sizzles through the sky close by. Lucy opens her eyes, just as the brilliant light is fading.

A boom of thunder like bursting cannonballs rattles the window.

Lucy instinctively steps away.

The scurrying gets louder. Something that has been climbing the wall enters her room. It stands before her.

Lucy gasps. It is the figure of a man. He is tall with ice-blue eyes that bore into her soul, pinning her to the spot. His white-blond hair reminds her of an animal in a storybook—a wolf, she thinks. But it is his skin, slick with rain and deathly pale, that sends a chill traveling from the roots of her hair to the very tips of her toes.

"Lucy, come," he says in the same voice she's been hearing in her dreams. Her mother's voice, but not her mother's figure.

She shakes her head slightly. No. This cannot be.

"Lucy, Lucy," the creature says, in a singsong, mocking voice. Then he throws back his head and laughs, a sharp howling sound like the hyenas Lucy has seen at the London zoo.

A single tear escapes Lucy's eye. She stands firm and does not brush it away.

"Who are you?" she asks in a shaky voice.

"That is not the question." His voice is deeper than she expected with a hint of an accent. "The question, dear Lucy, is who are you to become?"

# *Chapter One*

In the Frying Pan pub, on the corner of Thrawl Street in London's East End, Polly Nichols pours the last of her doss money down her throat.

Inside the pub, it's warm and noisy. Outside, it's cold and dark and damp. Polly doesn't want to go outside. She's been sleeping rough the last few nights, and tonight she'd planned on sleeping at Wilmott's lodging house with the other women who could earn enough for a bed. She vastly prefers the single sex lodging house to some of the others that allow men and women. And anything is better than the workhouse where she'd been confined for several months.

Polly entered the Frying Pan with enough doss money for three nights at Wilmott's—if she could have held on to it. But the demon drink was too much for her tonight. Her compulsion has been getting stronger and stronger. She can no longer control it. At one time, she could stop just before oblivion overtook her and reason left her entirely.

Not tonight. She hands her last three pennies to the

bartender for a large glass of gin and throws caution to the wind. She needs the release that comes with alcohol. It relaxes her limbs and frees her mind momentarily from the harsh reality of her life—begging for money, tramping on the street, or going back to the workhouse. When she drinks, the world opens up to possibility. Good luck is just around the corner.

She'll figure out the money and find a bed somehow. She always does.

Polly stands up to leave and the floor lurches to the left. Then to the right. She realizes she might be sick and holds her hand to her stomach. Slowly, she regains her balance and walks out into the inky night.

Just outside the pub, Polly presses her hand to the slick stone wall to steady herself. She's hungry is all. She's not had anything to eat but a bit of bread and tea yesterday morning.

Polly closes her eyes and leans against the cold, damp wall. She needs to rest for a bit and stop her head from spinning. She can still hear the sound of laughter from inside the pub, and for a moment, she instinctively turns back towards the warmth and light before remembering she has no money. She can't go back inside.

Could she return to Wilmott's and beg for a bed from the deputy lodging-house keeper? She will. She just needs to rest first. She's so tired she could sleep standing up. She hears a man's snickering voice as he leaves the pub. He calls out something lewd to her. Polly must move soon if she's not to get more verbal assaults—or worse. She reluctantly opens her heavy eyelids.

Polly is no longer young, no longer pretty. Her long brown hair is streaked with gray, and her face shows the years she's spent sleeping rough on the streets, punctuated by stays at the Lambeth workhouse. She may be alone at night and drunk, but she is not a woman who would trade her body for a few shillings.

After a few minutes, Polly rights her black straw bonnet on

her head as best she can. She's quite proud of this jolly bonnet. It was given to her by her last employer, the kindly, though strict, Mrs. Cowdry. Perhaps she shouldn't have left her position as servant, but she could no longer abide the abstinence from alcohol that her employer insisted on. Nor could she stomach the Bible reading and church services. She was as imprisoned as she ever had been in any workhouse.

When she left the Cowdry home, Polly took goods and clothing, enough to pawn and give her lodging for a couple of weeks, but they are long gone now. Only the bonnet remains. She'll have to sell that too to get money for a bed, though it's unlikely she'll be able to sell it at this late hour.

Polly feels the cold seep into her bones from the stone wall. The thick East End fog slithers against her skin and threatens to engulf her. She pulls her brown overcoat closer around her to keep out the damp and, unsteadily, begins to walk. The steel tips of her men's boots echo on the street as she walks in the direction of the lodging house.

Polly is barely aware of the other rough sleepers out tonight. Her eyes glaze over at the many men and women sleeping on cold stone steps or in the recesses of doorways. She only pauses briefly when she sees a few children, shoeless, bundled together in a heap to keep warm.

Images of her children, the five who lived, come flooding back. She can still feel the weight of her last baby in her arms, and a single tear escapes her eye. She thinks of William, the handsome man she married at eighteen. How happy they were then. It was a long time ago. Just one more time, she'd like to feel William's strong arms around her, leading her to bed, telling her he loves her.

But no, that could never be. William had started carrying on with their harlot neighbor. How dare he fall in love with someone younger and prettier after she bore his children? It was intolerable to be married to him and feel his lack of love for her. What woman could bear it?

She walked out and left them—eight years ago now. Another lifetime ago. She feels a spark of anger rise in her chest at the harlot who stole her husband. What could she do? Stand by and watch herself be replaced?

Polly shakes her head to dislodge the memories, the good and the bad. She does not want to think about the family she once had and lost. She has chosen her hard path.

The church clock strikes one as Polly teeters towards Wilmott's lodging house. She pauses every few feet to steady herself and gather the strength to carry on.

Finally, she reaches Wilmott's. But when she knocks and shouts to wake the deputy keeper, he shoos her away. No credit tonight.

Polly Nichols is turned out. Where can she go? She follows Whitechapel Road towards the White House, the lodging house on Flower and Dean Street that allows men and women to sleep together. It is not the doss house she prefers, but at least there she can perhaps barter her bonnet for a bed and rest her bones.

Despite the fog and chilly night air, Polly feels just as intoxicated as she was when she left the pub. She had more glasses of gin than she could count. Her limbs are as heavy as anchors.

Polly has been on her own for many years, and endured more hardship, heartbreak, and hard work than many women in her forty-three years. She's not easily afraid. Yet suddenly, she feels a dark sense of foreboding.

"Polly?"

Out of the fog, a figure appears before her. Polly steps back and almost trips. Then she connects the familiar voice with her friend, Ellen Holland.

"Aye, Ellen. What are you about so late this night?" Polly slurs her words. She can't make her tongue work the way she wants.

"There was a fire on Shadwell dry dock, and I've been to

see it. Quite the spectacle it was. Flames shooting high into the air. Ships called from all over to the harbor to help put out the fire. Where are you off to? I'm going to Wilmott's. Will you come?"

Polly shakes her head. "Nay. Not me. I'm going to White House now. I won't go back to Wilmott's."

Polly won't be humiliated again a second time by being told she can't sleep at Wilmott's. She has her pride. It was her pride, and her bruised heart, that caused her to leave her family, after all. Polly is the one who leaves—not the one who gets told to go elsewhere.

Ellen tries to convince her friend again to go with her, but Polly waves her off. She needs to keep walking or she will fall down from drink and exhaustion right there on the corner of Whitechapel Road and Osborn Street and never get up.

The clock strikes half past two. After one last appeal, Ellen wishes her good night, and heads off.

The night has gotten even darker. Polly stumbles through the thick fog, feeling her way. When she's in her cups, she sometimes gets the Whitechapel streets confused, but she'll find her way, eventually. She mustn't stop. Mustn't take a rest.

When she gets to Buck's Row, it's so dark that Polly feels as if a black cloak has been placed over her eyes. She's carried around a blackness inside of her for so long and now it's outside of her too.

She hears a rustling sound and peers into the darkness. A chill goes down her spine, despite the large Ulster coat she wears.

"Who's there?" she calls out.

Polly feels more than sees a presence close by. Is someone following her?

She wills herself to pick up speed, but her legs won't obey her brain. She's more awake now and sobering up. Her heart beats faster. The color rises to her face with the exertion. She has a sudden memory of William stroking her hair and her face, softly, gently, when he was in love with her.

She hears a lone howl and turns around. She can't see. She hears a rustling sound but no footsteps. Is it a man or a beast closing in on her?

"Help me," she tries to scream. But the words won't reach her lips. Besides, there is no one to help. Polly is alone. Truth be told, other than a brief period in her marriage, she's always felt alone. There's another sharp howl. Then a flash of silver illuminates the darkness. In an instant, Polly Nichols sees no more.

**EAST LONDON ADVERTISER**
Saturday, September 1, 1888

### GREAT FIRE AT THE LONDON DOCKS

A fire broke out shortly before 9 o'clock on Thursday night in one of the huge warehouses of the London Docks. The docks were closed as usual at 4 in the afternoon, and there are then few persons except the night policemen and firemen left on the premises. At about half-past 8, a smell of fire was noticed and shortly afterwards there was an immense burst of flames from the top of one of the vast buildings right in the centre of the docks.

The volume of the fire was terrific, but at 9 o'clock the authorities of the fire brigade had heard nothing of the occurrence. Shortly afterwards an alarm was given at the Whitechapel Station, and the officials of the brigade instantly ordered every steamer to proceed to the scene, and the circulation of the news amongst the other stations caused steamers to be sent on from every district in London.

On arrival of the engines it was found that a fire of enormous strength was raging in the upper floors of a great building about 150 yards long and half as broad. The flames could not have broken out in a more dangerous part of the docks than the site of this fire— the South Quay Warehouses. They were crammed with colonial produce in the upper floors, and brandy and gin in the lower floors. Through the great iron-barred windows the fire could be seen raging like a furnace, and the enormous tongues of bluish and yellowish flames which constantly burst up with great roars pointed to the fact that spirits were aiding the progress of the flames.

Gradually steamer after steamer was got to work, for it was seen that only a great body of water would subdue the fire.

By 11 o'clock the fierceness with which the fire was burning began to be diminished, and presently the firemen were able to circulate the official "stop" message, stating that the two top floors of the provision warehouse had been nearly burned out and part of the roof destroyed. At midnight, however, the great force of firemen and extinguishing appliances were still at work.

# *Chapter Two*

Lucy Rutherford leaves her father's house wearing only a thin white gown. It is long past the hour of the night when any virtuous woman would be out of doors at all. With silk slippers on her feet, she glides down the front marble steps of her family townhouse in Mayfair and is swallowed by the dense London fog, which wraps her in its chilly embrace.

Lucy shudders against the night air. She is unaware of her movements. Her body is propelled by a force larger than herself. Her eyes are fixed straight ahead, yet she sees nothing.

It's the voice calling to her again. A sweet voice. A woman's voice that whispers inside her head, "Come, Lucy. Come now." She must obey.

She was just an infant when her mother died, but Lucy knows this is her mother's voice. All her life she's longed to be held by the woman who gave birth to her, to have her mother stroke her hair, kiss her cheek, tell her she is loved.

How is it possible that tonight of all nights, her mother is calling her?

Lucy doesn't pause at the next street corner but continues to follow the beckoning voice down far away from the safety of her father's house. With every step she takes, the voice gets louder and more insistent.

The moon is hidden behind thick fog tonight. No other pedestrians are out at this early hour of the morning. They are all home and snug in their beds, as Lucy should be.

Suddenly a cry, a howling sound, cuts through the air. Lucy stops. Shivers. Someone or something is in pain.

Lucy knows she must hurry to the voice now. Her slippers are soiled. Her gown is wet with moisture. "Wait. Wait for me. I am coming," she whispers. There is no response.

Onward Lucy continues her journey through the streets of Mayfair, propelled by some dark force. She is unsure of her destination. She only knows she must obey. Soon she is far from the glowing gas lamps of Mayfair and is lost in the blackness of the night.

### MORNING ADVERTISER (LONDON)
September 1, 1888

A horrible murder was discovered early yesterday morning in Whitechapel. Constable John Neil on his beat discovered the dead body of a woman lying in Buck's Row. Her throat was cut from ear to ear, and she bore other wounds of a revolting description. The body has been identified as that of Mary Anne Nichols, who was formerly a domestic servant, but who has lately been living a wandering life. No arrests have been made.

The particulars of the latest dreadful murder in the East End of London will horrify the public. The outrage is almost unequalled in the annals of crime. It is fiendish in conception and revoltingly cruel in execution. Our civilisation is a wretched mockery while crimes like this are committed in our streets.

*Chapter Three*

"There are to be no more nocturnal wanderings," Lord Rutherford pronounces at breakfast. "I forbid it. Lucy, you are not to leave this house." His voice rolls down the table like thunder to where his daughter is seated.

Lucy says nothing. Tea and toast lie untouched before her. Her father's plate is heaped with kippers, eggs, and sausage; the morning papers, freshly ironed, are at his elbow.

There's no point in challenging her father when he's in such a foul mood. And more often than not lately, his lordship is in a foul mood.

Lucy had not planned to walk in her sleep. She's had strange dreams for several weeks—dark, disturbing nightmares she cannot remember when she wakes. But last night was the first time she rose and actually left her bed. She has no memory of where she went. But this morning, she feels a weariness in her limbs and mind, and a new presence inside herself. As if she's not quite herself but inhabited by someone —or something—else.

It was only by sheer good fortune that she was brought back to her house last night unharmed and still unaware. Lucy had been found by her maid, Sally, who'd gone outside to see if she could view the fire at the docks; supposedly, it lit up the night sky. Sally was walking back to her employer's home when she unexpectedly came upon Lucy on Mount Street.

Shocked, Sally guided her mistress home. Lord Rutherford was not home late last night when Sally raised the other servants. His Lordship was only made aware of the commotion this morning.

Lucy would have preferred to keep her rambling secret from her father. She herself isn't sure what to make of it. One moment she was in bed, the next she recalls being led up the stairs back to her bedroom by Sally.

Indeed, she feels as if the entire incident happened to someone else.

"And you are not to read the papers nor any of those sensationalist novels you're so fond of. Indeed, that may be the root of the problem, Lucy." Lord Rutherford shoves the papers away, where they're picked up by a servant. "You are too excitable. That is the long and short of it. You're at a delicate age, and I should have insisted on a new governess when Mrs. Parker left us. I can see now that you need looking after. You need a woman's influence. But for now, I'll find a doctor to come and examine you. In the meantime, you are to rest and calm your nerves. I'll have Sally see to it."

Lucy's nerves are calm, but she does not resist her father. Yes, she was the one who insisted at the ripe age of eighteen that she was too old for another governess when hers found a new position closer to her ailing mother.

Lord Rutherford is right on one account. Lucy keenly feels the lack of female companionship. She's had a series of nannies and governesses, yet none of the maternal love she has so desperately wanted. Not one of the women her father employed has been what she would call motherly.

It's time for Lucy to enter into society, yet Lord Rutherford has always been too busy with politics to attend to his daughter. Now, as Home Secretary, he is busier than ever. He had talked recently of shipping her to the country, to stay with his sister. But Lady Dorothy is unmarried, unwell, and uninterested in taking on the job of introducing Lucy to society. Nor is she willing to help her niece find a suitable husband, having never been successful in that endeavor herself.

Suddenly the pocket doors open, and Lord Rutherford's butler enters, bringing him a note on a silver tray.

Her father reads it, then rises from the table, pushing his plate, still half full with his breakfast, aside.

"What is it, father?"

"Nothing that concerns you, my dear. I have urgent business. You are to rest until I can summon the doctor."

Lucy has no intention of resting. Despite her late-night sleepwalking, she feels well enough. But her interest is piqued by her father's abrupt rise from the table. She too waves away her breakfast and follows him quietly out of the large dining hall.

Fortunately, Lord Rutherford does not turn around but walks directly towards his morning study.

Lucy lingers in the hallway and prays that no servants spot her. She presses herself against a wall behind the central staircase. From her hiding spot, she sees two men. One is certainly a police constable because he's in uniform—dark woolen trousers and blue-black tunic with large, shiny buttons down the front. In his hand is a police cap.

The constable seems to sense Lucy's presence and turns to look at her directly. Lucy blushes, both from his gaze and from the first thought that passes through her mind—that he is young and somewhat handsome. Thankfully, the constable does not give her away but turns his back, blocking the others from seeing Lucy. Is this intentional?

Lucy recognizes the voice of the other man: Sir Charles

Warren, Chief Commissioner of the Metropolitan Police. Lucy has met Sir Charles several times before; he comes frequently to the house to meet with her father. She likes the Commissioner, with his bushy flaxen mustache and kind grey eyes. He always makes polite conversation with her. Compared to Sir Charles, Lucy has been nowhere and seen nothing. And yet, every time she exchanges pleasantries with the man, he asks about what she's reading and seems genuinely interested in her life.

The three men enter her father's study, and the door is shut.

Glancing around, Lucy thankfully does not see Sally or any of the other servants. She is hoping her maid has gone up to her bedroom, thinking Lucy is there.

Dare she proceed further? Lucy tiptoes to her father's study and places her ear against the door. She thinks of her father's orders at breakfast. No, she will not go quietly to her room and rest.

The men's voices are muffled through the thick oak door. Lucy presses closer.

She hears the sonorous voice of Sir Charles and then another, younger voice that must belong to the police constable.

She catches his name. Neil. She blushes again, wondering why she should care.

Lucy can only make out certain words. Butchery. Knife. Killer. The police constable is talking, describing something. Lucy wishes she could hear him clearly, but she cannot.

It's frustrating to be always on the outside looking in. She's had this feeling her entire life—that she's being kept at a distance from the world, almost as if she's so fragile she would break otherwise and must be kept locked away under glass.

Her father has only tried to protect her, she knows, but from what? Life itself? Lucy understands that it must have been terribly hard for her father to lose his wife days after Lucy was born. And that Lord Rutherford fears that he'll lose her too somehow.

"Nonsense," she wants to tell him.

Lucy is so wrapped up in her own thoughts she doesn't realize at first that the voices have stopped. The next thing she knows, the door swings open with Lucy on the other side of it. She flattens herself against the wall and holds her breath, as if that would make her invisible.

It does not—the police constable spots her. Thankfully, he closes the study door so the others do not see her in the hallway.

He's older than Lucy first thought, and not as handsome as Sir Charles, if she is to compare. The constable has a mustache too, not nearly as bushy. His hairline is receding in a V-shape, but his eyes are a warm brown and filled with amusement as he beholds Lucy.

"Miss Rutherford, I presume?" His voice sounds Irish, lilting.

Lucy flushes. He is standing close to her.

"Constable Neil at your service," he says, bowing slightly. "Your eavesdropping is safe with me."

With that, he tips his police cap at her and takes his leave.

Lucy stares after the constable, momentarily at a loss for words. The man isn't handsome, she tells herself. Not really. Her face feels warm. She must get to her room before her father or Sir Charles emerges and catches her standing there.

Upstairs, she restlessly paces around her room, chafing at her father's pronouncement that she's too excitable and nervous. Hah! She's nothing but bored here, entombed in this large townhouse with only the servants for company. No wonder she is struck mute by the sight of a strange man in her house.

Lucy circles the room again, picking up the final volume

of the triple decker she'd borrowed from Mudie's Library. She is tired of Mrs. Oliphant. Mr. Gissing might be more like it, but her father would certainly disapprove of novels called *The Odd Women* or *The Nether World*.

As she tosses the book aside, her mind settles on something her father said at breakfast. She whirls around and presses the button installed over her dressing table. Lord Rutherford has a passion for new inventions, and enough money to indulge that passion, so he recently installed electricity in his home. Now Lucy can summon a maid with a simple touch. She waits impatiently, crisscrossing the thick Oriental carpets layered on the floor.

"Sally, my father will have finished with the morning papers by now," she says when the maid appears. "Please bring them all to me." Lucy puts some extra imperiousness into her voice, in case the maid refuses.

Lucy is deliberately defying her father. But there must be something particularly interesting in the morning editions if her father has forbidden her to read them.

What's more, there is something afoot. Not one but two policemen, if you count the Chief Commissioner, have come to speak to the Home Secretary this morning. What could this be about?

Lucy has always had a taste for knowledge, the kind of knowledge her father specializes in. From his hushed private club to the teeming streets at the heart of the City, there's an entire world out there that Lucy longs to know about.

The sense that important events are unfolding elsewhere, in rooms she has never entered and to people she has never met, has grown stronger as she has come of age.

When Sally reappears with a stack of neatly folded newspapers, looking nervous, Lucy thanks her and pounces on them. Here is the real world, delivered to her door!

She spins back to her bed and spreads the pages across the

coverlet. *The Times of London*, *The Pall Mall Gazette*, *The Daily News*, and *The Morning Advertiser.* With a sigh of satisfaction, she settles back against the pillows for an edifying day. Lucy's stomach rumbles. She's hungry but wants to be left alone. She'll send for a lunch tray later.

# Chapter Four

KENSINGTON, SEPTEMBER 1

"Madam?" The soft voice comes from behind her, but Maude Hepworth does not look up. Her hand continues moving smoothly across the page, the pen scratching slightly. The grandfather clock tick-ticking in the corner is the only other sound in the room.

"Your tea."

Maude hears the rustle of a cambric skirt and petticoat as feet approach across the carpeted floor. Her writing desk faces the bay windows, which in turn face the back garden of their narrow townhouse on Charles Court. The room isn't large, and the dark paneled walls make it seem even smaller, claustrophobic even.

Two heavy armchairs frame the fireplace, one pushed slightly off center from when Edward stood up for his smoke. The mantel holds her collection of crystal paperweights. Casement bookshelves on the south wall house books all the way to the ceiling. Reading is Maude's favorite—perhaps only —pastime. The bay window, with the delicate writing desk she chose herself, faces north. Even scrubbed clean every week, the glass allows only the weakest light through to illuminate her correspondence.

The maid sets down a tray on the desk beside her hand.

"Thank you, Emily." Maude continues writing, the words flowing from her pen without any effort.

"Madam." The voice is even softer now, if possible. Emily clears her throat.

Maude looks up. The maid is standing with her hands behind her back, shifting from foot to foot. Her eyes stay on the ground. "I..." She turns around to leave. "Never mind, ma'am."

"Whatever is it, Emily? Sit right here and compose yourself." Maude points to an upholstered stool.

"It's me...my sister. She's a thorn in my side, but she's family. More like a mum to me than our own mum. She sang me to sleep when I was still in swaddling clothes. And she needs a place, ma'am." She bites her lip. "I was wondering if maybe you and the doctor need someone for heavy work, like. A charwoman or laundress? She's strong, ma'am." Finally, Emily looks up and there is a tortured sort of plea in her expression.

"I see." Maude puts down her pen and considers her maid. She too looks sturdy. It occurs to Maude that she doesn't really know this person who lives in her home. "And her character? What of that? Can you vouch for her?"

Emily's shoulders sag and her spine seems to curve in on itself. "Annie means well," she admits at last.

"I'm afraid good intentions do not make a good servant, Emily. She must work hard and be reliable, as you are. You know how stringent the doctor's requirements are."

Their eyes meet for a moment and Emily rises from her stool.

"Yes, ma'am. I do know." She retreats back across the carpet and closes the door behind her silently.

Maude sighs as she looks at the closed door. It's a pity, but it wouldn't do. She picks up the pen again.

*Condolences for your loss... Michaelmas in Devon... Wrap a flannel cloth around your neck to prevent dry coughs. Cook will send her recipe for a warm tonic...* Maude turns the page over and continues, then turns it again to finish across, signing her name with an illegible scrawl. There. One down. She folds the pages carefully into the engraved envelope. DR. EDWARD HEPWORTH. ROYAL ACADEMY OF MEDICAL SCIENCES. 16 CHARLES COURT. KENSINGTON 12. She pulls the next letter from her portable secretary and grimaces, since no one is looking. Only five more to return today. Between her own family across the home counties and her husband's relations and acquaintances in Edinburgh, sometimes there are as many as sixteen letters to write before the noon post.

Maude lets herself pause to look out the window for just a moment. A cloud passes, and the small tended yard behind the house is briefly illuminated by a diffuse golden light. The flower beds need weeding. She will speak to Owens before Edward notices. The flagstones are well swept, she notes with relief.

Maude feels a frisson of alarm as she thinks of her husband—and she glances around the room to check for any other abnormalities. *Abnormalities* is a word she learned from Edward.

Lucy cannot banish the image from her mind of that poor woman found dead in Whitechapel. Alone in her bedroom, she read several reports in the daily papers describing how Mrs. Nichols's throat was cut from ear to ear.

The unfortunate woman was still warm when Constable Neil came upon her body in the early hours of the morning— the same time that Lucy herself had been wandering in her sleep. The reporter had also alluded to other "shocking wounds" upon Mrs. Nichols's person. Is that why the police constable and commissioner came to see her father?

And what could those wounds be? A chill runs down Lucy's spine. To think that the person who had found poor Mrs. Nichols was here in her house. If she could, she would ask the constable: Who could commit such a heinous crime against another person, and a woman at that?

Lucy was miles away from Whitechapel when the murder took place, but what if something like that had happened to her while she was sleepwalking? She shudders at the thought.

In devouring the news, Lucy also learned about a fire at the docks the same night that poor woman was murdered. Were the two related somehow? Lucy didn't see how they could be.

Lucy hoped no one was hurt in the fire. What if she had walked as far as the docks in her sleep? Would she have woken up? Or could she herself have been engulfed in the enormous flames?

Perhaps her father is right. Lucy needs to be cured of whatever caused her to leave her bedroom and wander into the night. And yet, though she knows nothing of the circumstances of Mrs. Nichols's life, Lucy feels an unexpected kinship with the woman who was out in the early hours of the morning walking alone, just as she was.

Lucy sits on her bed and closes her eyes. She's suddenly overcome with weariness in body and mind. With her eyes closed, she feels something dark looming just out of her vision. What is it?

"Don't be a silly goose," she tells herself. Is she really as impressionable as her father thinks all women are? Has her reading about the murder imprinted itself on her character and unhealthily excited her imagination? Her father would say yes.

Lucy lies down. Her eyelids are suddenly heavy weights.

She wills herself to open her eyes but cannot. The effort is too great. Her limbs sink like anchors into the bed.

She doesn't want to fall asleep. It is too early for bed, and yet a bone-deep lethargy has taken hold of her. Maybe the effects from last night's walk?

Lucy should summon Sally but cannot rouse herself. Darkness covers her mind like a thick, heavy cloak.

Lucy wakes with a start. It's ice cold in her room. Has a window been left open? She glances at the fireplace and sees the fire has gone out. How long has she been asleep? Where is Sally?

Lucy looks down to find she is wearing a nightdress, but does not recall changing into one. Her long red hair has been released from her chignon and hangs down her back. Had Sally helped her out of her gown and changed her whilst she slept? Had she combed out her hair? Sally must have. How could Lucy have been so deeply asleep as to be unaware of her maid's actions?

Though the weariness has not entirely left her body, Lucy's mind is now alert. Where is the cold draft coming from? It's as if an icy wind is sweeping through the room.

Lucy shivers as she gets out of bed. Even with a thick rug, the floor is frigid on her bare feet. Soft white light seeps in through an opening between her thick, velvet curtains. Is it dawn or dusk?

Lucy walks towards the window, then pauses, suddenly afraid, and steps back.

What is there to fear? Her heart beats faster, though she doesn't know why.

She shakes her head to dispel her foolishness. Perhaps she's had another nightmare that she can't remember.

Yet how strange she feels. How very unlike herself. Maybe her father is right. She needs to see a doctor.

Lucy pushes the heavy fabric of the curtain aside. The window has indeed been left open. There's light in the sky coming from a fat, full moon and from the amber glow of the gas streetlight below. From nearby, a dog howls, a mournful sound. Lucy shudders.

She raises her arm to pull the window shut, but suddenly stops. Something compels her to lean further and look out of the window.

Lucy hears a soft voice, almost a whisper, calling to her.

*Come, Lucy,* the voice says. Lucy looks down into the garden. There is no one there. Is she imagining things? Is she still dreaming?

The voice whispers on the breeze. It's a woman's voice, soft and soothing. Her mother. She is calling to Lucy again. And Lucy must heed the summons.

The windowsill is not high, and Lucy can easily hoist herself to sit on it. She swings first one, then the other leg to dangle outside the window. She does not look down. If she did, she would see nothing but cold, hard stone below.

Lucy has no fear for her safety. She has one overarching desire —to be reunited with the mother she's longed for all her life.

*Come, Lucy, dear. Come to me.*

Lucy's heart beats faster. Her breathing is shallow. A dog howls, louder this time, but Lucy is not afraid.

Her body and mind have been taken over. Lucy spreads one arm wide to envelop the night air. She can almost feel her mother's loving arms in the breeze that ruffles her hair and nightgown. She will go to her and fly into the night.

Just then, scudding clouds cross in front of the moon, extinguishing the moonlight. Lucy pauses for a moment. Her arm drops to her side. Her mind begins to clear. Where is she? What is she doing?

Then the moon emerges from the clouds, and the voice calls softly again. The clarity she had for a moment, like the clouds, vanishes.

Lucy loosens one of her hands from its grip on the windowsill and teeters on the edge. She is ready.

Suddenly, there's a commotion behind her and a scream.

"Miss Lucy! What are you doing, my lady?" Someone rushes behind her.

Lucy hesitates for only a second. She releases her hand to jump.

But it is too late. Strong arms wrap around her waist from behind and pull her back from the ledge.

"No. Let me go!" But the urge to follow the voice into the night is leaving her even as she protests. Sally is stronger than Lucy and carries her mistress away from the window and back to her bed.

After she deposits Lucy, the maid rushes to the window, slams it shut, and fastens the latch securely. Sally pulls the curtains across, covering the moon from view.

Lucy collapses. She is shaking. What was she about to do? Was she really going to jump from the window?

"I'll get a doctor. You're quite pale, my lady."

"No!" Lucy insists. "No. No doctor. And do not tell Lord Rutherford about this. Please. I beg you."

A look of fear crosses Sally's face. Lucy grabs her maid's hand, pressing it firmly. "This is to remain between the two of us." Lucy wants to explain to Sally, to offer some reassurance to her maid, some excuse. But what can she say?

Reluctantly, Sally nods slightly.

"Thank you, Sally. I need only to rest now."

"I shall stay with you" Sally pulls the bed covers over Lucy.

What is happening to her? First she wanders outside at night, and now she has a waking dream—for that's what it must have been—about her mother calling to her. Lucy cannot explain it. And she is too exhausted to think much more. She will follow her father's advice and meet with a doctor.

Sally makes up a bed on the rug at Lucy's feet. Lucy is relieved that her maid offered to stay with her. It is not something she would have asked. As soon as she closes her eyes, Lucy falls into a deep slumber.

*Chapter Five*

John Neil wakes with a start, bolting upright in his narrow bed. His chest heaves for air. Air, air. He searches the darkened room wildly. Is this his room? His home? The vision is so real—the crumpled body, the mangled flesh.

He presses a hand over his eyes and feels the clammy damp of his skin. He closes his eyes and reopens them slowly.

By reflex, his brain kicks in, checking for evidence and verifying impressions. Yes, he is home, in his own bed. There is his pitcher and basin, his shaving brush, razor, and strop, just as he left them on the side table. There is his own comfortable armchair, worn to the shape of his backside. There is the familiar, faint scratching in the wall. A mouse. No surprise there.

Wheels lumber by on the street below, audible through the half-open window. A wagon, likely laden with produce and heading to Covent Garden in the quiet pre-dawn hours.

The dream. No, not a dream. A memory of the night before. Finding the body. That was real. Gruesome even for him, going on thirteen years on the force now. He'd seen things. But this—the lads hadn't said a word when he walked in yesterday. No slaps on the back, no elbows. He must have looked clouded over because Anderson had given him tonight off, gruffly, shaking his head. That never happened before neither.

He slumps back against his pillow, heart still hammering, and makes himself wake up. He shakes off the thin sheet covering his bare chest. He sleeps hot and thrashes about. Always has.

Something is bothering him... He makes himself remember. He told it all already.

Walking that beat, same as ever, coming upon a shape on the ground. Then the shape was a body, a woman, dead.

He shudders again and tells himself to buck up. It's a job, this is. And a good one, especially for an Irishman in London, isn't it? Decent pay, and steady, with a chance to jaw with folks as you made the rounds. Stop for a smoke or get stood for a pint, some nights. With no missus at home, he'd take all the companionship he could get, apart from the other peelers. He closes his eyes and puts himself back there, under the black night, standing on the worn cobblestones, pointing his bull's-eye at the pile of lifeless limbs. No one should suffer like that. No one should maul another human being like that, like an animal. It was unnatural, for certain.

He surveyed the scene with his mind's eye. *Too clean*, that's what it was. No blood on her clothes. No bloody footprints on the paving stones. For all her injuries, there was not near enough blood.

**Daily News (London)**
September 2, 1888

## BRUTAL MURDER IN WHITECHAPEL

A murder of the most brutal kind was committed in the neighbourhood of Whitechapel in the early hours of yesterday morning, but by whom and with what motive is at present a complete mystery.

Viewing the spot where the body was found, however, it seems difficult to believe that the woman received her death wounds there. The body must have been nearly drained of blood, but that found in Buck's Row was small indeed.

Mayfair September 2

"What do you make of this?" Lord Rutherford slaps the *Daily News* down on his broad mahogany desk and then pushes it towards Sir Charles Warren.

The Commissioner glances down at the headlines but does not pick up the large black and white broadsheet. He's seen it already, as well as half a dozen other newspapers.

"It is an unspeakable tragedy." His voice is grim. "And we will find this monster."

"Yes." Rutherford twists the whiskers of his bushy mustache and glares at him. "I'm talking about the lack of blood in particular. Do you think it has anything to do with our mutual enemy?"

Warren hesitates. It had crossed his mind, but he chose the more logical explanation: one or more merciless men preying on helpless women.

"We suspect Mrs. Nichols might have been killed elsewhere and the body moved to Buck's Row. That would account for the lack of blood at the scene—"

"But not for the lack of blood on the clothing."

"There are other explanations, my lord."

"I thought we had taken care of this monstrosity with the fire."

"We can't be sure. As you may remember, while I said that fire was one way of eradicating the…" Warren hesitates, searching for a term he has not used in conversation, "the ungodly cargo. I suggested but did not condone the setting of a fire, especially so close to a warehouse full of spirits."

"Is that a criticism, sir? We did not know at the time about the spirits. And I trusted your advice. With your vast knowledge of archeology and ancient secrets, as well as your years in Bechuanaland, I would have thought you could have resolved this matter by now."

Warren ignores the insulting tone. Lord Rutherford appointed him Police Commissioner, and he serves at the Home Secretary's pleasure. But he does not believe the Whitechapel murder to be the work of the demon Rutherford fears. Humans are also capable of unspeakable evil.

"We will do everything to find the murderer and bring him to justice," Warren assures Lord Rutherford.

"You will have all the men and resources you need. Robert Anderson has been appointed commissioner of criminal investigations to help. But your primary job, need I remind you, is first and foremost to destroy that demon who was transported on my ship. I expect that next time we meet you will have happier news to share on that front—as well as the Whitechapel murderer."

Lord Rutherford looks distinctly uncomfortable.

"One other matter. It concerns my daughter." There is a long pause before the Home Secretary continues. "She has been having nocturnal wanderings."

Warren raises an eyebrow. He's always been fond of Lucy, thinking her a bright young woman, and, truth be told, feels a bit sorry she has to live with a bear of a father.

"Walking in her sleep. It is most unusual. And I'm sure a

knowledgeable doctor can get to the bottom of this, but I want one of your men to keep an eye on her."

"Excuse me, Your Lordship?"

"Keep an eye out. Stand guard at night—not all the time, mind you—but I would rest easier knowing you have someone watching outside." Lord Rutherford gestures toward the windows. "To make sure that Lucy does not leave and wander out of the house again. That is all."

With a curt nod, Warren departs. He deeply regrets ever getting entangled in Lord Rutherford's "matter," as he calls it. Now he must devote one of his men to watch Rutherford's daughter.

He has enough on his hands with the murder and being tasked with finding this creature, this undead thing that his Lordship's greed had disturbed. Rutherford wouldn't tell him what had happened in Kimberley, but it must have scared the man. He returned to London rattled, and his Lordship didn't rattle easily.

Warren didn't want to know any more about the lord's dealings in diamonds, or his investments in certain clubs in the East End, for that matter. All he knew was that the demon had followed Rutherford here in one of the lord's own ships and they devised a scheme to destroy it. He'd heard tales of such creatures in his worldly travels, but never expected that this knowledge, such as it were, would be put to any kind of practical use.

Now he has been tasked with finding the unfindable and destroying him. It. Warren doesn't know what to call the demon. He knows of other names. Obayifo. Vrykolakas. Bloedsuier. Vampire.

*Chapter Six*

BETHNAL GREEN, SEPTEMBER 2

It is almost dawn and still Jonathan Hinton cannot sleep. He softly paces his small sitting room, keenly aware of not wanting to disturb his kindly landlady, Mrs. Cavendish, who lives below.

Since the murder of Polly Nichols, Jonathan has spent hours roaming the streets of London's gritty East End. Like any journalist worth his salt, Jonathan has trusted sources inside Scotland Yard. He knows many of the H-Division inspectors and the detectives at the Criminal Investigation Department by first name. He also cultivated sources among the working men and women in the area, sources he's found useful in the two years he's been working for the Central News Agency.

Whitechapel is a rough part of town, yet despite his dress and manner, which signal Jonathan doesn't reside in this neighborhood, he's known to many of the inhabitants as a trusted and responsible journalist.

The night Mrs. Nichols was killed an enormous fire had

broken out at the London dock. Jonathan wrote about that, too, for the newspaper, and this time didn't have to rely on eyewitnesses. He was there. He saw the yellow and orange flames shoot up into the dark sky and illuminate the night. A great billowing wall of fire crackled and roared when it caught the warehouse. The heat and noise were unlike anything Jonathan had ever experienced.

There were shouts from the fire brigade and calls for help.

"Is anyone in the warehouse?" Jonathan had asked a dock worker.

"Nay. It's full of spirits and feeding the fire. Quick man, we need help." The dock worker tossed a bucket at Jonathan.

Despite the man's assurance there was no one in the building when the fire broke out, Jonathan thought he saw a figure near the warehouse, not twenty feet from the flames. A tall figure in a long coat staggering away from the fire.

Jonathan had stood paralyzed for a moment. Should he go and help him?

Despite the fierce heat from the blaze, the hair on the back of Jonathan's neck stood up. The man turned towards him, as if aware he was being watched.

Jonathan saw a flash of white-blond hair, and two eyes that seemed to glow red with some internal fire. Then the figure was gone. Had Jonathan imagined it? Were his eyes playing tricks?

Jonathan didn't have time to think because he was soon pressed from all sides into action.

Though he'd gone to the docks to record his impressions, he joined the ranks of firemen, policemen, dock workers, and other passersby working to extinguish the flames. Every hand was needed to hoist buckets of water. Steamers had come from all over, great vessels summoned to help quench the flames. The noise of the steamers pumping water and the crackle and roar of the fire was deafening.

Even now, days later, Jonathan can almost feel the hot

flames and hear the men shouting as they worked to extinguish the flames. Finally, near eleven o'clock, the fire began to
abate.

But alone in his room, Jonathan replays the events of the
night of August 31—the fire and the early morning butchery
of a poor woman in Whitechapel thereafter.

Though his brain and his body are tired, Jonathan can still
feel the adrenaline rush through his veins. So many policemen
and firemen were drawn to the docks that night that there
must have been few night watchmen in Whitechapel. Did
Mrs. Nichols's killer know that? Is that why the murderer
chose that moment to commit his brutal act?

Mrs. Nichols was not young—forty-three years of age,
according to her father, who identified her. Twenty years older
than himself. His mother's age.

What if his mother or one of his sisters had died under
similar circumstances... But no. It's unimaginable, and he
pushes the thought aside.

On his father's deathbed, Jonathan had promised to look
after his mother and his three sisters. And yet here he is in
London, far from his home in Bath, trying to make a name for
himself as a journalist.

It was his sisters who insisted he go to London to fulfill his
dreams. A natural journalist, Jonathan had been recording his
observations since he'd been a boy. He'd dreamed of being a
writer, and now here he is, though he misses his family desperately at times.

What would they think if they knew how often he
traversed the dark and grimy streets of Whitechapel? What if
they knew he had visited the mortuary, looked on the face of
death, and written about it?

His family knows little of his life in London. He sends his
mother money every week from his small wages and forgoes
all luxuries—even some necessities, such as eating three meals
—to provide for them. His father had a small military pension,

and this, along with Jonathan's support, keeps the family afloat.

Jonathan pushes his hand through his hair and sinks into a hardback chair at the small table where he composes his articles in longhand. He has made no presumptions about Mrs. Nichols and what she was doing in the early hours of the morning, alone and on the streets, though his other colleagues have already called her a prostitute.

He recalls the police commissioner's orders last year on this very subject. "The police are not justified in calling any woman a common prostitute," Warren had decreed, "unless she so describes herself, or has been convicted as such."

Yet that did not stop most members of the police force and the press from assuming that Polly, like many of the unfortunate women in London's East End, were prostitutes when they were out late or in the early morning hours. Certainly Polly's love of alcohol, by all accounts, and her rough sleeping reinforced this belief.

But can Jonathan blame Polly for wanting to drink? No. He doesn't judge these women for their unfortunate circumstances.

In the last few months, he's spent countless hours walking the streets in London's East End, where hardworking men and women live cheek by jowl in cramped doss houses if they're lucky, or sleep outdoors on the cold steps or in corners of verminous alleyways if they're not.

Many times Jonathan has seen unhoused children wearing rags and sleeping in doorways or on benches as well. He can hardly believe his eyes at times. How could there be so many poor, unhoused souls in this great city?

Many of the poor inhabitants of Whitechapel now recognize Jonathan. And for his part, he can't quite get the grit and the scents of this poor section of East London out of his mind. It doesn't take much prompting for him to vividly recall the particular smell of Whitechapel he encounters on his night investigations—the fetid smell of urine, feces, and filth that permeates the streets and alleyways.

If he closes his eyes, he can hear the noise, the constant drunken brawls, the bickering between men and women, the crying children, and the sense of overwhelming human misery that is part of the very fabric of this neighborhood of London.

And now there is a fiend, a butcher, in Whitechapel. Why target the unfortunate? The question pops into Jonathan's mind and he quickly returns to his desk and dips his pen in ink to capture the phrase. Of course, a woman like Polly is easy prey, but Jonathan wants to find the deeper answers.

His sisters would be proud of him, though he hopes they have not gotten wind of the murder from the newspapers. They would only worry. Jonathan has been well schooled by his sisters to believe that women are equal to men—hardly the view that society holds—but he wants to spare them, if possible, from knowing about such evil.

Jonathan decides to go to Scotland Yard and talk to the police again. He grabs his black top hat and coat, both worn to a softer shade of black after many years, and heads down the stairs. He descends as quietly as he can, knowing his landlady, Mrs. Cavendish, will hear him and ask about his health.

The woman means well. She is always inviting him for tea, and Jonathan suspects she knows how precarious his finances are, and how often he forgoes meals. Sometimes he takes her up on her kind offer and listens to her stories about her late husband and his travels with the merchant marine. She likes to hear about his investigations too. But he has business to do now. He manages to make it out to the street without interruption.

Once outdoors, Jonathan's pulse quickens. The hunt for a story makes him feel alive—mind sharp, senses alert. He will stalk the Whitechapel butcher, at least in print, and try to bring the killer to justice.

*Chapter Seven*

KENSINGTON, SEPTEMBER 2

Maude has already eaten a solitary dinner and is sitting in the back parlor when her husband comes home. She hears the faint rattle of a hansom cab on the cobblestones out front and rustling sounds in the entryway as Edward hands his hat to the butler. Next, she knows, he will set his heavy black bag on the sideboard, then proceed up the stairs. Maude glances at the clock.

Nine o'clock. Despite herself, she feels her breath quickening. One footfall on the carpeted stair. Another. Lightly, Maude presses her fingertips against her cheeks to smooth out any sign of expression, then bends her head over her embroidery.

"There you are." He pauses in the doorway and surveys her closely. What does he see when he looks at her? She is small and feels even smaller. She pulls the light woolen shawl around her shoulders. She had asked Emily to light the fire, even though it is only September.

Maude raises her eyes but avoids her husband's. "Here I am."

What is his mood tonight? She tries to look calm, but she quivers at attention, searching for clues in his posture, his tone of voice, the very air surrounding him.

From the corner of her eye, she surveys his familiar figure, her husband of five years now. He looks just the same as he did when they met at Godinton House. He cut a fine figure then, as now, though there is nothing flashy about him. He has regular features—a square jaw covered by a well-trimmed beard, a long narrow nose, angular cheekbones that flush easily when he is angry. His sandy hair is combed back to reveal the high forehead of an intellectual. A pair of wire-rimmed spectacles completes the impression of a distinguished medical man.

At eighteen she had known only the carefree younger sons on their neighboring estates, and the doctor's seriousness had appealed to her. She had known nothing of London, nothing of the world outside Kent, nothing at all.

Edward sweeps his gaze around the room as he enters. "And?" Maude can feel him cataloging any changes made during the day. Had she moved a pillow? She thought she had put everything back in its place.

"I answered seven letters. I ate adequately. My meals were nutritious. I took several turns around the back garden for my afternoon constitutional." She is careful to keep her voice even.

He takes the chair across from her and taps his fingers on its upholstered arm. His eyebrows rise. "Several? How many is that?"

She watches as he reaches one pale hand toward the afternoon post to sift through it. His hands, his long and bony fingers, unnerve her now. "Five, of course. Three is too few for proper exercise and seven is excessive."

"Quite right." His mouth curves into a smile, though his

attention is clearly on the envelopes in his hand. "You will be an asset to me yet. A doctor's wife must be the very picture of health. You still look pale though. Did you take your cod liver oil?"

Once upon a time, Maude had thought that her fiancé's concern for her well-being was a sign of his love and affection. No more.

"Of course," she repeats. And she had. But her bones ache with the effort to keep her posture perfectly straight in her chair.

Thank goodness he couldn't see under her skin to her bones. Or her weary heart. *Aweary.* The word reminds her of Mariana in the moated grange, though her mother had named her after a different Tennyson poem. Once she had known all three parts of *Maud* by heart.

> In the shuddering dawn, behold,
> Without knowledge, without pity,
> By the curtains of my bed
> That abiding phantom cold.

For a few moments the only sounds in the room are the barely audible swish of her needle pulling thread through a piece of damask and the tearing of paper as Edward opens his mail.

"Well, you shall soon have an opportunity to reflect well upon me. We are summoned to Lord Rutherford's for dinner tomorrow night." Edward flings the note onto a side table and turns to look at her speculatively.

"Indeed?" Her husband did not like direct questions, but he sometimes responded to murmured prompting.

"Indeed. He has asked me to attend to his daughter's health. It appears he has concerns about her."

Maude can't help it. She looks up at her husband's face, her surprise showing.

"And for some reason, his Lordship would like my wife to attend. He believes that his daughter is also in need of female companionship. I trust you will be a worthy model for Miss Rutherford."

Maude holds her breath for him to continue. She has never met Lord Rutherford or his daughter. She knows that he is the Home Secretary, but nothing else. She has never been invited to a dinner hosted by one of her husband's acquaintances. She does not even know how he knows Lord Rutherford. It is a very odd request. If Edward regularly attends such affairs, she has no knowledge of them.

The fire in the hearth suddenly sends out a spark and crackles with energy. Her husband stares into the flames, stroking his chin with one hand.

"Wear your grey silk. You must be well dressed but draw no attention to yourself. You must eat carefully. Sample every dish but do not finish any course. Do not hunch your shoulders. Lord Rutherford's patronage is important to me. I am honored that he has chosen to consult with me about his daughter's nervous condition. He knows my reputation as a man of science and an alienist at Bethlem."

"But how would he have heard…" Maude stops herself but it is too late.

His hand grabs her chin, hard, pulling her face around to meet his cold gaze. "Must you doubt me at every turn? Must your own incompetence and stupidity color every word you utter? My devoted helpmeet—" he sneers. She has gone too far. She knows better. She closes her eyes in fright.

Edward stands abruptly, his chair creaking from the sudden movement. "I trust you will not disappoint me tomorrow." Without waiting for a reply, he whirls around and leaves Maude alone in the room.

# Chapter Eight

So now he's watching over young ladies, acting the nursery maid. That's the return he gets for finding Polly Nichols's body on Buck's Row, for having a bit of the blue devils since then.

Constable Neil unwraps a meat pie from a wad of newspaper and settles in for a long night outside the toff's mansion. Warren told him nothing had better happen to Rutherford's daughter on his watch. And nothing would. It isn't her fault her father was a right arse. He could tell even the chief didn't like the man.

Neil shrugs and takes a big mouthful before glancing up at the lady's window. Shameful this is, observing her window like a common peeper. But orders are orders.

Instinctively, he assesses the ways in and out of the building. Windows too high up to reach without a ladder. No balconies in front. A full house of servants, judging by the electric lights that blazed on every floor when he first got here.

No mews or alley between the homes either, so horses and carriages must be kept out back, discreet-like.

Neil wondered what it took to land a great house like this one. Five hundred quid a year? More? He swallowed. That was as high as he could imagine.

Sleepwalking, they said. He chews on that word for a bit. Poor girl. He has his own nightmares and they aren't pretty. Neil takes another bite and wipes his mouth with his sleeve.

He thinks about Miss Rutherford. Yes, she is pretty, with that red hair and pale little face. He stares at her window for a few minutes, wondering what is going on in there. Is she already dressed for bed? He feels his cheeks flush and scolds himself. None of that, now.

A light wind rustles through the plane trees of Hyde Park as clouds scud across the sky. A carriage ambles down the road, sedately. A few minutes later two drunken sods stumble down the pavement, arm in arm, singing incoherently. The bobby at the corner watches them and swings his stick, but keeps his distance.

Neil stifles a yawn and crumples up the soiled wrapping. That night in Buck's Row was just like this one, he thinks. The air heavy, the city sleeping fitfully beneath low clouds. And a charge in the atmosphere, like this one, like… He straightens, looking around. What was that sound? Like a whisper or a brush at his elbow. All around is silent. Not a noise, maybe, a feeling. A premonition of evil envelops him like a miasma. He must be over-tired. His eyes feel sunken.

Something nags at him too. Did he see anything else that fateful night? The fog of memory seems to cloud his brain.

Suddenly, from every direction, he hears birds screeching and a whole pack of dogs howling and barking. Neil jumps to his feet, startled. What on earth…?

A flock of crows wheels around the Rutherford house, carrying on in loud abrasive tones. The dogs whine and moan nearby, unseen. A dark cloud passes before the moon, pitching the street into total darkness, and with it a terrible chill descends.

Neil shivers and watches in wonderment as nature seems to revolt against some strange invisible intrusion. Then, as soon as it arrives, it is gone and Neil is left staring stupidly at Miss Lucy Rutherford's bedroom window, heart racing.

# Chapter Nine

KENSINGTON, SEPTEMBER 3

*My dearest sister,*

*You will perhaps be surprised to hear from me this morning as I replied to your note yesterday. Do not be alarmed!* ~~There is no reason to worry about me~~*. I have little time to spare this morning but I feel somehow compelled to reach out to someone on this cloudy day, as the sun struggles for purchase in the sky. Someone familiar from our dear home, from bygone, more innocent days. I will dash off this missive before attending to my real duties.*

*The household is in quite a state this morning as we are to dine at Lord Rutherford's tonight. The invitation arrived only yesterday, so Emily will have to work hard to make me presentable. Edward has insisted I rest this afternoon and take no exercise at all, to preserve my stamina for a long evening. It is true that I rarely go out in the evenings and I have been feeling listless. You know how* ~~insistently~~ *solicitous my husband can be.*

*I have a strange confession that I shall share only with you, the elder sister I have relied upon so completely since our mother's death. Poor mother had such a gentle soul and was so easily moved by fanciful phrases. When she was alive, I hardly understood her passion for poetry, but now I find these familiar lines echoing through my head at all hours of the day. You know the poem as well as I do:*

> Come into the garden, Maud,
> For the black bat, night, has flown,
> Come into the garden, Maud,
> I am here at the gate alone;
> And the woodbine spices are wafted abroad,
> And the musk of the rose is blown.

*It is illogical, dear Cordelia, but I feel these lines pulling at me like ~~the tug of an actual rope~~ an omen. I am not a dreamer, like our mother was, but I can picture this scene as vividly as if it were happening before my eyes: a young woman at a window…and who is beckoning her to leave the safety of her bower—? I can't tell, but already we know no good will come of it. ~~Flown becomes blown! I don't like it, Cordelia!~~ I shudder even now, in my own parlour, in my own home, at the presentiment of danger. It is this, perhaps, that led me to write you this morning, before I submit myself to my afternoon rest and my evening's entertainment. ~~I am sure~~ I hope it is indeed entertaining. ~~I will know no one there but my husband.~~ I shall send you a complete report, of course.*

*Do you remember when we were children how you used to call me a fox terrier, small but determined to find her quarry? I chafed at your teasing then, but now I only wish I had some of that fierceness left. But ~~I am a fool.~~ what nonsense! The young girl you once compared to a hunting dog is long gone and in her place is a well-settled matron, which is exactly as it should be. Ah, I hear the tea bell and I must be off. My regards to your brood, especially young Alfie—*

*Your loving Maude*

≈

Mayfair, September 3

.  .  .

"Sally, bring me some cutting shears," Lucy says when her maid comes into her bedroom.

Alone in her room, Lucy has taken to devouring the newspapers these last few days—against her father's wishes. As if he could keep her from knowing about the world.

She has taken matters into her own hands, literally, she thinks, as the black ink from the newspapers stains her fingers. She has been collecting a scrapbook of stories about the Whitechapel murder—Lucy doesn't know why exactly she feels called to do this. Now she has another piece to add to her collection.

When Sally returns with the scissors, Lucy reads out loud, "Female detectives." The two words sound odd together.

"What, miss?" Sally asks.

Lucy puts down the shears. "Listen to this from the *Illustrated Police News*, one of the papers you brought me from my father's study."

#### ILLUSTRATED POLICE NEWS
September 2, 1888

#### FEMALE DETECTIVES!

This is the latest idea for solving the Whitechapel murder. Metropolitan Police Commissioner Sir Charles Warren has been urged to enroll women in his force, and the suggestion has the support of Miss Frances Power Cobbe, whose philosophical musings have appeared in the Westminster Review. In a letter to the Times she says that a female detective would pass unsuspected where a man would be instantly noticed; she could extract gossip from other women much more freely; she could employ for whatever it might be worth that gift of intuitive quickness and mother wit with which her sex is commonly credited.

We are bound to assume that Miss Cobbe wrote her letter in sober earnest and after mature consideration. But the communicated certainty reads more like a grim joke than anything else. It is the female employment question carried to a ludicrous extreme.

Lucy tosses the article back onto the bed. "What do you think of the idea?" Her maid cannot read, but Sally is perceptive and will understand the message.

"It's true what that writer says," Sally answers after a moment. "Many women, specially like me, go unnoticed. Nobody gives me a second look when I'm out and about. But I don't know anything about policing." Lucy observes the maid's sharp-featured face. The girl's skin is pockmarked and her eyes are shrewd.

"Do you believe that the idea of a woman police force is a joke?" Lucy cannot keep the anger out of her voice, though she tries not to color Sally's reaction.

"No, miss. But it's not for the likes of me to say."

Satisfied, Lucy asks Sally to keep bringing the rest of the day's newspapers to her after her father reads them and before his manservant disposes of them. Lucy isn't sure what machinations Sally has to go through to follow through with this request—perhaps her maid is already engaged in confidential work, though she might not see it that way.

After Sally leaves, Lucy rereads the piece. This Miss Cobbe must be very clever. She herself would never have thought of the idea. Imagine women detectives! It is not a "grim joke" at all. She makes a mental note to ask Sir Charles his thoughts the next time she sees him—without her father nearby, for she can already guess her father's position on the matter.

*Chapter Ten*

MAYFAIR, SEPTEMBER 3

Maude looks out her carriage window as they approach the aristocratic Mayfair townhouse. She cranes her neck to take in the grandeur and counts four stories of stately white marble rising high into the sky. Two impressive white Corinthian columns flank an ornate doorway with some kind of crest above it. Bow windows face the street, but nothing can be seen behind the thick drapery. Freshly painted black railings and a high row of hedges divide the property from a long stretch of paved sidewalk. Maude was unaware that such a home could exist in London.

Maude gazes at her husband, wondering if he is similarly awestruck. He is leaning forward, his face tight. The horses snort and the carriage shakes from side to side as they get nearer. She trembles. She is nervous and hopes Edward is too preoccupied to notice. It is too late to do anything now but see this strange evening through.

In the entryway, Maude hands her cloak to a silent butler and looks around discreetly. Despite the electric lighting, the hall seems dark, the interiors stuck in an old-fashioned solemnity.

In the drawing room, the furnishings are of the finest quality, and newer than they first appear. She turns to discover Lord Rutherford himself suddenly at her side, murmuring something as he bends politely over her hand. He straightens into a tall, slightly stooped figure with bushy eyebrows, and a mustache to match. For some reason, Maude fights a shiver as she meets his dark eyes.

As she murmurs her greetings, she casts an eye around the room. Are there no other guests? No, from here she can also see a young woman at a window seat, almost hidden by curtains. Her face is turned away, so all that is visible is her red hair and bared shoulders. She is wearing a dark green evening dress.

Maude has heard some rumors about Rutherford, born a cash-strapped aristocrat but now quite wealthy after amassing a fortune in mining of some kind. Coal from the north? Or was it gold and diamond mines in the Cape?

Edward did tell her that Lord Rutherford is a widower, his wife having died shortly after childbirth, and that Lucy Rutherford is an only child who has been left too much to her own devices. Did Lord Rutherford tell her husband that? Or was Edward editorializing, as was his wont?

With a sharp gesture, Rutherford beckons his daughter, who rises and approaches silently. The poor thing, Maude thinks, watching her glide toward them. She is like a wraith, too slender and too pale.

"Doctor. Mrs. Hepworth." Miss Rutherford nods a polite greeting, but her mind seems elsewhere.

Under Edward's watchful gaze, Maude responds exactly as she ought, then folds her hands again and casts her own eyes to the floor. Edward prefers her not to speak unless spoken to. Maude accepts a glass of wine that she does not intend to drink and listens as the men make conversation.

Two servants open the pocket doors at one end of the drawing room. With an elegant sweep of one long arm, Rutherford directs the small party toward a long rectangular table ablaze from an electric chandelier hanging overhead. Floor-to-ceiling windows line one long wall, but heavy swagged curtains obscure the view outside. Along the facing wall, a small army of footmen stand at attention, ready to spring into action. The guests find their seats amidst the clink of silverware and the scrape of chairs against the parquet floor.

At the head of the table, Lord Rutherford raises a hand and the footmen advance, bearing plates of poached white asparagus, then tureens of fish soup. For several minutes there is only desultory conversation as the plates are cleared to make room for a roast capon. Then Rutherford dismisses the servants with a wave and leans back in his chair, his plate untouched.

"My dear guests," he begins. "I have an ulterior motive for tonight's dinner party. I thank you for your presence, and now, your indulgence, if you please. It is driven by a fond father's concern for his only child."

A small choking sound comes from the other end of the table, and Maude glances from her host to Miss Rutherford, who freezes in place, her eyes downcast.

"My Lucy has not been well, and her behavior has not been all it should be. I've heard of your work, Dr. Hepworth, at the hospital where you are studying and treating nervous conditions in women. My dear Lucy, like many of her fair sex, feels sentiments deeply, imaginatively, and it is my hope that you can treat her."

Maude notices Lucy's eyes tell a different story. They shine with barely concealed fury. The young woman lifts her napkin and wipes her lips.

"Sadly, my daughter has been without a mother's tender influence since her first year," Lord Rutherford continues. "I thought perhaps the sympathetic or intuitive understanding of another female might also bring her back to the pink of health." He smiles at Maude, showing sharp teeth.

Maude glances up in alarm. Surely he did not mean for her to impose on Edward's case? Her eyes briefly meet Miss Rutherford's, and she sees her own recoil mirrored in the younger woman's expression. Dinner was agonizing enough. Now she is to be enlisted as a companion? Dear God, Edward would be... She feels more than sees her husband's tension from across the table. A roar fills her ears.

"Of course, Lucy is to be treated at home." Lord Rutherford looks at Dr. Hepworth, who nods in understanding.

"I am perfectly fine," Lucy says. It is the first complete sentence she has spoken all evening, Maude thinks. "My dear father worries too much about my health, but I am not such a delicate flower."

"I beg to differ." To anyone else, Edward's words sound polite, but Maude hears the frustration behind them. "A rest cure is highly beneficial for calming nerves and restoring health."

"A rest cure? I am to be sentenced to bed then?"

"Why don't we let the good doctor examine you first, Lucy, and make his recommendations?" Lord Rutherford's voice softens a bit. He stands up, signaling that the dinner portion of the evening is over.

Lucy throws her serviette on the table and rises as well. "I would like Mrs. Hepworth to accompany me."

Maude's throat suddenly constricts. She doesn't have to look up at Edward to know he is furious.

"Very well," Lord Rutherford says. "Doctor, we will have brandy later in my library afterwards."

Maude has no choice but to follow Lucy up the wide staircase to her bedroom. She can feel Edward's eyes boring into her back with every step. Part of her expects him to push his large, black medical bag into her back. She would pay for this unexpected turn of events later, though she had nothing to do with it.

Lucy's bedroom is on the third floor. It is a very pretty room, large and well decorated, much more feminine than the rest of the townhouse. Lucy sits on a pale yellow daybed by the window. Maude wonders if she has a view of the gardens below.

"I would like Mrs. Hepworth to stay during my examination." Lucy pats the space next to her.

Edward nods. Maude can see his thin lips sealed in a tight, angry line.

Maude dares not meet her husband's eyes but keeps her gaze on her own clenched hands. She watches while Edward taps Lucy's limbs with a small rubber-tipped mallet and measures her skull with a metal contraption. He presses his long fingers into her neck; Lucy swallows visibly, her face rigid. Maude makes an effort not to check her own throat for signs of Edward's hands.

When he is done with his brief examination, Edward announces he will speak to Lord Rutherford about his findings.

"Maude, you may stay with Miss Rutherford. I trust you will model good habits." He closes the door with a sharp snap.

Lucy waits for the doctor's footsteps to retreat before turning to study his wife. Mrs. Hepworth is much younger than she seemed at first. She has dark blond hair pulled back into a tight bun and a round face with a small snub nose. The overall effect is cherubic, except for the weariness in her blue eyes. Those eyes and the wispy voice age her.

"Thank you, Mrs. Hepworth."

"Please call me Maude."

There is silence in the darkened room. Sally had lit a fire, and the warmth starts seeping back into Lucy's chilled limbs.

"What am I to do?" She speaks more to herself than with any hope of advice from the doctor's wife.

Maude clasps her hands together in her lap and surveys the room. "We are safe up here," she murmurs. "Will you tell me what has been bothering you? I am no doctor, but…"

"Forgive me, but I fear your husband cannot help me. You see, I have been having such strange dreams. I hear a voice calling to me." How to explain without sounding mad, Lucy wonders. But Maude looks at her sympathetically, so she continues.

"Though I cannot recall all the particulars, in my dreams I hear a woman's voice, and I feel certain that it is my mother. I was but two days old when she died, so how can that be?" Lucy hesitates. But Maude says nothing. She is listening intently and nods her head slightly.

"The voice—my mother's voice—tells me I must come to her. And I do. I want nothing more in the world. I feel such an urgent sense of yearning and then foreboding. Twice my maid Sally has found me walking in my sleep. Once when I was outside at night and another when I had gone to my bedroom window." Lucy shakes her head.

"I remember nothing upon waking. Just a vague feeling of dread. My father does not know about the nightmares. He was alerted to my sleepwalking, and it is for that reason he called your husband."

Almost as if reading her thoughts, Maude whispers, "Come into the garden—"

"Yes. Exactly!" Lucy sits upright and grabs at Maude's hands with both of her own. "Do you have these feelings, this urge to…this pull that happens between sleep and waking?" She feels a sense of hope.

Maude meets her eager gaze and shakes her head slowly. "Not exactly. No. But I have been hearing words in my head, in my mother's voice, though she is long gone. She used to quote Tennyson's poetry to me."

"But you knew your mother. Her voice. I have no memory of mine," Lucy says softly, through the sadness." I don't think my father has ever forgiven me for my mother's death in truth." Lucy has never expressed this feeling out loud to anyone, but there's something about Maude that invites her confidence.

"Why, that's absurd," Maude says.

Has Lucy revealed too much? Embarrassed, she changes the subject. "I have only just met your husband. Tell me about him."

There is a long pause as Maude worries her hands in her lap. Finally, she says, "I cannot."

Lucy sharpens her gaze. "Cannot what?"

"He would not like it." Maude slowly raises her eyes to look tentatively into Lucy's green ones. "Miss Rutherford…"

"You must call me Lucy."

"Lucy," she says more firmly now.

Maude's voice is so low Lucy has to bend closer to hear her. The woman sounds afraid. Why? There is another silence that feels pregnant with possibility to Lucy. It feels companionable, like they are on the same side.

"There is much we don't understand about these dreams and nightmares, about somnambulism. Maybe you can be of more help than your husband. Some dark force is at work in my dreams. I know not what. But I feel it. Does that sound strange to you? Or do you think I am going mad?"

"No," Maude says firmly. "You mustn't ever say that you are mad. My husband…"

"Do go on," Lucy implores Maude. "Whatever you tell me is safe with me."

"My husband runs a ward for women. In an asylum. Have you heard of Bethlem Hospital?"

Lucy shakes her head no.

"It is…" Maude stops herself and looks towards the door, as if worried someone may be eavesdropping on the other side of it. "I don't know much about my husband's work, but I fear that these poor women are treated more like laboratory subjects for my husband's research than as patients needing to be cured. Indeed, my husband believes our sex to be weak and in need of correcting."

"Correcting?"

"I have said too much." Maude looks down again at her hands, twisted in her lap.

"You don't believe that, do you?" Lucy's voice is a whisper.

Maude shakes her head.

"Nor do I. And I won't let my father dictate what I should read or do. He has his work, as your husband has his. I believe that we are capable of much more."

Lucy offers the other woman a tentative smile. Is this woman a friend? Is this what friendship feels like?

Maude smiles back, and the small movement transforms her face into youthful prettiness again.

"Did you know that my father forbids me to even read the newspapers?" Lucy says. "But I have disobeyed him. I've read all about that poor woman murdered in Whitechapel."

Maude shudders.

"Have you not heard?"

"I have heard the account, but it is hard to read of such things. And Edward would not like it either if he knew."

"Pff," Lucy waves her hand as if dismissing Dr. Hepworth.

"I have met the police constable who found poor Mrs. Nichols." Again, Lucy fears she is revealing too much. But once she has started she finds she cannot contain herself.

"Constable Neil." Lucy blushes when she says the name, something she is certain her new friend has noticed. "And Sir Charles Warren came to speak with my father."

"About the murder?" Maude is pale. She looks truly shocked.

"I do not know," Lucy confesses. "I tried to eavesdrop but I was not entirely successful."

Maude smiles. "You are quite the detective, Miss Rutherford."

Suddenly, Lucy jumps up from the daybed and rubs her hands together, excitement seeping into her veins.

"I have an idea!" She rummages through a pile of newspapers scattered across a dainty desk on the other side of the room. "Here!" Lucy seizes one and flips through its pages. She spreads out the page and leans over Maude, jabbing a finger at one corner.

"Miss Frances Power Cobbe invites curious-minded young ladies to attend a public lecture on FEMALE DETECTION. She will advance a modern theory of criminal investigation that makes use of the particular talents of the female sex. Hosted by the Victoria Street Society on the nineteenth of September at three o'clock. Light refreshments served. No men or police invited!" Lucy reads, her voice rising in triumph.

"This"—she points again—"is exactly what we need. We can attend this lecture together and learn something about detective techniques!"

Maude gazes up at Lucy with wide eyes, and Lucy wonders if she has completely shocked this virtual stranger. She can almost see the struggle in Maude's blue eyes. Her timidity and fear wrestling with something else. The light of possibility? Lucy takes Maude's hands in hers and squeezes them.

"Please," she begs. "We can keep this between us. My father wants me to have a companion. You can accompany me. No one need know. I will go mad if I'm to be shut up in my room all day."

Lucy looks pleadingly at Maude. Lucy knows how to use her power of persuasion to get what she wants. Even her father isn't immune. Not always, anyway.

"What do you say, Maude? Shall we go to Miss Cobbe's lecture and listen to her radical views? It would so help me to take my mind off my own troubles."

Maude doesn't respond. Lucy does not take her eyes off Maude's. Then Maude nods ever so slightly.

"Let's do it," Maude says. "But we must be very careful that my husband does not find out. He would…" Maude does not finish her sentence.

"No one will ever find out," Lucy says. She hopes she can keep that promise.

# *Chapter Eleven*

*Dear Maude,*

*I write in haste so that my maid, Sally, may post this for me this morning and you will not have to wait too long for my response.*

*I hardly know where to begin, dear friend. My mind is in a whirl.*

*Last night, Sally, who now sleeps in my room, says that she found me again wandering down the staircase. She'd heard a noise at the window, which woke her, and was startled to find that I was not in my bed. Sally quickly hurried to find me, and says that I was descending the staircase towards the front door. She tried to lead me back to my room, but I resisted, instead continuing my path down the steps.*

*Sally says I was quite resistant, and that I kept repeating that I had to meet "her," but who? I don't recall any of it. Sally was able to lure me up the stairs by saying that the person was waiting for me in my bedroom. And once there, she locked the door and pocketed the key. She says that I struggled against her and did not want to go back to bed.*

*How can I have no memory of this? It is a mystery that I could act so unlike myself. I have only you to confide in about this. Sally I have sworn to secrecy. In any event, she is not keen on telling my father, who would, no doubt, blame her for allowing me to leave the room.*

*We must meet!*

*I overheard my father talking about a new committee that he, as Home Secretary, is forming. Now I believe it may be connected to the murders in Whitechapel. I will try to investigate further—*

*One other thing. I do not recall how my father and your husband met. Only that my father had heard of your husband by reputation, perhaps at his gentlemen's club, and thought your husband—a man of science and reason, my father called him—could help rid me of my sleepwalking affliction. Now I doubt that your husband or any doctor can help me. But your friendship will do me a world of good better than any man of science.*

*I think it is best if we meet in person. If I may be so forward, and it is agreeable to you, may I come to your home? I will let my father know, of course, and I think he will be pleased, for he regards your husband— and, by extension, yourself—very highly. Of course, it will be easiest if your husband is not home at the time.*

*We can contrive to attend Miss Cobbe's lecture. Female detectives are such a forward-thinking idea. If you agree, I will visit as soon as I can.*

*I eagerly await your reply!*

*Yours,*

*Lucy Rutherford*

*Chapter Twelve*

BETHNAL GREEN, SEPTEMBER 5

*"I was proceeding down Buck's Row, Whitechapel, going towards Brady Street. There was not a soul about."*

Jonathan Hinton is in his sitting room at his desk, reviewing his notes from the inquest into Polly Nichols's murder. He has been attending the inquests that have been held every day for the last few days at the Working Lads Institute in Whitechapel, hearing testimony from Mrs. Nichols's father, the doctor who was summoned to the scene, a police inspector, neighbors, and a police constable, John Neil, who discovered the body.

"I had been round there half an hour previously," Neil testified. "And I saw no one then. I was on the right-hand side of the street, when I noticed a figure lying in the street. It was dark at the time. I examined the body by the aid of my lamp and noticed blood oozing from a wound in the throat."

Jonathan wonders what kind of monster could cut a woman's throat. There were also other terrible injuries to Mrs. Nichols's body, including violent knife wounds along her abdomen. Jonathan is not a doctor, and yet even he knows from the ghastly reports that there should have been more blood both at the scene and on her clothing. What exactly happened to all the blood that should have flowed from these vicious wounds?

Police Inspector Spratling testified that, following the removal of the body, he made an examination of Buck's Row and Brady Street but failed to find any traces of blood. "It's a curious thing," the inspector testified. "We at first thought the murder had happened elsewhere, but we ruled that out."

Jonathan pauses from his notes and looks up. What kind of killer is this? What monster could be so brutal, towards a woman no less?

Jonathan won't soon forget the ghastly sight of the woman's corpse lying in the mortuary at Old Montague Street. There were bruises on her hands. Had she tried to fight off her attacker? Was it a robbery that provoked such a vicious attack? Hardly, for by all accounts, Polly Nichols was penniless, a rough sleeper, who would have little on her person worth stealing, never mind something worth killing for.

"Her bonnet was off and lying to her side," Constable Neil testified. But there was nothing on her person, other than a piece of comb, a bit of looking glass, and a white handkerchief in her pocket, the policeman recounted.

Jonathan rubs his eyes as he sits at his desk. He's tired. He's hardly slept the last two nights as he's rushed to get his articles into the Central News Agency where they could be distributed to newspapers, such as the *East London Advertiser.* He's pleased that his articles are being widely circulated. And he has made it his mission to attend every inquest and write as much about the murder as he can.

After day one of the inquest adjourned, Jonathan interviewed Neil. He replays the interview with the police constable in his mind.

"Must have been a large knife," Neil told him. "Never

seen such carnage to a body. This fiend could be a butcher or a doctor, someone who knows human anatomy and how to use a blade."

Buck's Row is a rowdy and busy place at all hours of the day and night. And yet, according to Constable Neil, no one heard a thing. No piercing screams filled the night. No one saw a woman brutally murdered in the early hours of the morning.

"I was never far away from the spot," Neil said at the inquest. And yet he'd heard and seen nothing. The killer was certainly stealthy.

Through one of his sources, Jonathan was introduced to the barman at the notorious Frying Pan public house, the very pub where Polly Nichols had been drinking the night of her murder.

"She kept to herself, mate," Paddy Smith, the barman, told Jonathan when he'd asked about Mrs. Nichols. "She was a quiet woman. I'd never known her to quarrel with anybody. In fact, she seemed to be weighed down by some mighty trouble. Whatever it was, she never did say, not even when she was in her cups. God rest her soul, the poor thing."

Whatever her troubles and the source of her grief, Polly Nichols took them to the grave with her. Yet Jonathan imagines that the forty-three years of Polly's life were filled with many sorrows. Her rift with her husband and children, her stints in the workhouse, and living rough on the streets were more than enough to weigh her down with grief and unhappiness.

Jonathan looks down again at his notes from William Nichols, Polly's husband, who was also at the inquest. He'd testified that he hadn't seen his wife in years, and that she'd left him and the children of her own accord. He said if it hadn't been for Polly's drinking, they would have gotten on well together.

Most of the testimony from the inquest will not make its

way into Jonathan's article. But he has a journalist's curiosity about Mrs. Nichols and feels he is doing some justice by being thorough in his interviews and notes.

Jonathan sighs loudly. Then he gets up from his desk and paces his room. He needs to eat something. His meals have been irregular, hastily grabbed pieces of bread and cheese as he goes back and forth to the Working Lads Institute, and then out into the streets of Whitechapel. When had he last had a proper tea or rested a full night?

He can't remember. He's driven by his urge to both cover Polly's death and to uncover a clue to the identity of this silent killer.

Jonathan sits back down and reads his notes again. He had spent an afternoon going door to door interviewing the neighbors in Buck's Row.

A Mrs. Purkiss told him, "I hadn't yet as gone to bed but we didn't see nothing out of the ordinary." Her husband confirmed, "If there'd a been any screaming in Buck's Row, we'd have heard it." Furthermore, a Mrs. Green mentioned she was up early that morning and looked out her window, "But I couldn't see anything on account of a thick fog. Very strange and thick on the ground it were, so if a body were a laying there, I couldn't of seen it."

After four days, the inquest was adjourned for a fortnight, and Jonathan still had more questions than answers.

Jonathan took to the streets of Whitechapel once again. "He's evil, that man," a woman known as Widow Bessie told Jonathan about the murderer. She was sure that the same man who killed Polly also went after her the day before the murder: "He come at me out of nowhere with this long knife, threatening to rip me up, just as I was crossing the square near London Hospital."

"What did you do?" Jonathan asked, writing furiously in his small notebook.

"I screamed for me bloody life," Widow Bessie said. She

said that other women had seen a tall threatening figure wearing some kind of leather apron or cloak. Jonathan wrote down every word to piece together a description.

*The man's expression is sinister, and seems to be full of terror for the women who describe it,* Jonathan writes in his notebook in preparation for his story. *His eyes are metallic and seem to glow. His lips are usually parted in a grin, which is not only disturbing, but excessively repellent. He also carries a leather knife, presumably as sharp as leather knives are wont to be. His name nobody knows.*

The strangest thing, many women confirmed, was that "Leather Apron" never makes any noise. He emerges out of the shadows and leaves without a sound.

Jonathan puts down his notes, sighs, and closes his eyes. He is so weary. His left eyelid twitches, a sure sign he is exhausted and in need of sleep. But he cannot rest. He needs to get a story to the Central News Agency in a few hours' time or he'll miss the morning editions. He has so much information, but how to piece it all together?

Jonathan puts his arms on his desk and lays his head down. He'll rest just for a moment. After a few minutes, he begins to grow sleepy. He's in a half state between waking and dreaming when he suddenly sits up straight and rubs his eyes. He knows where to begin. He picks up his pen and writes.

*The fog in Whitechapel hangs like a shroud. It wraps around buildings, softening the edges of hard brick and limestone. It causes shrieks of surprise when pedestrians come upon each other suddenly in the street without warning. It somehow amplifies the harsh shouts and drunken arguments that always erupt in the early morning hours when downtrodden men and women who've spent the last of their pennies on drink and have nowhere to lay their heads take out their frustrations on one another. And it allows a killer to come and go unseen, stealthily, cloaked by a thick fog that conceals his movements.*

*Chapter Thirteen*

Count Vloeken had not intended to settle in London's East End. He had not intended to come to England at all and would have gladly remained peacefully in his vault under the mountain if not for the greed of one English industrialist. The English tormented him while he was living and then desecrated his tomb where he intended to lay for all eternity. Undead. He hates all Englishmen, but his wrath is reserved in particular for one man. Lord Rutherford, who destroyed what was most precious to him. In return, he will take what is most precious to Rutherford. Vengeance is simple.

In Whitechapel, Vloeken has found a fertile field already planted for his needs, brimming with humanity, ripe for the taking. At first, he didn't even have to hunt. That work had been done for him.

He'd arrived weak from his months-long journey, narrowly escaping a fire that had almost destroyed him. Weak and pale, with a dreadful thirst, he'd managed to crawl away from the flames engulfing the docks and the warehouse where he'd hidden himself. He was unfamiliar with the streets of this strange, new city but was drawn by a potent scent. Could it be?

Yes, it was. He could hardly believe his luck. After feeding, he'd almost thrown back his head and laughed. He felt his power again. Karlien would have been pleased. No, that's not quite right. Karlien would not have been pleased, but she at least would not have been horrified by what he'd done.

But he cannot think about his lost love now. Everything he's done has been for her. He had made a pact to be with her forever, sealed deep underground, where they could be at peace. It had been Karlien's idea. She could not bear what they had become. And he would never have hunted humans again, just for her. But she is gone now. Killed by that Englishman's greed in the blast. He is awake now and will avenge her death.

It is after 2:00 a.m. when the Count knocks on the heavy wooden door of number 19 Whitbourne Street. There is no sign indicating what goes on behind this door at one of the better looking tenements in this section of East London. But gentlemen in the know are schooled in discretion and understand the secrets behind this unprepossessing facade. And the Count's thirst for vengeance has led him here.

The door is opened by a burly manservant in white and black livery who bows before him and beckons him to enter. The Count knows what the man would see if he dared to look at him directly. He'd notice the long black dress coat, with a ruffled carmine shirt, and long leather gloves. He'd see a clean-shaven face with pale bluish skin that gives off an unearthly sheen, a long, straight nose with flared nostrils, thin red lips, and blond, almost white, hair that curls just below his chin.

The manservant motions the Count in and shuts the door against the icy chill he has brought with him. The temperature does not warm even when the thick wooden door seals out the chilly, foggy night.

The Count hears the tinkle of glasses and the hearty laughter of men who like their pleasures. He can use men like that. He will find one to provide what he cannot do without.

How easy it is in this cold, foggy city, where the prey is already behind bars or sleeping unawares in the street. He can move more freely too, covered by the yellow fog that he can summon and hide within at will. Still, he will not be here long before he sails back to Johannesburg with his precious cargo, his revenge complete.

He pulls off his gloves slowly, one finger at a time, as he scans the interior. The dimmed lighting. The heavy curtains. The air stale with cigar smoke. He floats through the rooms, ignoring anyone who tries to speak to him. He maps the space with his eyes, committing its nooks and crannies to memory.

After prowling through every floor, he descends some dank stairs to the basement. The sound of giggles and the clink of more bottles suggest servants below, sneaking a squeeze or a swallow.

The Count slips around a corner into the furthest reaches below ground. His eyes easily adjust to the dark and he heads toward a coal chute set in the low ceiling. Soundlessly, he clears the debris from the opening and looks up at the trap bolted shut on the inside. Yes, this will do nicely for a crypt. He can come and go as he pleases. And he will be right under Rutherford's nose. How satisfying.

# Chapter Fourteen

Lucy feels restless. She should be sleeping, but she's not at all tired. What time is it? It must be late. She heard the grandfather clock in the hall chime eleven and that was ages ago.

Sally must be wondering why her mistress hasn't sent for her to help her undress. Lucy was a bit rude earlier when she turned her maid away and now she drifts around her bedroom, picking up objects on her dressing table and putting them down again, unable to settle.

Since her introduction to Mrs. Hepworth—Maude—Lucy feels hopeful. She's buzzing with energy. Surely her father can't keep her locked inside her house when it was he who arranged for female companionship. She is to visit Maude tomorrow and her head is full of plans.

Lucy stops her pacing when she reaches the window. She pushes the curtain aside and looks through the glass. There's no moon tonight. All is inky blackness outside. Then someone lights a cigarette under her window. The flare briefly illuminates a man's face, looking down, broad shoulders hunched together against the night chill.

It's the policeman, Lucy realizes. Constable Neil who had come with Sir Charles to visit her father. She'd read that he was the one to find that poor woman's body in Buck's Row. What is he doing outside her father's house?

She shivers again, watching the man straighten and stare out into the dark as he smokes, all alone. As if sensing her gaze, he turns to look up at the house, head cocked. Their eyes meet for the second time in their acquaintance, and Lucy holds her breath, waiting for something, but she's not sure what. She tucks her hair behind her ear and realizes that it is loose, and she is in her white nightdress, silhouetted by the light behind her. She draws back in confusion.

Just then, something smashes against the window. Lucy recoils in fright. She brings her hands to her mouth to scream but no sound comes out.

Again, something throws itself at her window.

A bat, she thinks. Just a bat that has lost its direction and flown into the window, attracted by the light. She glances back outside and sees the policeman has gone. Has she imagined him? She is beginning to doubt her own senses.

Lucy's heart beats fast. She will summon Sally and go to bed. Sleep is what she needs. And yet she fears the dark curtain that closes over her in the night. What if she walks in her sleep again? What if the voice calls to her? Lucy has come to fear the night and that is why she cannot settle tonight. But she must get to bed.

Just as she is about to summon her maid, she hears someone call to her. A female voice. Her mother's. But louder and clearer this time.

"No," Lucy says out loud, startling herself. She cannot heed the call. Who knows where it will lead her?

"Sally!" She rings the bell. Then she puts her hands over her ears and paces her bedroom. Is she going mad?

"Are you all right, miss?" Sally suddenly stands before her.

"Do you hear that, Sally?" Lucy takes her hands away from her ears and lets her arms fall down to her sides.

"Hear what?" Sally cocks her head to the side.

Lucy can hear the voice. It's a whisper in her ear commanding her to come. She must not appear to be going mad before her maid. Sally is still in Lord Rutherford's employ, after all, and might tell her father.

"It is nothing," Lucy says at last. "I thought I heard something outside."

"Let us get you to bed."

Lucy allows herself to be undressed. As Sally chatters away about the lateness of the hour and the need for rest, Lucy thankfully can no longer hear the voice.

She sits at her vanity as Sally brushes her hair. The motion of the brush through her long curls soothes her.

But what she sees in the mirror startles her. Her face is so pale against the dark red of her hair. And there is a haunted look in her green eyes.

"Sally, will you stay with me tonight?" Lucy asks. "I don't wish to be alone."

"Of course, miss."

Sally makes up a bed on the rug next to Lucy's bed. Her maid has taken the small blanket from the daybed as well as a pillow, at Lucy's insistence.

Sally is the first to fall asleep. Lucy listens to her maid's rhythmic breathing and then soft snoring. She herself is wide awake. The clock strikes two. Then three. Lucy closes her eyes, but sleep does not come.

Though her body is so very weary, her mind is a hornet's nest of thoughts. It will not let her sleep. She is afraid of what might happen if she succumbs to slumber and her thoughts keep her too busy.

Lucy hears something stirring outside. Carefully, she steps over the sleeping Sally and walks to the window. She pushes aside the curtain and looks down below at the courtyard. It is almost dawn. The sky is not black but a dark gray. In the twilight, Lucy sees her father step out of his carriage. Why is he returning so late? Or so early in the morning? It is unusual for Lord Rutherford to come home at dawn.

Lucy pulls the thick velvet curtain across the window. She's suddenly overcome with weariness. Her limbs are so heavy, and she is less careful this time as she steps over Sally. Her foot brushes against her maid as she climbs into bed. Sally stirs but does not wake.

In the early dawn, Lucy feels calmer. She lies in bed and pulls the thick covers up to her chin. A moment later, she is fast asleep.

# *Chapter Fifteen*

Annie Chapman warms her hands at the large kitchen fire at Crossingham's lodging house. It is after midnight, and she knows that if she cannot get the money for her bed she will soon be out on the streets.

She looks up anxiously when the kitchen door opens and another potential lodger enters. Her heart sinks. It's not someone she knows. If it were an acquaintance, she might be able to beg a few pennies. The disheveled man who enters the kitchen joins the large number of hopeful lodgers. In his face she reads the telltale signs of a rough sleeper who knows he, too, will soon be asked to pay up or leave.

Annie sits quietly. She's too ill to move. The pain in her chest is bad tonight. She tries to hold back the cough that threatens to explode from her lungs but cannot. The bit of muslin she uses as a kerchief is tinged pink from blood when she wipes her mouth. She puts it in her pocket and crosses her arms across her chest to stem the pain. She is feverish and longs to lay her weary body down.

But as much as she needs sleep, she needs drink more. Instead of using the five pennies she's begged from her brother, Fontaine, for a safe place to rest her head, she's asked someone to fetch her a beer from the pub around the corner.

The urge to drink wins tonight as it does every night. In her nearly five decades of life, Annie can't remember a time when the lust for alcohol was not top of mind—ahead of her children, husband, sisters, and mother who all pleaded with and prayed for her to stop. Yet the demon inside her has only grown stronger.

Annie gathers her thin black coat and pulls it tightly around her. She is chilled to the bone despite the warm fire.

Lately, in her sickness, as her body has forced her to slow down, she's had more time to think, and she finds she's thinking about the past. She tries not to dwell on what was taken from her. Five of her six children dead from sickness, punished for her sins. A sixth who lived but was born with palsy. Her beloved husband, John, dead now for two years, though she'd left him several years before that. She'd only known he was gravely ill when she'd stopped receiving the ten shillings he arranged for her every week.

John had been an army man who'd always taken good care of Annie and her children. She had never wanted for anything. He had even risen to the rank of private coachman and groom for a wealthy family in Windsor. For him, Annie tried once to live a sober life. Her sisters had even arranged for her stay at a sanatorium. She'd been there a year, and can recall the joyous homecoming with John. How long ago that seems.

Annie hangs her head in shame when she recalls how, soon after, she began to drink again. Then she left, the need for drink a more consuming force than anything else in her life. And she found herself on the crowded, dirty streets of Whitechapel.

When the man returns from the pub with her beer, Annie

downs it in a few gulps. Though she much prefers the heavy, sweet taste of rum, she makes do. The beer settles, but she is hungry. Her stomach rumbles. When has she last eaten?

Was it just two days ago that her only friend, Liza, had seen her walking past Christ Church in Spitalfields and remarked on how ill she looked?

"Why, Annie. When have you last had a cup of tea?"

Annie shook her head. She can't recall.

"You take this." Amelia had put two pennies into Annie's hand. "And mind you don't spend it on rum but on tea and bread."

Annie had assured her friend she would, but Liza had no sooner walked away than Annie headed to Britannia's Pub to buy herself a drink.

If she can only hold out a few more hours then Ted, the man she now considers her husband, will be back.

Annie pictures meeting Ted on Brushfield Street, as she has every weekend these past few months. The two of them are well known in the area as a couple. Ted will have gotten paid. He'll take her to the pub. Then afterwards, they'll lodge together in a double bed at Crossingham's for the weekend until Ted has to leave for his job at a brewery. He will give her some money for a bed for the coming week.

But this week, Annie has already spent it all at the pub.

She'd thought to get more money, wrangling linens or hauling coal because she was strong for her small size, but she'd felt too poorly to work. Her sister said she'd put in a good word for her with her employer, a fancy doctor. Annie wants no more to do with doctors. Why can't Emily spare a few pennies instead?

Annie eats one of the cold potatoes left in the kitchen at Crossingham's. It's the only thing she's eaten in three days.

Feeling somewhat restored, she goes upstairs to the lodger's office to beg for credit for the night. Ted will be here tomorrow. He is good for it.

"Please trust me for tonight," Annie pleads.

"You can find money for beer, and you can't find money for your bed," Tim Donovan, the deputy keeper, tells her. His voice is harsh. "I cannot allow you to stay, Annie. You have made your choice."

"Don't let my bed," Annie tells him, lifting her chin. "I shan't be long before I am in."

When Annie leaves the lodging house on Dorset Street with the other unfortunate men and women whom Donovan has kicked out, she knows that she won't be back tonight.

Though dark and foul-smelling, Dorset Street is full of cheap lodge houses. None of them will take in a penniless woman for the night.

Annie has no choice but to make her way slowly back towards Christ Church, Spitalfields. She has slept outdoors here many a night, and knows of a secluded spot on Hanbury Street. In truth, it's only a gap between a house and a wrought iron railing. She hopes it will be vacant, as it usually is.

Annie can't walk very fast. Her chest hurts even to breathe and she must pause many times in the dark, cold night to cough and try to catch her breath.

She has been to the hospital, where she was given medicine for the consumption that has wasted her body. It didn't help. The only thing that helps to numb the pain in body and mind is the alcohol that she craves more than life itself.

As she walks through the benighted streets, Annie does not look back. A rat crosses the road before her.

At times, she steps over excrement, or hears the moans of couples fornicating against a building. There are no streetlights. The only light is that which spills out from pubs.

Annie's pulse quickens at the soft, yellow light and the sound of voices and clinking of glasses, but she knows she can't go into the pub. She has no money and no way of getting any. Nothing to pawn. She has never sold her body. Not in that way.

When she finally makes it to Hanbury Street, Annie is relieved to find her secret spot is empty. She will curl up for the night, her back against a wall, her head resting on her arms.

As she starts to fall asleep, she feels a dark presence and hears a swishing sound, like something in the wind.

"Who's there?" Annie calls out. The fog is thick, the night icy. No one answers.

She is too weary to keep her eyes open anymore, the pain in her body almost too much to bear. As she drifts off, Annie makes plans. Tomorrow she will see Ted. Tomorrow she will sleep in a bed. Tomorrow she will feel better.

Tomorrow never comes for Annie Chapman.

Before she can even cry out, she sees a sharp blade before her eyes. She raises one hand to fend off her attacker. But it is too late. She feels a sharp stab in her neck. And then Annie Chapman feels no more.

**MORNING ADVERTISER (LONDON)**
September 10, 1888

### ANOTHER MURDER IN WHITECHAPEL

On Saturday morning, about six o'clock, the neighbourhood of Whitechapel was horrified to a degree bordering on panic by the discovery of another barbarous murder of a woman at 29 Hanbury Street (late Brown Lane), Spitalfields. The circumstances of the murder are of such a revolting character as to point to the conclusion that it has been perpetrated by the same hand as committed that in Buck's Row.

The murdered woman, who appears to have been respectably connected, was known in the neighbour-hood by women of the unfortunate class as Annie

Sivvy, but her real name was Annie Chapman. She is described by those who knew her best as a decent although poor looking woman, about 5 feet 2 inches or 5 feet 3 inches high, with fair brown wavy hair, blue eyes, large flat nose; and, strange to say, she had two of her front teeth missing, as had Mary Ann Nichols, who was murdered in Buck's Row. When her body was found on Saturday morning it was miserably clad. She wore no head covering, but simply a skirt and a bodice and two light petticoats. A search being made in her pockets, nothing was found but an envelope stamped "The Sussex Regiment."

# Chapter Sixteen

KENSINGTON, SEPTEMBER 10

At her breakfast table, Maude gives a little gasp as she reads the horrific account in the newspaper. She cannot help it. For a moment the print seems to swim before her eyes.

"What?" Across the table, her husband lifts his head in annoyance from his own newspaper to bark at her.

"It's no matter. I am sorry for disturbing you."

Another woman murdered. And this time, Maude knows the victim. Or she thinks she does. She swallows and inhales a calming breath.

"Where is Emily this morning?"

Maude is surprised her husband notices her maid is not by her side.

"She is attending to a family matter." It is not a lie. Emily Mackie begged off this morning with tears in her eyes, saying she needed to be with her mother and sisters. Though she didn't give her a reason, Maude is sure that the latest murder victim must be Emily's sister.

Maude feels herself flushing under her husband's stare. Thankfully, he returns to his newspaper, and Maude continues reading:

*No knife or other weapon such as would inflict the wounds borne by the deceased was found on the premises, but police speculate that the monster who perpetrated these crimes may have knowledge of anatomy, such as a butcher or a surgeon.*

This time, she's able to suppress her tiny gasp. She steals a glance at her husband. He is not handsome, Maude knows that. His nose is long and aquiline, his eyes are too closely set together, his cheekbones high and thin. He has a hawkish, predatory look to him.

Maude suddenly feels a chill travel down her spine. She doesn't know why.

Like a child, she asks to be excused from the breakfast table, but not before asking what time her husband would like dinner.

"I'm dining out tonight. I suggest you eat a light supper and get to bed early. You seem to be in need of rest."

Maude nods and quickly leaves the room. She has no intention of going to bed early.

Kensington, September 10

*Dear Lucy,*

*I write in great agitation, please excuse the spots of ink! My hand is shaking.*

*I hardly know what to think or write. A moment while I compose myself—*

*Here, I shall try again.*

*There has been another murder in Whitechapel! That is the gist of my great alarm. Did you hear of it this morning? I was sitting at the breakfast table and it took all of my willpower to preserve the appearance of calm as I read the news.*

*But what of it, you wonder? What is it to me or to us, in our comfortable beds in our comfortable homes? I know not, Lucy, but I fear. Yes, I admit I fear some Evil approaching. It approaches even us, who are so well protected, as well as those poor souls on the streets. And Lucy, I am almost certain that this latest poor victim was known to me—was indeed our own maid's sister. I underscore the lines to convey my utter confusion.*

*I will tell you what I know on these pages before I post them to you myself at one of the pillar boxes on the corner. Forgive my haste!*

*Someone came to our servant's door one Saturday morning, about a week ago. I heard raised voices downstairs and went to investigate. I was astonished to see a woman arguing with our Emily, huddled together in the doorway. The stranger had an unprepossessing appearance. Her face was quite florid and she was missing teeth, but her clothing was neat and she was well spoken. That was all I noticed before the woman tore herself away and ran out into the street. Emily would say only that the woman was her sister Annie and insisted the dispute was nothing important. I should have questioned her more closely but just then my husband appeared and asked sharply about the "vagrant" at our door. As I stammered and stumbled to explain, Emily slipped away and I forgot to pursue it. My pulse quickens just from the memory!*

*I press on.*

*Early this very morning Emily requested leave, crying that she must be with her mother and sisters. She left before dawn, red-faced and sobbing. Then I read the newspaper.*

*I cannot help but conclude that Annie Chapman is my own Emily's sister! Emily had asked me once if I could find a job for her in our household. And I refused! Oh, Lucy, if this is indeed the same poor soul, how my lack of charity will haunt me!*

*Now, I have questions spinning helter-skelter through my brain that I must release.*

—*Why did your father invite me and my husband to your home that evening? It always struck me as strange. Is there an unknown connection between my husband and your father??*

—*Why is Lord Rutherford personally supervising the investigation into the Whitechapel murders? Oh yes, I recognized the names Neil and Warren from the press!*

*I am not usually so frantic, Lucy, I assure you. Though I admit to being sometimes headstrong, I am quite known for my calm and rational ways! And I know I take liberties with our short acquaintance in writing this though we've only met twice. I'm sorry that your visit to my home was shortened by my fear that Edward would return early. Still, I believe I can address you in this candid and emotional manner.*

*Lucy, <u>what shall I do</u>? I feel at such a loss. So helpless in the face of evil. Do you really think we should attend the lecture by Miss Cobbe together? Is this detective work really something women can do? Do write and let me know.*

*My husband has left for his office in Harley Street and makes his rounds to patients this evening. I will make haste to post this now—*

*I await your response in a state of the greatest turmoil!*

*Your new friend,*

*Maude*

*Postscript—My goodness, I forgot to inquire about your sleep!! Have you rested well without sleepwalking? I am eager for your reply. Excuse my scrawl!*

Note by return mail, noon

*Dear Maude, How truly awful about your poor, poor maid's sister! I have not yet read of the murder in Whitechapel but will ask Sally to bring me the papers so that I, too, may be fully informed of this horrible tragedy. It is really too unimaginable to think on. How do you bear it? I wish that I could comfort you in person, dear Maude. What monster is preying on vulnerable women like Annie? I shall find an occasion to call on you tomorrow! LR*

*Postscript— it is more important than ever that we attend Miss Cobbe's lecture!*

*Chapter Seventeen*

Constable John Neil crouches down on the pavement and eyes the bloodstain from several angles. With more than ten years on the force, Neil has learned to trust his instincts and collect every scrap of information that might someday be useful to him—who knows when? These greyhounds, now, this is new, but they might be useful. Just look at the nose on this one, quivering already. He pats the dog's neck, waiting while he takes in the scent.

"Now, Barnaby, this here is blood, presumed of Annie Chapman, dead these last two days. What you got for me, old fellow?"

He pulls a piece of fabric from his pocket and puts that too beneath the dog's nose. "Give it a whirl and lead on."

Neil stands, feeling the strain in his calves. He pictures, not for the first time, the toff's daughter with the red hair. He grimaces and watches the dog, which is tugging him down the street, nose on the ground. "That's it, old boy!"

The strange events in Whitechapel disturb him. First Polly

Nichols, now Annie Chapman. And why is Lord Rutherford, that right piece of work, concerned with his daughter's safety when she's in posh Mayfair? Why have Neil watch her house? Are the murders of these women somehow related to his Lordship that he fears for his daughter's safety? But how??

Neil needs to collect more evidence. When in doubt, take another look, do another round, read another article, even.

He takes the international police papers just for that, to read about the latest in crime-solving. There are even some gents who spread dust all around a room and look for finger marks! Not that they know whose they are, but maybe some-day, they could preserve those marks and identify a perpetra-tor. Not this Whitechapel murderer, though. Whoever he is leaves nothing behind to examine. Curse him!

Neil gives Barnaby his head and keeps trailing him, ignoring the curious looks of passersby.

He waves at Mrs. Whitcomb standing in the doorway of her pawnshop and makes a mental note of the five McVay children out on the street again. The tykes all scatter when they see him. Neil sighs. For better and worse, he knows this pocket of Whitechapel like the back of his own hand. And they know him. That is a help and a hindrance in a case like this. They might talk to him, or they might protect their own. Too soon to say.

The dog leads him around a corner onto Commercial Street. Had Annie traveled this way? She must have as the dog seems certain of the scent.

"Good dog!" Neil takes the bit of sausage from his coat pocket and unwraps it to reward the bristling animal, who is shaking with excitement. "Well done, mate."

Then Barnaby picks up a scent on the wind again and Neil hurries after the hound, unsure of where they're going.

Constable Neil follows for several streets until the dog abruptly stops in front of Christ Church cemetery.

"What is it?" Neil looks around. Surely Annie Chapman

did not go through the cemetery? She might have tried to find a quiet spot to rest, but the night watchmen are vigilant about chasing rough sleepers off the benches here.

The dog stiffens and the hair along the ridge of his back stands up. Neil is puzzled. There are no other dogs in the vicinity. No rats. Nothing but a small graveyard with thick yellowish fog hugging the tombstones.

The dog snarls and bares his teeth.

Neil looks again. There is nothing. And then he sees it. A black carriage with two coal black steeds heading down the street.

Once it has passed out of sight, the dog's fur relaxes.

Odd, Neil thinks. The dog must be picking up something, but what?

# *Chapter Eighteen*

KENSINGTON, SEPTEMBER 11

Lucy clutches her dark plum-colored cloak, pulling it closer to her body. It is a cool September day, with a low, heavy sky. More rain is coming. She hopes to get to Maude's home before it does. Sally is accompanying her, walking slightly behind, trying to keep up with Lucy's rapid pace. She's given her maid both an older bonnet and a gray cloak that has gone out of style so that Sally appears respectable, as befits a lady's maid.

The sense of dread Lucy has felt since waking this morning has abated somewhat as she walks with Sally through the busy streets of Mayfair. It's comforting to see men going about their business as if it's an ordinary fall day.

Lucy does not feel that it is ordinary. For the fourth night in a row, she's gone to bed and woken up less refreshed than the previous evening, and with a vague cobwebby nightmare still clinging to her brain. She hasn't been able to make out its shape nor see the spider in the middle, but she feels certain something is hovering, watching her, just out of reach.

Even now, she feels a sense of foreboding, a dark presence near her. Lucy pauses and looks around. Men wearing high, black top hats and long tailcoats are walking with purpose. A stylish carriage and two horses pass by. A news agent's boy is hawking his ware on the corner. And yet, she feels as if she's being followed. Is it her father? Has he sent someone to spy on her?

She told her father that she had received another invitation to tea at Mrs. Hepworth's, and Lord Rutherford seemed pleased and not at all concerned about her going.

Why does Lucy feel as if eyes are watching her? Another carriage passes by, painted black with two black as night steeds, very near where Lucy and Sally are paused on the sidewalk. As it goes by, Lucy feels a rush of cold air sweep across her. A sudden fog descends like a dark cloud. Every hair on the back of her neck rises.

She looks towards the carriage and can make out one sole occupant, a man with startling white-blond hair, clean-shaven, with an aquiline nose, and an intense stare. He seems somewhat familiar, but she cannot place him. His eyes are piercing. They aim straight at her, burning with a metallic fire that seems to look into her very soul.

One of Lucy's hands instinctively goes to her throat. Suddenly she's unable to breathe or cry out for help. She feels as if she might faint. She leans on her maid, who seems unaware of any outside disturbance.

Then the carriage and the strange man are gone, taking with them the icy air and the feeling of suffocation. Is she getting ill? Taking a chill?

"Murder in Whitechapel! Leather Apron strikes again. Read all about it!" The newsboy's cry interrupts her thoughts.

Lucy rushes across the street to where the newsboy is selling papers and asks for the latest edition of the *Daily Telegraph*. Sally offers to carry it for her, but Lucy declines, unconcerned that her dove-colored gloves will be stained with ink.

She skims the front-page article. She has never heard the name Leather Apron before. Is he the murderer of these poor women? She reads the description of the man who soundlessly comes upon his victims with a large knife and feels a sense of alarm.

Lucy then hands the paper to Sally. She is anxious to see Maude and will tell her about the strange man in the carriage. No doubt her friend will set her mind at ease.

Leather Apron preys upon vulnerable, destitute women in London's East End, those who are out in the middle of the night. Surely, he's not riding the streets of Mayfair in a carriage looking for his next victim in the fashionable West End.

Yet as she continues walking, Lucy can't shake the fact that the man had seemed as if he knew her. Not just her outside features but even more than that. As if he could peer into her thoughts and dreams.

As she turns on South Audley Street, Lucy sees the small cemetery next to Grosvenor Chapel. A shudder goes through her when she sees a black carriage stopped by the graveyard. Is it the same one carrying the strange man? She thinks it might be. The horses are dark as ink. The carriage itself is glossy black.

Lucy cannot be sure. But she will find out. She hurries towards the carriage, half hidden in mist though it is the middle of the day, Sally almost running behind her to keep up. The carriage has been following her. She is sure of it.

A white flash of anger rather than fear races through Lucy. She will confront this man and ask what his business is with her. But before she can reach the carriage, the coachman whips the horses and the carriage flies off.

"Miss Lucy, where are you going?" Sally asks when she catches up to her.

Lucy looks around. It's as if the carriage has vanished. She can't hear the horses' hooves on the cobblestones nor see the black carriage anywhere.

"Did you see that, Sally?"

"See what, Miss Lucy?"

"That black carriage that was just over there?" Lucy points to the church and the graveyard.

Sally pauses and looks toward the chapel.

"There's nothing there but that church and cemetery."

"Before. There was a carriage and two horses. It paused right there." Lucy points again.

Sally shakes her head. "Ay, it could have been, Miss Lucy. I was not a looking that way."

Lucy's hands are shaking. The sound of her heartbeat pulses loudly in her ears. She is being followed. She is sure of it. She is not going mad.

"Never mind, Sally," she says at last.

The sky has suddenly darkened. Lucy looks around. A dense fog has descended, obscuring the church from view. The air is heavy with moisture.

"Come, we are late." Lucy tries to keep her voice even, but she is suddenly very afraid.

### Evening Standard (London)
September 11, 1888

## THE WHITECHAPEL MURDER

The scene of the murder on Saturday morning in Hanbury street, Spitalfields, was visited again yesterday by crowds of sightseers, and there was a good deal of excitement throughout the district, due chiefly to the arrests and the many rumours of arrest. About nine o'clock yesterday morning a detective constable arrested a man he supposed to be "Leather Apron."

Altogether, seven people have been detained since Saturday night. So far, however, no trace seems to have been found of the actual culprit.

Sir Charles Warren resumed his duties at Scotland yard yesterday, and during the day conferred with some of the chief officials respecting the murders. Great indignation prevails in the East End because no reward has been offered for the discovery of the murderer.

Dr. Forbes Winslow has communicated to the police his opinion that the murders are the work of one person, who is either a discharged lunatic from some asylum, or one who has escaped from such an institution. He has suggested that all the asylums should be communicated with, and particulars requested respecting the recent discharge of homicidal lunatics, or of persons who may have effected their escape from such institutions. The present whereabouts of such lunatics should, in Dr. Winslow's opinion, be at once ascertained.

# Chapter Nineteen

"Miss Rutherford has arrived," Emily announces from the open door in the back parlor. Though Maude had given Emily time off to be with her family, her maid insisted that working was what she needed. But Emily's tear-stained face has not escaped Maude's attention.

Maude springs to her feet and rushes toward her new friend, then pauses.

"Lucy, you look agitated. Emily, bring us some tea!" Maude takes Lucy's cold hands in hers and peers into her face, which is flushed with color. Emily must have already taken her wrap. "Has something happened?"

Lucy passes a hand over her hair to smooth out the flyaway strands that have come loose. "I am so glad to be here." She continues to hold tight to Maude's hands as she glances over her shoulder.

Maude is suddenly aware of the smallness of her parlor. The attached townhouses in Kensington are tall but narrow, and none of the rooms have the sort of space and light found at the Rutherford's Mayfair mansion. But Lucy does not seem to be looking at the room.

"It's nothing, I'm sure. Or something. I don't know. Just these terrible feelings and a black coach and a strange man." Lucy shudders.

Maude leads her to an armchair by the low fire and waits for more details.

"But Sally didn't see it. Where is Sally?" Lucy seems confused.

"Emily probably took her to the kitchen for her tea." Maude has a sudden realization that she must be the sensible one. At home in Kent, she had been an indulged younger daughter, but now that she is a young matron, she will need to be the practical one with Lucy, who seems so young to her and so very distraught.

Maude listens as Lucy describes her restless nights, her shadowy dreams, and her foreboding about the man in the carriage. Maude nods and murmurs "go on" as Emily comes in with a tea tray and leaves again. Maude pours two cups and hands one to Lucy. They both pause for the rituals of stirring and sipping.

"How very odd," Maude says. "I believe that there must be a rational reason for what you describe, but I'm afraid. I can't account for it."

Lucy's flush has receded, and she looks too pale again, as she had the evening of the dinner party. She shakes her head slowly. "I know what I saw," she says. "Even if Sally did not. I'm so glad that you are taking my terrors seriously though. I doubt myself otherwise."

Maude rises from her chair and retrieves a small leather notebook from the writing desk in the bay window at the back of the room. "Of course I will be on your side, Lucy. We are a team now. Here. Let's be methodical then and list our questions to pursue. My governess, Miss Taylor, always recommended a systematic approach to all inquiries."

Maude smiles at the memory of that lady's shrill lectures. Back then, she had been impatient with lessons and eager for life, but now she wishes she had more people to talk with about books and ideas. Maybe Lucy would be that friend, too.

The women are bent over the notebook, in the middle of composing their list, when Emily reappears in the doorway, looking uncertain.

"Yes?" Maude says.

"There is a man at the door, ma'am."

"Is he looking for the doctor?"

"No, ma'am. He asked for the lady of the house, and he said he'd also like a word with me, with your permission." Emily looks as confused as Maude feels.

Maude frowns. "Is he a gentleman?"

"I don't rightly know, ma'am. He said he was a journalist. He gave me his card." Emily advances hesitantly and hands over the plain white card.

"Central News Agency," Maude reads aloud. The reverse has an address written in pencil. The women exchange a glance and Lucy gives her a tiny nod. "Please show him in, Emily."

They sit in silence as the clock ticks in the corner and footsteps retreat, then near again with a heavier tread. The man who appears at the doorway seems genteel enough to Maude. In fact, he seems unremarkable in any way—of middling height and with nondescript features. His sandy hair is already receding, though his face looks young. The visitor gives each woman a slight bow and remains near the door, as if uncertain whether to enter the room without permission.

"Thank you for receiving me, Mrs. Hepworth. I fear I am interrupting a social call." His voice is cultured at least. Maude gestures for him to enter the sitting room.

"I confess I am curious about your reason for calling, Mr...Hinton." Maude glances at the card in her hand, then gestures toward Lucy. "This is my friend, Miss Lucy Rutherford. And you have met my maid Emily. You say you'd like a word with her?"

"Yes, Mrs. Hepworth," Mr. Hinton says. "My business may perhaps involve her."

Maude feels some indignation rising in her chest. Emily stands in the doorway, her face looking firmly down at the floor. The maid shrinks as if she is trying to escape.

"Mr. Hinton, I hope you are not here to cast any aspersions upon anyone in this household. I do not know you and am inclined to have you removed."

Mr. Hinton rushes back into speech. "No, no, I am not explaining myself well. Please, it is not at all like that. Just bear with me for a moment. I am a writer with the Central News Agency and I am investigating the Whitechapel murders." He looks directly at each woman in turn, assessing their reactions. "You may not know in this part of town that there have been—"

"Yes, yes, we do know." Maude recovers her poise, but she is afraid to look at either Lucy or Emily. "We read the newspapers, though I have no idea if I have read your articles." She gestures toward a chair and waits while he pulls one closer to them. "But what does this have to do with us?"

Should she serve him tea? Maude wonders. What is the etiquette for social calls with a journalist? She has a fleeting thought that Edward would be absolutely livid if he knew about this visitor—and that she has invited him to sit.

But at this nearer distance, Maude can now see that the cuffs of the journalist's coat have been turned inward to hide some fraying. His wrists poke out awkwardly. She suddenly feels protective of him.

Mr. Hinton clears his throat. "The latest victim two nights ago was named Annie Chapman. I believe she is your maid Emily's sister."

Still standing at the doorway, Emily looks up. Tears run down her face.

Mr. Hinton pulls a notebook and pencil out of a worn leather satchel, licks the pencil, and jots something down. "If I may ask a few questions?" Jonathan Hinton looks at Emily and then at Maude.

In a brief exchange of glances, Maude feels that she and Lucy have agreed to collect as much information as possible without revealing any of their own. She waits for the journalist to continue and invites Emily to take a seat. The maid does so reluctantly, twisting her hands in her lap and keeping her gaze on the floor.

"When did you last see Annie? What can you tell me about her?"

They all turn to Emily, who raises her head to reveal a face smeared with drying tears. "We…my other sisters and I… were estranged from Annie."

Maude sees Emily is shaking. She pours her maid a cup of tea and hands it to her. Emily looks surprised to be served by her mistress, but takes the cup and wraps her hands around it.

"She is…she was a good soul, but the fondness for drink is what caused her to be set against us. We are teetotalers. All except Annie. She couldn't abide to be sober."

The journalist nods and writes something in his notebook.

"Annie came to our door last Saturday," Maude adds gently. Emily nods, and Maude waits for her to finish the story.

"She were asking for money…"

Jonathan pauses and looks at Emily, then at Maude and Lucy.

"I heard arguing," Maude prompts.

Emily nods. "My sister wanted money. We had words." Emily places the untouched tea on the table in front of her. "I don't like her coming to my place of employment. It isn't right."

"I don't mean to speak ill of the dead." Emily's voice is thick with tears. "Annie had her troubles but she was a good woman. She slept rough but she wasn't..." Her voice catches in her throat. "She only pawned things not..."

Emily's meaning is clear. Maude nods. "Is this helpful, Mr. Hinton?" she asks.

"My condolences for your loss," the journalist says, looking at Emily. "It is helpful in that it gives me a more complete picture for my articles."

Mr. Hinton pauses. "I'm not sure if you're aware, but the neighborhood is mounting a volunteer patrol now to prevent another attack. The Metropolitan Police are doubling their force there."

"They say the murderer comes and goes like a mist," Lucy adds. "That he's as silent as a jungle cat. And that he may have some anatomical knowledge."

"Yes, on all accounts."

Emily stands, clearly wanting to escape the conversation. "May I go now, madam?"

"Of course," Maude says. "Is that all, Mr. Hinton?"

The journalist shifts forward in his chair. "I do have a question for you, Mrs. Hepworth."

Maude raises her eyebrows at this young man. He's very forward, and she's not sure she approves of him. "I think I've told you everything I know about poor Annie Chapman."

"It's not necessarily about Annie but about your husband, Dr. Hepworth."

"What about him?" Maude is glad her voice sounds even to her own ears. She feels anything but steady at the mention of her husband. She cringes to imagine what Edward would do if he knew of this visit. He will surely find out...

"He is the doctor in charge of a ward for women at Bethlem hospital, is he not?"

"Yes, but if you have further questions about Dr. Hepworth's work, you must speak to him directly."

Maude's cheeks are warm. What could this journalist want to know? Does he know something she doesn't about her husband's work? She wants more information, but she isn't sure how to ask.

Instead, Maude looks down at the notes she and Lucy had been composing and leans forward to adjust her tea cup, closing the notebook as nonchalantly as possible, though her hands are trembling.

The journalist regards the two women steadily. "There is something else." He stops.

"Outside…" Mr. Hinton twists his hands together, looking uncomfortable. "Outside I saw a dark carriage with its curtains drawn just down the street. I had the strangest sensation, a sense of foreboding, a chill…" The journalist seems at a momentary loss for words.

Lucy gasps. Maude jumps to her feet and dashes to the parlor window.

"You saw it?" Lucy asks.

"Yes. But it's gone. It departed just as I approached your home." He frowns. "But whoever was inside made haste to leave with the horses pulling like they were chased by demons."

He looks blankly at his hand for a moment. "But it was odd. I felt as if I were being watched. By something or someone. And there was a strange chill…" He shakes his head. "Forgive me. I am usually a rational man, and I did not mean to disparage your guest."

"We do not know the occupant of that carriage," Lucy says emphatically. "Nor where it came from. But I, too, felt what you describe. The carriage was near the cemetery when I spotted it, and I must confess, I'm relieved not to be imagining things. Will you promise me something, Mr. Hinton?"

"If I can. I have sisters near your age," the journalist says. "You can rest assured that whatever you ask of me, I will keep my promises."

"Very well. If you see that carriage again or find out more information, will you inform me and Mrs. Hepworth?"

"Yes. If I can ever be of service to you, I hope you will consider me an ally. You have my card." He appears about to say something else, then changes his mind and shakes his head.

The journalist comes slowly to his feet and gazes down at them solemnly. Suddenly he seems a little taller than when he had arrived, and friendlier too. Then, with a little bow, he departs, leaving Maude and Lucy alone.

"Should we have trusted him?" Maude wonders. She must have said it out loud because Lucy shakes her head.

"I don't know. He seemed sincere and he too saw the carriage and felt what I did. I think we should cultivate his friendship. Perhaps I should cultivate one of those policemen too!" Lucy smiles, and she seems younger all of a sudden.

Maude frowns at her teacup. The tea has gone cold. "What should we do next?"

"I think we should start where we are. And conduct our own investigation! You haven't said so, Maude, but I fear, with the journalist's line of questioning, that there is some information he must know regarding your husband. Do you have any idea what it could be?"

Lucy leans forward and grabs Maude's hands as Maude shrinks back into her high-backed chair and shakes her head no.

"Does your husband have an office at home?" Lucy asks.

Maude's heart skips a beat, but she nods her head yes.

"Then you must search his rooms, Maude. I see your face. I know your feelings. Are they not my own? I fear my father, too. I quake in his presence at times." She gives Maude's hands a little squeeze and lowers her voice.

"But we can be brave together! You search your husband's belongings to see if you can find out anything about the journalist's suspicions. And in turn, I will search my father's desk to see if there is something connected to the murders. Maybe we will even have a reason to consult Mr. Hinton or Constable Neil again."

Lucy's blush when she mentions the policeman's name is not lost on Maude. Nor her friend's bravery.

"Alright," Maude says at last. "We will investigate together."

∾

Kensington, September 11, dusk

As the heavy air turns into drizzle, Constable Neil stands under a streetlamp, lighting a cigarette. He pulls his hat down low over his brow. The yellow light bathes him in shadow and anyone watching from a window—or a carriage—would have been hard pressed to identify him later. He had stood unobtrusively as the well-dressed young lady in a plum cloak entered the home across the street.

He had stood very still as the unmarked black carriage that had been idling at the corner suddenly jolted into motion and dashed away in a clatter of wheels and snapping whips. And he had watched in silence as a young man had walked up and down the street several times, and entered the same house after her. He lingers until the young man departs again. Then, with one last glance at the home across the street, he stubs out his cigarette and saunters off.

**EVENING NEWS (LONDON)**
September 11, 1888

THE POLICE AT FAULT

Although the utmost vigilance was kept by the large

force of detectives around the district in which the murders took place, no further arrests have been made either in connection with the Buck's Row or Hanbury Street tragedies up to eight o'clock this morning. The search, which has now extended over the greater part of East London, has been, as far as the attainment of any real evidence is concerned, futile. There is only one man under detention at Leman Street Station, and all those who were brought to Commercial Street and Bethnal Green Stations have been released.

# Chapter Twenty

WHITECHAPEL, SEPTEMBER 12

It is late, and Jonathan hurries toward Leman Street Police Station. He still feels unnerved by the visit with Mrs. Hepworth and Miss Rutherford the day before. The sun was shining and the day quite warm when he took his leave, but still he felt cold inside.

Now the temperature has dropped precipitously, and there's a chill in the night air that signals the changing season. There is no moon, but Jonathan makes his way by the gas streetlamps, which cast small pools of light onto the otherwise dark streets.

He walks quickly, anxious to learn about the man the police have in custody, a man they suspect could be Leather Apron.

Jonathan has his doubts. There has been talk of little else in Whitechapel than of the identity of Leather Apron, and he's heard at least half a dozen different names from his sources. Rumors are spreading like wildfire. The Spitalfields district is known for its cabinet and shoemakers, so it's not at all unusual for men to wear leather aprons.

What's more, the district is full of men who fit the vague description of Leather Apron—tall, thin, with mousy hair and deep-set eyes. Jonathan has always felt the area around Mulberry Street, with its two-story brick houses, to have an air of industry about it, and the inhabitants he's met are hard-working men. But now, there's a terror of foreign-looking men in general and those who wear leather aprons in particular.

In Osborn Street, Jonathan even came across an old woman who told him that Leather Apron was probably responsible for the death of a woman last year during Christmas week.

"Her body was found right here," the older woman said, pointing a little way towards Wentworth Street. "Aye, the police never did learn her name, the poor woman, God rest her soul."

Jonathan thanked the old woman for her information. The woman's killer didn't sound like Leather Apron, but now that they had a moniker for the murderer, he was accused of doing all kinds of things—from harassing women and men to brandishing a knife and chasing people down alleyways, threatening to rip them apart.

It was even said that Leather Apron was spotted south of London Bridge and in other far-flung parts of the city. He was everywhere.

The terrified inhabitants of Whitechapel could talk of little else. They gathered in groups on corners to discuss the murders and speculate about the killer. There was always a crowd at the spot where Annie's body was found, Jonathan noticed.

So, he is not surprised when he approaches the police station and finds a small crowd talking outside, even this late at night. Word has spread quickly that the police have a man in custody, and there is a good deal of excitement among the men and women in the group as Jonathan walks by.

Jonathan hopes that Sergeant Thicke, with whom he is friendly, will talk to him about the man in custody. At least, as a journalist, Jonathan could dispel the rumors that were so widely circulating and help calm people's fears—or so he would tell the sergeant.

When Jonathan enters the police station, there is more commotion. A man of slight build with dark hair and a small mustache is just being released. Jonathan notices the man walking with a limp, as if with some kind of infirmity. And though he is told by the constable that he is free to leave, the man looks around anxiously and says he prefers to stay in the precinct.

"I cannot go out there," the man says, waving his hands towards the street. "They will set upon me."

Jonathan thinks this is true. The crowd outside is hungry for blood. They would clearly harass the man and follow him home, taunting him, if nothing else. The fellow can't be Leather Apron. The man seems not at all well in body or mind.

Just then, Jonathan catches sight of Sergeant Thicke and approaches the policeman.

"His name is John Piser," Thicke tells Jonathan. "He has an alibi for the night of Annie Chapman's murder—his step-mother and sister. Recently released from hospital and, while we found a knife on his person, the man's a boot finisher and doesn't use the type of knife we suspect in the murders."

"So you're releasing him?"

"We're still making inquiries, but Mr. Piser is free to leave. You can put that in your article, Mr. Hinton," Thicke says.

"So you don't think he's the Whitechapel murderer?" Jonathan wants the Sergeant to say the words so he can quote him.

Instead, Thicke glances over at Piser, who is wringing his

hands and refusing to leave. The man appears even smaller and frailer, hunched over, as if preparing to be attacked.

Thicke just shakes his head. "That's all the information you need, Mr. Hinton."

Jonathan has seen enough. He is already crafting the description of Piser in his mind and planning his article as he leaves the police station. Piser, with his graying hair and short stature, is a far cry from the description of Leather Apron others have given.

Jonathan fears there will be many more men like John Piser detained and questioned by the police. Just yesterday, he'd attended a meeting of local tradesmen in Whitechapel—respectable men, who'd formed a committee and offered a substantial reward for information leading to the capture of the murderer.

The frenzy and accusations are only going to increase as the citizens of Whitechapel, hungry for justice and anxious that the killings cease, now have a monetary incentive.

The wind has died down but a thick fog is settling in the streets, obscuring his way as Jonathan walks towards home. The sun has disappeared, blocked out by the fog. It's as dark as night.

The voices of the small crowd still gathered outside the police station grow fainter and fainter. After a while, the only sounds he hears are his own footsteps on the pavement.

Jonathan thinks of the neighbors who claim they'd heard and seen nothing the night of the murder. And of one woman who heard something, one set of footsteps—Polly fleeing her killer, in all likelihood. How is it possible that this man—or men, though Jonathan is more and more convinced there is only one murderer—is able to come and go so silently, so stealthily?

For some reason, an image of Lucy Rutherford pops into his head. She was certainly lovely to look at, with her masses of red hair and intelligent green eyes. His sisters would say so and tease him. Jonathan does not feel stirred that way towards Lucy—or any woman.

He picks up his pace, anxious to get home and write his story. He's upon a cemetery before he realizes it, the high stone gate rising out of the fog when he's practically upon it.

Jonathan shivers. A blast of cold air rushes over him. The fog is thick tonight, like a curtain, encasing him in its shroud.

Just then, something darts in front of him. He steps back, shaken. It must be a rat. There are plenty of vermin all over the city. The East End, with its filthy streets, especially seems to breed them. He's seen the creatures everywhere, even traveling over the unhoused as they sleep in the doorways. He shivers again and pulls his top hat down on his head, though it doesn't cover his ears.

There's a slight rustling behind him, and he turns. He peers through the fog, seeing nothing. He is imagining things, letting the hysteria of the day get to him. The murderer kills only women. He has nothing to fear.

Just as he turns to cross the street, he hears a loud swishing sound. Then he's pinned by something or someone. Jonathan cannot move. He's frozen to the spot.

He feels hands on him. Holding him. An urge like he's never felt before surges through his entire body. He longs for something he cannot name or say.

In the next moment, he sees a man's face. Pale, almost white blond hair and blue eyes that darken with a metallic gleam The man has an aristocratic look to his brow and nose. Jonathan thinks he knows him. He has seen him before. But where?

Every fiber of his being is telling Jonathan to run. But he's not given the chance.

The man pulls him closer. Jonathan does not fight the desire that suddenly surges in his loins at the man's touch though his brain is telling him to flee.

Jonathan's breath comes fast. Faster and faster.

Help, he thinks, weakly, but cannot get the word out.

The man bends towards him. And instead of fleeing, Jonathan pulls at his shirt collar instinctively loosening it.

Then he feels a piercing so mixed with pleasure and pain that he cries out loud.

One moment he is in bliss, the next he is released, and there is nothing there. Only darkness.

Jonathan crumples to the ground.

### North London Standard
September 12, 1888

## MYSTERIOUS MIASMA COVERS TOWER HAMLETS CEMETERY

Our correspondent in Mile End reports a most puzzling phenomenon on Friday night last. A thick yellow fog was seen to cover the local cemetery, normally a haven of greenery in environs known for the noxious airs of distilleries. Several passersby noted that the fog did not appear to descend from above but rather lifted from the consecrated grounds themselves, and hovered as if formed and manipulated by a divine or diabolical!—hand. Mr. Robert McCrae, grocer residing at 14 Houndstooth Crescent, said, "I seen plenty of fog and this weren't fog. It were more like sticky stuff that you could lose yerself in. It weren't natural. It set my horses off, it did." Miss Ebenezia Lagrange of Ladderly House said that she was dusting the tombstone of her esteemed father, which she does after every evening service at Saint Middagh's, when the sickly vapor gushed out of the earth as if emanating from an open grave, though there was none. "I shrieked and made the sign of the holy cross," she said. "But not a single soul came to my assistance! It made me cold all over like I had an attack of ague. Nor do I yet feel like myself." Our correspondent found several other witnesses to this strange meteorological issuance who agreed that the fog appeared and disappeared suddenly at dusk that evening and has not been seen since.

# Chapter Twenty-One

MILE END, SEPTEMBER 13

Jonathan is woken by hands going through his pockets. He reaches for the hand and grabs hold of a man's upper arm instead. The thief, startled, pulls back. Jonathan cries out for help. It's a weak, croaked cry that sounds foreign to his ears and which he can't quite get out of his throat. But it's enough to scare the thief, who abandons his mission of searching Jonathan's pockets and takes off with his worn, but serviceable, black top hat instead.

He's disoriented. Though his limbs are weak and heavy, Jonathan manages to sit up. Where is he? He's on the cold pavement outside the Tower Hamlets Cemetery. It's early morning, just after dawn. The sky is brightening. The fog has dissipated, but the color of the air is a sickly yellow, not uncommon in London.

The fog. Jonathan shakes his head. He remembers walking home from the police station. The fog was so thick he could barely see his own hand if he held it out in front of him. He recalls a rat, or some creature, crossing his path.

And then? Then there was a swooshing sound and something came up on him from behind. He closes his eyes and sees a man's cruel face. Or is he imagining this? He's had little sleep these past few weeks and is unsure of whether to trust what he thought he saw.

But what is too shameful to remember is the sense of longing, of desire that stirred in him. He shakes his head again and puts the thought out of his mind. It's preposterous.

Had he fainted? Probably. He must have imagined the man who came upon him as silent as the Whitechapel murderer. He must have been a thief, and Jonathan fainted. He's had only a few, light irregular meals.

Besides, Jonathan has thought of little else but this killer for almost two weeks. His work has cost him much-needed sleep—and perhaps his sanity. After all, he's spent more time on the streets of Whitechapel than he has in his lodging or anywhere else. He needs sleep and nourishing food, that's all.

It takes more effort than he would have imagined to stand. His head is still woozy. He has lost strength in his limbs. What would his sisters say if they could see him now, weak and having fainted? They'd scold him certainly, and fuss over him and feed him tea and meat stews to nurse him back to health.

For a moment, he thinks of his sisters and his mother and longs to be with them in Bath, hearing their chatter and being cared for. But the journey is too far, even if he had the time and the strength to visit. He does not.

The sky is getting lighter. It promises to be a fair day, he thinks. He longs for sleep, and wonders how he is going to be able to walk the rest of the way home.

Fortunately, he spots a hansom carriage with a single horse and driver, no doubt on their way to start work for the day. He waves his arm to signal the driver. Then he plunges his hand into his coat pocket. Thank goodness, the thief did not get his small pocketbook. Though he must look a fright with no hat and rumpled clothing, the driver stops in front of Jonathan and he tells the coachman his address.

It is only when he is home, upstairs in his lodging house, that Jonathan looks in the mirror to assess his state. What he sees shocks him. Not only is he pale, almost white in color, but there's a spot of red blood on his shirt collar. How did it get there? Did he hurt himself when he fainted?

Loosening his collar further, he sees a mark on his neck. Two tiny dots. He puts his fingers on the spot. His neck is tender there, yet he feels his blood pulsing underneath, beating rapidly.

How odd, he thinks. Was he bitten by an insect? Or had the robber done this? Again, Jonathan sees the face of the strange man before him. Suddenly, his head spins. His vision narrows. Blackness closes in. He needs food. Water. Rest. He forgoes the first two as he stumbles towards his bed. Fully clothed, he collapses into a heap and falls into oblivion.

When Jonathan wakes for the second time that day, it is early evening. His landlady is knocking at his door, a sound that has infiltrated his dream. Whatever dream he had is slipping away. He longs to hold on to it, but the knocking has chased it away.

Mrs. Cavendish is standing by his bed, holding a tea tray. Jonathan struggles awkwardly to sit up. She is a tall rectangular woman and seems to loom over him.

"I've brought you some tea," she says, looking at him, her eyes getting wider as she no doubt takes in his disarray. "Are you ill?"

Jonathan's hand instinctively goes to his throat where he found the strange mark. He turns away slightly, in case his landlady can see.

"No," he says. "Just a bit tired. I've been very busy with my work." His words don't sound convincing to his ears. "I very much appreciate the tea," Jonathan continues, looking down at the teapot, cup, and saucer. There's bread and cheese, and it's all Jonathan can do not to grab the hunk of bread and stuff it in his mouth. He's ravenous.

"You're very kind," he says, taking the tray from her.

Mrs. Cavendish continues to stand there, examining him. She seems on the verge of asking him something, but then shakes her head and changes her mind.

"I have some cod liver oil downstairs," she says.

"No. Thank you. This is sufficient. I'll bring the tray down when I'm done."

Jonathan is relieved when Mrs. Cavendish closes his door and he hears her light tread on the steps.

Then he eats as if he's never tasted food before, washing down the bread and cheese with hot tea that he hasn't even bothered to mix with milk.

His rest has restored him. After he eats, he'll wash, and then go to the Central News Agency. He's late with his story about Mr. Piser and his detention at the precinct. How long ago that seems now, ages ago, but it was only last night. Less than twenty-four hours.

Jonathan pushes the tea things aside. He vows to take more care with his health. He can't have another episode like last night.

# Chapter Twenty-Two

He had endured the soul-shredding metamorphosis of becoming a demon when he was abandoned for dead on the fields surrounding the Orange River. Yet he had survived, and when his blood had been drained from his wounds by an inhuman predator, he had awoken changed. Stronger. Stealthier. And when he convinced his beloved Karlien to join him, she too was changed. But not entirely. She could not abide what they had become. It was his love who had convinced him to hide themselves away forever. He had. But no longer.

Now Karlien is gone. And he is immune to human concerns, which now seem to register so faintly as to be imperceptible. What use is love, when he has none himself? What need for gentleness or sympathy, when these emotions interfere with his own survival, his nightly feedings?

Count Vloeken extends a languid hand to the table and picks up a folded linen serviette. He dabs at the corner of his mouth, then studies the red blood staining the perfect whiteness. She had been delicious. Almost as sweet as that young man in the cemetery who had struggled and resisted. He appreciates some resistance.

Vloeken stands and stretches, feeling the energy coursing through his limbs. There is nothing like a good feeding.

He strides to the heavily curtained window and refocuses his energies. It takes a bit of effort, calling humans to him. Animals are easier, and mist and fog the easiest of all. He has the most power at night and under cloud when the smoke from factories thickens, as it often does in Whitechapel, and the least at dawn, as light breaks and drains his strength.

He closes his eyes and directs his will, like a steady beam of light, outward into the London night. With his mind's eye, he can see forms hustling down the busy streets of nearby Whitechapel, pulsing with fears and desires and compulsions.

He wheels away mentally, over mansard roofs, beneath which people dine and sleep, unaware of his telepathic presence. He casts a net for his prey—and waits. The muffled sounds of glasses clinking and card games from the floor below create a steady backdrop, punctuated by the occasional moan or giggle from the floor above. With his heightened senses, the Count hears it all.

He would come. It was time. Vloeken smiles as his mental net closes on another victim. Any moment now... He can be patient when he needs to be, a lurking presence in a tangled web. Tick tock tick.

The door bursts open and crashes against the wall as a tall man in evening clothes stumbles into the room, breathing hard.

"What is the meaning of this?" he bellows into the room. His dark eyes are wild and his greying hair mussed. He stops short as he sees the Count Vloeken straighten and move away from the window. Vloeken's footsteps are silent on the thick carpeting of the gentlemen's club.

"Good evening, Lord Rutherford."

"You! You fiend... You monster!" Rutherford splutters

with rage and advances on the Count, but an invisible hand jerks him back into place, standing in the middle of the room, shaking.

Vloeken smiles thinly. "I have a few words to say to you. Then you may leave."

"I have a few choice words for you, too. Get the hell out of England! How dare you follow me here! What possible purpose—"

This time, an invisible string yanks the lord into silence and his mouth closes.

"I will speak. You will listen." Count Vloeken raises one finger and draws a circle in the air.

Lord Rutherford coughs and clutches at his throat, throwing murderous looks at Vloeken.

"As you see and feel, you have no power here. Your laws and your money—your pathetic scruples—mean nothing to me." The Count waves a hand and Rutherford gulps in air.

"I am the dead arisen. I am the eternal life force." He stills, his arctic eyes ablaze. "And I Am Vengeance."

Rutherford's eyes bulge in his pale face. Again, he tries to rush toward Vloeken and an invisible hand prevents him. His body shakes with the effort to resist.

"You interrupted my repose. Your unholy excavations disturbed my slumbers and murdered my beloved. You have been tried and judged by me. And now I will sentence you. *I will take from you what you have taken from me.*" The last words ring out with chilling severity and echo around the room.

"I have found this secret club of yours." The Count glances around with disdain. "And I have everything you care about ready to crush in the palm of my hand."

"Now, go." The Count turns his back on Lord Rutherford and bows his head.

The window clatters open and an icy wind sweeps through the room. Outside, a flurry of bats weave and squeal in excitement.

Lord Rutherford opens his mouth, his expression wild, and then another blast of cold air pushes him backwards out of the room. The door slams shut behind him.

Mayfair, September 13, midnight

Lucy shivers as a cold draft whistles past her neck. The servants' staircase has bare wood steps, and the cold seeps in through the thin soles of her slippers. She clutches her white gown closer as she creeps down to the kitchen and through the back hall. If she avoids the front rooms, she will miss her father. If she runs into a servant, she can always pretend she was sleepwalking again.

Lucy is perfectly awake now, though, her heart pounding and her mind racing.

For several nights in a row she has tried to search her father's desk, but each night he thwarted her by staying home, smoking in the library and subjecting her to an impassive stare whenever she addressed him. His mind has been so preoccupied of late that he barely notices her.

Her father has never truly cared for her, Lucy thinks bitterly. He blames her for her mother's death, of this she is sure.

She feels her way carefully past the dining room toward the library door. After dining at home last night, Lord Rutherford has finally gone out, which was more his usual wont. Judging by the servants' talk, he's not expected till the wee hours of the morning, which is also typical of him.

By discreetly questioning her maid, Lucy has learned that her father lets himself in with a key rather than disturbing the servants. In the morning, they often find traces of dirt on his dressing room carpet or stains on his evening clothes. The servants, of course, do not ask any questions.

There is no light coming from under the library door, so Lucy gently turns the handle. Locked! How very frustrating!

Undaunted, she tiptoes back to the dining room and squeezes behind the nearest velvet curtain. She's enclosed in shadows now, as the night outside is black. Groping with her hands, she finds the window latch and eases it open. Instantly, a rush of cold spreads over her body and rustles the curtain.

She quickly sneaks through the opening, leaving the window a bit ajar so she can get back in. Her feet sink into the flowerbeds as she hastens to the flagstone terrace that the library windows open onto. She had prepared even for this—by unlatching one window when browsing for a book earlier. She hopes the butler did not check each one when he did his rounds.

No, she is in. With a feeling of satisfaction, Lucy climbs in the unlatched window, rubbing her arms to get her blood moving again. The complete lack of moonlight makes the night seem even colder.

Lord Rutherford's desk would be locked, of course, but she has thought of that as well, over the days and nights since leaving Maude's home. She hasn't heard from her friend yet, but she knows that Maude too would be waiting and plotting, plotting and waiting for the right opportunity to do some sleuthing.

Lucy takes a key from the pocket of her nightgown and inserts it into the top drawer of the desk. In the morning, she will return it to the housekeeper, who will be none the wiser. She makes sure all the curtains are closed and lights her candle. The drawer sighs softly as she eases it open and rummages through the papers within.

Lucy examines one of the papers. It's a receipt for deliveries to a building on Whitbourne Street. Where is that? Her father owns a great deal of property—mines in South Africa, the mansion they live in, an estate in the country that he can't bear to step foot in since her mother died. But why is he paying a victualler for crates of wine and buckets of oysters to an address she's never heard of? She places the receipt back with the other papers.

Lucy holds still and listens for any noise that may signal her father's return. There is nothing, within or without, except the faint stirring of trees and the hooting of night birds.

She searches a bit more but finds no evidence of anything that doesn't look like official government business. Time to leave, she thinks.

Lucy stands. Just before she turns to go, she glances down at the desktop with its embossed leather writing surface. She notices a bit of white paper sticking out from under it. She pulls gently with her finger and one of her father's engraved visiting cards comes loose, a little dented. LORD VINCENT RUTHERFORD. PARK LANE. MAYFAIR. She flips the card over absently and freezes at the sight of her father's familiar handwriting, the letters blocked out in capitals. SOUTH QUAY WAREHOUSES. And a date. August 31.

Lucy remembers that date. It was the night she first walked in her sleep. The night Sally found her. It was the night of a fire on the London docks. And it was also the night that poor woman was murdered in Whitechapel. Does any of this have to do with her father?

Lucy stands, unable to move. Then she hears it. The sound of galloping horses breaks through her paralysis. She shoves the card back under the writing pad and blows out her candle. Someone is approaching at a fast pace.

Now the jingling of reins and the scrape of wheels on cobblestones make her hasten back to the library window.

In a moment she is through it and huddled against the corner of the house, where she can see a carriage rocking from side to side as it careens towards the front door. A driver in a great black cape flogs the horses to greater speed as they make the last curve. A flock of large, dark creatures trail through the sky above the vehicle, their great wings flapping furiously. Are they bats? What on earth?

Lucy scrambles back to the dining-room window, shaking with cold and fear, and takes one last look as she eases the window shut behind her. She gasps as the carriage jolts to a sudden halt in front of the house's entrance. The horses spin and rear as Lord Rutherford leaps from the vehicle and waves the driver away again with an out-flung arm. The great door opens with a loud bang as her father stalks into the house, his breath coming in noisy gasps. He seems angry, very angry.

With growing alarm, Lucy hears the sounds of servants scurrying to greet him. His loud arrival has woken the house. There will be no quiet, unseen return to her bed now. She takes a deep breath and unfastens her hair from its braid. After a swift glance around the room, she takes the key from her pocket and hides it in a decorative vase on the mantel-piece. She removes her thin slippers, soiled with dirt, and tucks them in an oversized urn. She shakes out her limbs and closes her eyes, inhaling deeply and exhaling again, trying to slow her heart rate.

Mustering her courage, she glides through the open pocket doors to the front drawing room and arranges herself as quietly as possible on one of the sofas. Then she waits to be found.

# Chapter Twenty-Three

At half past nine in the morning, Jonathan once again finds himself outside the red brick Working Lad's Institute building, with its soaring high-pitched roof, on 283 Whitechapel Road. He feared he was going to be late, and he'd hurried to arrive before the inquest began.

Since he is known to the constables stationed outside, they wave him in, though he hears the police tell several others to "Move along, please." Bystanders are not allowed inside the public hall today.

Jonathan is here to attend the coroner's inquest into the murder of Annie Chapman. When he enters the large, lofty hall library, he notices a few fellow journalists are already there. He mentally chastises himself for being late as he nods at his colleagues in recognition, and then stands behind them in the back of the room.

Jury members, about twenty men in dark morning coats and wearing serious expressions, begin trickling in and taking their places at a long table. No one says anything other than a brief hello. It is a somber affair.

Inspector Thicke and two other inspectors as well as two constables from the Metropolitan Police stand facing the jurors' table, ready to give their testimony.

Then the witnesses enter the room. Jonathan recognizes some of the same Whitechapel inhabitants he'd spoken to—women and men dressed in their Sunday best, or at least the best clothing that their circumstances allowed. One woman appears on the verge of tears. She keeps worrying her hands, turning them over and over, as if anxious to be gone. Jonathan cannot blame her.

Then comes the coroner's officer with a big black bag, and the coroner himself, who takes his seat at the head of the table. Above the coroner is a portrait of the Princess of Wales, which is only fitting since it was the Royal Highnesses, the Prince and Princess of Wales, who opened the building two years ago.

Jonathan usually enjoys looking at the variety of paintings that fill the walls of this light-filled space—there are several more portraits of the royal family, and many large, bucolic scenes of the English countryside. But not today. His thoughts are elsewhere.

Inspector Thicke begins his testimony by stating how, at ten past six in the morning, while on duty in Commercial Street, several men came running to tell him about a woman's body lying at 29 Hanbury Street.

Jonathan does not look at Inspector Thicke—he is too busy taking notes. He hears Thicke describe finding Annie's body and her personal effects, a small-toothed comb and a white envelope inscribed with the words "Sussex Regiment" on the outside. There were no signs of a struggle, Thicke says. The same was true with Polly Nichols, Jonathan writes. A leather apron, wet with water, not blood, was found near the body. But Jonathan stops taking notes and looks up at the burly inspector when he describes the examination of Annie Chapman's clothing and the crime scene.

Coroner: Were there any drops of blood outside the yard of number 29?

Inspector Thicke: No; every possible examination has been made, but we could find no trace of them. There were a few drops of blood in the immediate neighborhood of the body only. The largest was the size of a sixpence.

Coroner: Did you search the body?

Inspector Thicke: I searched the clothing at the mortuary. The outside coat—a long black one, which came down to the knees—had bloodstains around the neck and two or three spots on the left arm. There was little blood on the outside. The two petticoats were stained very little. No part of the clothing was torn. There were no bloodstains on the stockings.

Then Mr. George Baxter Phillips, divisional surgeon of police, gives his testimony, describing how Annie Chapman's neck was cut with a large knife, and her intestines disemboweled.

And yet, Jonathan thinks, shouldn't there be more blood found at the scene of such a vicious attack?

Despite the warmth of the room, Jonathan feels goosebumps along his flesh during this testimony. His hand unconsciously goes to his own neck. It has been a couple days since his fainting spell, and the two marks have faded considerably, but they are still noticeable. He quickly pulls his hand away, hoping none of his colleagues have noticed his reaction.

Jonathan's head swims as the coroner bemoans the lack of a public mortuary in Whitechapel. And how it is hardly fitting that Annie Chapman's body was brought to what amounted to a shed used by public officials.

Jonathan can't focus on the words. He hears witnesses being called about what they'd seen and heard, but he is finding it hard to breathe.

He feels as if he is being choked. His vision is tunneling

again. No longer is he in the light-filled room. Instead, the dark inky blackness at his peripheral vision is closing in. He starts to shake. He needs air. He wills himself not to faint again.

"Are you alright?" one of his colleagues asks. He is an older journalist, a man named Smith, who had been helpful to Jonathan when he first moved to London.

Jonathan barely shakes his head no, and Smith takes his arm to lead him out of the room. It is a generous gesture, for the journalist will miss the rest of the inquest if he is not allowed back inside.

Jonathan tries not to notice that all eyes are on him as he is led from the library. If he were feeling himself, he would have been highly embarrassed, but he is too ill to care.

The next thing he notices is that he is propped up outside the hall. The sunlight is bright, too bright. It sears into him and he feels weaker, not stronger, in the harsh light of day.

"You took quite a turn there," Smith says, not unkindly.

Jonathan nods. "I...I haven't been feeling well," he manages to say.

"There's a pub just down the street." Smith points down Whitechapel. "Lean on me, and we'll walk there."

"No. I'll be alright. I don't want to be a bother."

"Not a bother at all, mate." Smith is still holding Jonathan's arm, and seems reluctant to let go. The thought of sitting in a dark pub is much preferable to leaning against the red brick building, barely able to stand, and Jonathan is in no position to refuse help.

"Thank you. You're very kind." Jonathan allows himself to lean heavily on Smith as they walk towards the pub. He silently vows to repay his colleague for the kindness. He would think of some way. Journalists value information more than anything else, and if there is something he could share with Smith, he would do it, he told himself, when he was able.

There's no sign of Mrs. Cavendish when Jonathan walks upstairs to his lodgings. His landlady must be at the market, and he is glad for that. He's still feeling lightheaded and very weak, though the lager and shepherd's pie he had with Smith restored him enough to allow him to return home.

Mrs. Cavendish would no doubt ask about his health, and then she'd question him about his work. She, too, was not immune to the gossip and speculation about the Whitechapel murders, and she seemed very pleased that he was investigating and writing about the crimes. He had even heard her bragging to the neighbor about him and his close knowledge of the events.

Jonathan has only ever revealed his work to her in broad brushstrokes. He feels uncomfortable professionally and personally sharing the gruesome details he'd learned at the coroner's inquests with a woman, and his landlady, no less. He never wrote to his sisters and mother about the crimes, only that he was writing about the poor inhabitants of London's East End, though of course they too had probably heard of the murders by now. There was talk of little else in all of England, it seemed.

Jonathan lies down on his bed and closes his eyes. His heart is beating rapidly. He feels feverish and exhausted, and the side of his neck burns when he touches it. He wonders if he should consult a doctor. Perhaps he is in need of medicine of some kind.

He has yet to write his story and get it to the agency. He'll rest for a bit and then go back out. He is so very tired. He doesn't even bother to change but falls asleep in his day clothes.

It is just past dusk when Jonathan is awakened by a noise. At first, he isn't sure if he's still dreaming. A lone mournful howling pierces the silence. Jonathan tries to open his eyes but finds his eyelids are heavy and it takes several seconds before he forces them open. His limbs, too, are not under his control. They are heavy, weighted to the bed.

Is he in a trance, like those caused by the mesmerists he's seen? Not fully awake, but not asleep either?

The room fills with an icy wind. Jonathan shivers. Has he left a window open? He must have.

As he looks towards the window, Jonathan sees a figure take shape, emerging from a mist. Just like the other night, a strange mixture of hot desire and revulsion overtakes him. The figure solidifies. It is the same man from the other night. Icy blue eyes find his. The man shakes back his white-blond hair. And then he smiles, revealing two sharply pointed teeth.

"No. No," Jonathan cries out weakly. "Who are you?"

"I am your future," the man answers. He has a hint of an accent. Jonathan tries to place it. German? No. Dutch.

In an instant, the man is poised over Jonathan as he struggles to rouse himself from bed. One hand casts his long overcoat aside; the other he places next to the pillow supporting Jonathan's head.

An electric current rises through Jonathan's body. This is what he has been dreaming of. This is what he wants.

No. It is not, a small part of his brain tells him.

But it is of no use. Jonathan arches his back and curves in desire, just as the demonic figure plunges his teeth into the side of his neck. He sucks greedily. Jonathan moans in soft pleasure.

The side of his neck is burning, pulsing and burning, but Jonathan does not want the demon to stop. Then abruptly the pleasure and the pain are gone in an instant.

*No,* Jonathan moans. He reaches out a weak arm but comes up with nothing but icy air.

There is a knock at the door. It grows louder and more insistent.

"Mr. Hinton." The voice belongs to Mrs. Cavendish. "Mr. Hinton!" she calls again, louder this time.

Jonathan stirs. Was he dreaming? He struggles to open his eyes.

"In here," he says, his voice weak.

With difficulty, he sits up wrapping the bedclothes up to his neck. "Come in. Mrs. Cavendish. I am…indisposed," he says.

The key turns in the lock, and Mrs. Cavendish enters. "I heard you call out," she says. "And I thought you might be taken ill again."

In her hand is a bottle of cod liver oil. "You do look quite pale, Mr. Hinton. Shall I call a doctor?"

"No!"

Mrs. Cavendish does not turn around and leave, but reaches Jonathan's beside in just a few steps. She gasps.

Jonathan instinctively raises his hand to his neck. His landlady makes the sign of the cross.

"What happened to you?"

Jonathan shakes his head. "It is nothing. A bite. An insect."

Mrs. Cavendish doesn't move, though Jonathan wishes she would go back downstairs.

His landlady rushes to the open window, closes it, fastens the latches, and pulls the curtains firmly closed.

"I am not so easily fooled, Mr. Hinton," she says, standing by his bedside once again.

"Fooled?" Jonathan shakes his head. "It was just a bad dream." But the blood on his fingers says otherwise. He hasn't been dreaming.

Mrs. Cavendish sits on the edge of his bed. Jonathan is not shocked by her action. He is used to women ministering to him. If his sisters and mother were here, they would do the same, fetching hot water bottles and tea and forcing him to rest.

Mrs. Cavendish's ministrations take a different turn. "Shall I tell you a story?"

Jonathan looks at her with surprise. He is too old for bedtime stories. Too weak, in any case. He wants to be alone, but manners forbid him from being anything but polite.

In any case, his landlady does not wait for an answer.

"My late husband Stephen, God rest his soul, was a merchant seaman. He traveled far and wide, from India to Cape Town to places I had never heard of before."

Jonathan is listening, but he can no longer keep his eyes open. His head falls back onto his pillow.

"Go on," he says softly.

"We were never blessed with children." Mrs. Cavendish pauses. "But that is another story. In his travels, my husband met many strange things. He told me about the strangest of all, a being who came aboard the ship and sucked on the blood of the men. A ghastly, unholy creature. A vampire. I would not have believed it if I hadn't seen the marks on my own Stephen's neck. He was weak when he returned and died soon after, but he did not become the thing that he feared."

"What happened to the other men?" Jonathan asks.

"Stephen and a few others set fire to the ship, destroying the undead monster and most of their brothers who were too far gone."

"I see," Jonathan says, though he doesn't see at all. This cannot be real. It must be a nightmare.

"I see those same marks on you now," Mrs. Cavendish says.

Jonathan puts his hand up to his neck. He draws his fingers away. Two spots of blood are visible on his forefinger. So this is not a dream. Or a nightmare.

"You must be very careful," Mrs. Cavendish tells him. "You must not get bitten again, or you could turn into the very evil vampire who attacked you. I will give you something to carry with you that my late husband kept with him always."

The rational side of Jonathan's brain—the journalistic side—doesn't believe in vampires or the undead. There must be some other explanation. But though he racks his brain to think of what it could be, he can come up with no other explanation for the bites, the stranger who has sucked his blood, who both repulses and delights.

Jonathan gnashes his teeth, and a moan escapes him.

Mrs. Cavendish stands, alarmed.

"I have laudanum," she tells him. "It will help you sleep."

Jonathan hears his landlady descend the stairs. In a moment she is back again, and gives him a draught from a dark bottle, which he greedily drinks. Perhaps when he wakes, he will find out that he's been dreaming after all. Or that he's mad? He doesn't know which is preferable.

Then a strange weariness washes over him. The last thing he remembers is Mrs. Cavendish placing a large silver cross by his side.

**THE MUNSTER NEWS AND LIMERICK AND CLARE ADVOCATE**
Saturday, 15 September, 1888

### GHASTLY CRIMES

During the past few days a terrible map has been appearing in some of the London newspapers, indicating the exact localities of the "Whitechapel murders," as the ghastly appalling crimes are called, which have been committed in that locality within the past month. It is one of the most populous neighbourhoods in the City, and the butcheries were carried out in the very crowded parts, and at periods, too, when it seemed almost impossible they could escape detection. All the victims were women of the "unfortunate" class, and they were of the humblest description, whose deaths, poor creatures, could scarcely, one would think, benefit any person.

A few days ago, ANNE CHAPMAN was found murdered in the yard of a cottiered house in the same neighbourhood—her throat was cut, and her body so wantonly and frightfully gashed that one is led to the conclusion he must have been a very demon who did it, to have hacked and slashed the ill-fated woman as he did. No clue has been had to the devilish author of those murders. The police have entirely failed to hunt him down, and the people are in the wildest excitement about him.

Every other morning now, it is anticipated he will be heard of again through some similar sanguinary deed. The crimes are attributed to some insane but cunning wretch who is known as "Leather Apron," and who moves about with extraordinary rapidity and in a mysterious and noiseless manner.

He seems a kind of vampire, who has no regard for female human life, and the police have failed to find him, the residents of Whitechapel have formed a Vigilance Committee of their own to hunt him down.

# Chapter Twenty-Four

"It's true. He's no ordinary character," Sir Charles Warren tells Lord Rutherford.

The two men are sitting in Lord Rutherford's large office, the evening papers spread on the desk between them.

"We have constables patrolling every spot in Whitechapel every twelve minutes, Your Lordship. Still, our police have no sooner turned the corner, then this fiend emerges from the shadows to commit his brutal crimes."

"What are you implying?"

"As you said, this criminal is no ordinary man." Warren leans forward and lowers his voice. "You and I both know he is no man at all."

Lord Rutherford leans back from his large mahogany desk and crosses his hands across his vest.

"You believe that fiend is to blame for these murders?" Lord Rutherford slams his fist on the desk on top of the newspapers. The ink will stain his hand, and later his clothing, he'll realize.

"You were supposed to have taken care of that demon in the fire."

Warren opens his mouth to respond and then closes it. Rutherford knows he's at a loss for words. What can the Commissioner say? Still, there's a look of defiance in Warren's eyes. And if Lord Rutherford were to put words to the look, they would be accusing. It was his mining expedition after all that unearthed something unholy.

And what remains unspoken between the two powerful men is that this fiend found transport on a shipment of diamonds from South Africa—Lord Rutherford's cargo—that included not only the raw gems from his mine in Kimberley but also a monster worse than they could ever have imagined.

"We are not certain this Leather Apron is him," Warren says after a long pause.

"Don't call him that!" his Lordship shouts. "It's ghastly. And for my part, a hoax by some journalist trying to make a name for himself. The press is almost glorifying the killer. The newspapers have far too much free rein."

Rutherford is breathing heavily and suddenly feels too hot in his suit and waistcoat. He remembers the heavy pall that hung over his meeting with the cursed Count. The sense of power that filled that room at his club and his own utter powerlessness.

"I don't see it that way, Your Lordship," Warren says. "There is nothing heroic about this killer. But I do agree the letters in the press have stirred up an epidemic of fear and frenzy that makes our job more difficult. Scotland Yard is also under attack. The papers are full of this killer's ability to evade detection and our inability to stop him. Even the ones that speak of the force favorably only emphasize how this killer is able to move unseen, unheard, and leave without a trace."

"So who else could the killer be?" Rutherford snarls. "Who

else could evade Scotland Yard so thoroughly and butcher these women so brutally?"

"It is true, there was little blood found at the murder scenes…" Warren pauses. "Nosferatu," he continues, his voice low, "could account for that."

"I do not countenance that name either. Though you have heard of his kind in your archeological travels, this demon is beyond my ken. He presented himself to me as a nobleman at first. I did not—and I still do not—fathom the depths of depravity and immorality of this undead killer. It is your job to track him down and destroy him. And in that respect, I agree with the press."

Lord Rutherford's face is red and hot with anger. With a violent motion, he sweeps the newspapers onto the floor.

"We need more specialized resources to apprehend the fiend—whether he is human or inhuman" the Commissioner tells Rutherford. "And I must be discreet at all costs. I cannot very well alert my patrol officers to carry iron stakes, can I?"

Though he agrees with Warren's words, Lord Rutherford doesn't care at all for his tone.

"What do you propose, then?" Rutherford steeples his hands together and notices the black ink on his palms and fingers.

"We must develop a special force, a secret force, to combat the Whitechapel fiend. And this cannot be known to the press or the public. There would be untold ridicule I'm sure if the press knew what we were doing. And hysteria in the public if they suspected that the slayer of these women was not of this world at all."

"I will see that you get the funds," Lord Rutherford says. "And I expect a report on this secret force. I trust you will employ the utmost discretion when you recruit your team?"

Warren nods. "Of course, Your Lordship."

"Keep them in the dark as much as you can. And you'll continue with the patrols, of course."

"Indeed. I cannot rule out another killer, a copycat, or a lunatic who craves publicity. As I mentioned—"

"Yes, yes, different murder scenes. You do what you think is best. But I want this fiend apprehended before he commits another murder. And if there's a copycat killer, or lunatic, I want him stopped, too. That is all."

Lord Rutherford rings the bell for his tea. He does not invite Warren to dine with him. He's glad to see the Commissioner go and does not bid him farewell. He wants results, not theories of murderers and crime scenes and blaming the press. He will give Warren a few weeks, and if he can't deliver, well, Rutherford will have to find someone else to do the job.

He'd listened to Warren before, over a month ago. Fire would destroy the demon, he was told. Lord Rutherford was initially skeptical, but he went along with the Commissioner's recommendation. After all, Warren was an archeologist used to unearthing ancient secrets. Surely he must know about demons such as the one in Whitechapel?

Little good that did, he thinks. Perhaps he was wrong about Sir Charles from the start? Is he capable of doing the job?

Rutherford rings his bell again, louder this time. Then he stands up. He needs something stronger than tea. He hasn't been back to the club since the Count threatened him there. He rarely goes to the club he bought for a pittance. The memory of his last encounter there unnerves him still—and it was too humiliating to tell Warren about. The man better deliver results. And soon.

~

Kensington, September 18

*My dear Lucy,*

*What a week it has been since we met in this very room. I wonder at your determination—enduring the risk of discovery that night and awaking to your father's angry face. Do you think he suspects you of something? Pretending to sleepwalk was a stroke of genius! Are you sleeping at all?*

*I must make haste now to tell you my own discoveries, such as they are. Please excuse the scribble while I race to seal this letter before my husband's return this morning. He too may suspect…and his fury would be— My hand is shaking!*

*I must begin at the beginning.*

*I took your encouragement to heart and searched my husband's dressing room the very next day. That is a simple matter because our rooms adjoin, and I need only wait until he leaves for his office. Then I may retire to my room and search at my leisure, though I took care to leave everything exactly as I found it. Edward is quite particular about his belongings—about everything, really.*

*I found nothing of interest. Edward has the usual number of stockings and cravats, all folded meticulously. His collars are well starched. Indeed, I thought that if I were caught I could always claim to be checking on the upstairs maid's duties. That is Emily, whom you met. She appears to keep our linens in good order.*

*Really this campaign (Is that the right word? Do we see a battle ahead?) has already made me wonder at the sheer number of dead ends necessary to any fruitful inquiry. How curious. The only thing I noticed in Edward's dressing room was a surprising amount of ash in the grate. Does he keep his dressing room so well warmed or has he been burning papers there? (This reminds me, dear Lucy—please ~~destroy~~ BURN my letters after you receive them! I shall burn yours as well. I sound quite dramatic but if we are committed to this investigation we may go all in, as they say!)*

*I digress.*

*It took me several days to find an opportunity to search my husband's private desk. As you may have noticed, Edward does not have his own desk in our parlor with mine. Rather, he keeps a small office on the top floor, near the maid's quarters, where he manages his private correspon-*

*dence and accounts. He keeps that door, at the top of the staircase, locked and carries the key in his waistcoat. I was quite stymied as to how to enter it until I realized that the simplest solution is always best. I asked Emily if she had cleaned the master's office. She said, no, she dusts there on Thursdays when he leaves early for his supervisory visits at Bedlam. (I know I shouldn't use that common term for Bethlem but that's what I call it in my mind—Bedlam!) Emily said that the master does not trust her with the key but leaves the room open for one hour only, until he returns.*

*So I bided my time—in a state of some anxiety—until this morning, and when Edward left for the hospital and I heard Emily head up the stairs I waited a few moments, then followed. I found her with a mob cap and duster busily cleaning a room I had hardly ever seen. It was full to the brim with storage cabinets and massive volumes laid in stacks on top of each other. It was not at all like Edward's usual tidy ways. A small desk was crammed in front of a window overlooking our street, where I now realize Edward can view anyone coming or going from our house.*

*"Emily! My gloves need attending. The seam is worn though here," I said to her. I admit, Lucy, I had opened that seam myself with a darning needle. "I need them before my morning calls, if you please."*

*I do not like to take that tone with my servants, but I had less than an hour in the room and needed Emily gone. We had some back and forth in which she reminded me that I had other gloves but I managed to shoo her from the room and waited while she clattered down the stairs with my gloves.*

*Well, I must come to the point. The room was small but too full for me to search comprehensively. I raced from drawer to drawer, opening and closing them and scanning the room for anything that struck me as out of place when I saw it, among other identical bound volumes in a pile. The volume looked like an ordinary photographic album, like you might see on a drawing room table for visitors to peruse. But what is a photographic album doing in my husband's office?*

*Lucy, I blush to write this but the album was full of cartes de visite and cabinet cards of ladies in various states of undress. Some were quite nude. Many were posed on beds in contorted positions. Even writing this, I feel a wave of humiliation seize me. My own husband! I confess to you,*

*Lucy, that I have few romantic notions left about marriage, but I did and do believe in respectability, in the importance of moral principles. I had to force myself to examine this…evidence…in the impartial manner of an investigator. And I noticed something quite strange: they all bear the photo-graphic stamp of Bethlem Royal Hospital. Now, Lucy, I knew from bits of conversation overheard over years with my husband that the hospital employs a photographer to document cases of insanity for medical purposes. But this beggars the imagination. What do you suppose these so called men of science do with these indecent photographs????*

*One last line as I leave you to ponder the eternal mystery of the male brain. You won't believe this, but in another drawer I also found a bundle of hundred pound notes! I didn't have time to count them as I heard Emily on the stairs, but I am quite sure of what I saw. I hastily closed the drawer and scanned the room for any evidence of my search. Luckily, if Edward were to notice any disruption, he would blame it on Emily. That is not well done of me, I know. And I was just now talking of moral principles as I search my own husband's belongings for wrongdoing! I blush at myself. Ever since poor Annie's demise, I have felt like quite another person. To think that if I had but had the Christian impulse to give that poor soul a place, she might be alive today! Lucy, it tears at me. But that is a cross I must bear. Now I must face these facts too.*

*Oh Lucy, we must meet! I need a comforting shoulder to lean on as I cogitate these new facts and a trusted friend to speak plainly with!*

*Please let me know when we can contrive another tea. AND BURN THIS NOW!!*

*Yours in haste,*
*Maude*


*Postscript: Do you think we can glean any more information from that journalist if we were to meet with him?? Do we really dare attend Mrs. Cobbe's lecture tomorrow?? Stop—I hear my husband's carriage at the door! I must compose myself.*

# Chapter Twenty-Five

Suddenly, this seems a terrible idea. Maude reaches out a gloved hand and pulls open the heavy wooden door to the parish hall. A discreet plaque reading VICTORIA STREET SOCIETY tells her she is in the right place, but she still feels palpitations thumping in her chest. She'd asked Emily to accompany her, and though her maid was puzzled, she hadn't asked any questions on the ride to the meeting.

Maude enters a high-ceilinged room, filled with rows of chairs. A low stage occupies the far end of the room, where a tall lead-paned window lets in a bit of London gloom. There are women everywhere, settling into their seats, removing their hats, and conferring in low voices. There is not one man among them.

"There you are!"

Maude stifles a shriek as a hand grabs her elbow. She whirls around to find Lucy grinning at her, unapologetically.

"Oh, I...Miss Rutherford. Lucy, I mean." She tries to regain her composure. Lucy, of course, looks calm as could be.

She's dressed smartly in a walking outfit with a small bustle and a tailored coat with fringed epaulets on the shoulders. She looks quite the "New Woman" in this garb. Sally is by her side, and Lucy tells her maid to take Emily and find themselves some tea.

"At last. We are here! What an adventure! I told my groom to bring the carriage round in an hour. Let's find a seat in the front row," Lucy says.

Maude hurries after her friend, casting quick glances along the way. The assembled women range in age from spotty-faced girls to matrons, and span a range of social classes, she thinks. There are some whose threadbare cloaks may cover worn or outmoded dresses.

They huddle in small groups near a table outfitted with a large pewter urn of tea and a towering plate of iced buns. There are a few women in the rough homespun of the servants' hall or the plain gray wool of the sisters who tend the unfortunates in the East End, bearing nutritious foods or primers for the children. She has heard of those lady philanthropists and marveled at their courage and independence to venture so far east.

A cane raps against the floor as she and Lucy take their seats. "Attention!" a loud voice bellows. "We have much to cover! Take your seats, ladies!"

The woman on the stage is squat and gray-haired but has an undeniable energy. She has small eyes like raisins in a doughy scone, and flushed red cheeks. Her accent gives away her Irish origins as she orders several other women to move a lectern into position on the stage. She bustles toward it and raps again with her cane. Chairs scrape against the floor. Then the room quiets.

"I am Miss Frances Power Cobbe," the lady says.

She pauses and looks out from the stage, as if to let her authority settle on them. For a moment Maude feels her direct gaze, and then it continues down the rows of chairs. Maude shifts uncomfortably. She wants to turn around to see how crowded the room is, but she feels as embarrassed as a schoolgirl fidgeting before her governess.

"I believe women are as much God's creatures as men and deserving of equal rights before the law, as wives, widows, or spinsters. I believe animals have souls and feel pain so they should be treated with the respect we afford each other. I am a proud daughter of Erin and an unrepentant spinster myself." Here she pauses again and for a moment Maude thinks the woman's eyes actually twinkle.

"I founded the Victoria Street Society to advance the causes of women and animals, unfairly linked together as inferior creatures to the almighty MAN." The last word booms out and Maude hears a few murmurs, whether cheers or jeers she cannot tell.

Maude twists her gloves in her hand. "She seems quite the…firebrand," she whispers to Lucy, leaning in.

"Shhhh!" Lucy sits bolt upright, vibrating with attention.

"We are building an army, ladies, to fight for our just cause! These here are my lieutenants." She spreads her arms to either side to encompass the row of women on the stage behind her, all nodding approvingly as Miss Cobbe speaks.

"To be treated with respect we must have POWER." She gestures to herself with a smirk. "We must have AUTHORI-TY." She bangs her fist on the lectern. "And"—her voice drops to a lower, gentler register—"we must have *skills*, my muckers. Aye, indeed, we must educate ourselves and prepare ourselves for a battle against the forces of oppression. Are there men lining up to teach us what they know?"

She shakes her head as she peers around the room again. "Are there men inviting us into their institutions? The university? The church? The Inns of Court? Or now the new police force?"

She lets her unanswered questions sink into the audience. "That is why we must teach ourselves."

Maude believes Miss Cobbe is looking directly at her, staring into her soul. Or is she imagining it? Unconsciously, Maude has been holding her breath, so engrossed was she in listening to every word that this courageous woman spoke.

Suddenly, Maude thinks of her husband. If Edward knew…but no, he could never know that she was here. She shudders at the thought of what he might do. She searches the audience, fearfully, for Emily. Will she tell on her? She finds the maid standing with a clutch of other women, transfixed.

"You may have heard of the horrors in Whitechapel," Miss Cobbe says. "There is a monster at work preying on the most unfortunate amongst us. These women are our sisters as well. And what have the police done? Have they made any arrests? No. They have not."

Maude's heart beats faster. She feels a connection to Miss Cobbe's words and a connection to Annie Chapman, through her maid. Again, her guilt about Annie stabs her in the heart. But what can women such as herself or Lucy do?

"Women are ideally suited to police work," Miss Cobbe continues, looking out from behind her lectern. "We are verily invisible, wherever we go. We are trained by centuries of dependence to listen and observe carefully. And most of all we are *underestimated*."

Maude finds herself nodding in agreement.

"This is no idle dream, mates. We are already training women in stealth, weaponry, and self-defense. The working men have a Vigilante Association? Well, we have our own, my fellow females! So I ask you—are you with me?" Miss Cobbe's voice rises again, and she straightens her spine.

Suddenly she seems to Maude a veritable Amazon. All around her she hears women excitedly muttering and moving around. Yet she also hears heels retreat toward the entrance and then the heavy door slams shut behind a wave of women leaving in a huff.

This is risky, Maude thinks. She is very bold, this Miss Cobbe.

Lucy, she notices, still has her eyes locked on the speaker, her expression serious.

"What do you think?" Maude whispers.

Lucy turns to study Maude. "I think I've been waiting my whole life to do this."

Bath, September 19

*Dear Jonathan,*

*I write at the request of our dear mother, who is beside herself with worry about you. We all are, in fact. We think of you always, especially now having just learned the terrible news in Whitechapel. It has reached our local papers. What evil stalks the unfortunate women there?*

*However, I write not of the murders—the word is too awful almost to commit to paper but, as the oldest, you know I have never shied away from the unvarnished truth—but to find out how you fare. We have not heard from you for the past fortnight, and this worries all of us tremendously.*

*Are you well? I can only imagine that you are so busy with your journalism work that you have little time for much else. Are you taking care of your health? I hope so. Know that you are precious to all of us.*

*Mother even thought of making a visit to you soon to see with her own eyes that you are well. I have dissuaded her for the moment, but you know how she is once she gets a thought into her head.*

*I will not ask you more about your work. Instead, I will tell you the news from Bath in hopes that it may lift your spirits. For I know that you are working very hard and must be in the thick of it. Otherwise you would have written to us by now.*

*Our dear Elizabeth has accepted a position as a governess for two young children in Bristol. We will miss her, but the placement is with a good family and...*


Jonathan cannot read the rest of the letter. It is true he has not written to his family in the past fortnight, and yet, what could he say that wasn't a lie? His mother and older sister were too perceptive and would see through any attempts to assuage their concern.

He can think of nothing else but the Whitechapel murders and his own situation. Despite Mrs. Cavendish's tale, Jonathan cannot believe he was bitten by an unholy creature. And yet, he cannot deny that he feels something new inside him, something not quite himself. As a journalist, he's always been adept with words, but he has no words for this strange sensation.

And he can't help but wonder, is the same demon who attacked him killing women in Whitechapel?

Mrs. Cavendish had given him a heavy silver cross to wear. But being a rational man, he'd left it on his bedside table.

And since that awful night, Jonathan has a fear of returning to his room, a fear that someone—nay some *thing*—will visit him again if he sleeps. Now he thinks of his bed not with longing for rest, but as a place of terror where he is tortured by both desire and revulsion for something he cannot name.

So instead of sleeping, Jonathan spends his nights walking the streets of Whitechapel. He is more intimately acquainted with the streets, back alleys, and inhabitants of this section of East London than the vast majority of his journalism peers. And in his fevered state, he is producing article after article, about the murdered and the living, whose lives are more hellish than even he can describe. He is quite proud of this description in his latest article, which appeared in the *East and West Ham Gazette*.

**East and West Ham Gazette**
September 19, 1888

The Whitechapel tragedies have an aspect which
should not be disregarded, though only of the nature
of a side sight. The veil has been drawn aside that
covered the hideous condition in which thousands, tens
of thousands of our fellow creatures live in this
boasted nineteenth century. In the heart of the wealth-
iest, healthiest and most civilized city in the world we
have all known for years that terrible misery, cruel
crime and unspeakable vice—mixed and matted
together—lie just off the main thoroughfares that lead
through the industrial quarters of the metropolis.

Annie Chapman spent her last few days in a wretched,
narrow street, with houses of the most miserable class,
nearly all of whom are let off in single rooms or part
of a room. The house where the last murder was
committed had no less than six families, all toilers for
daily bread, some of questionable honesty or sobriety.
There is a continual going out and returning; some
work at the markets, some at the docks; one is a
cooper, another a carman, some of no occupation.

# Chapter Twenty-Six

WHITECHAPEL, SEPTEMBER 29

"You take this one. A journalist at Central News Agency forwarded it. It's addressed to The Boss." Constable Neil tosses a dirty envelope across a desk to Constable Shelley.

Since Neil found that wretched woman he's been off his beat and on "special assignment." When he isn't tailing a certain red-haired young lady, he is in a straight-backed chair that makes his arse ache, sorting a huge pile of post-cards, envelopes, and packages wrapped in string and brown paper.

Since August, these tips have arrived in a never-ending stream from local busybodies, amateur sleuths, and pranksters, all professing to help catch the murdering fiend. Almost all of them came in through the post, but some were dropped off and this one went to the press. The Commissioner wants them to read them all, though the task was what some wag had called *herculean*.

Neil reaches for a tin pot on the nearby hob and pours himself some more weak tea. He'd prefer a pint by this time of day but that wouldn't keep his eyes open, would it? Already past seven and tea time. He sighs. It will be another late one.

"Can't read the postmark," Shelley says. The letter had clearly been opened and read over at the Central News Agency, then passed along.

"*Dear Boss,*" Shelley reads aloud, smirking. "*I keep on hearing the police have caught me but they won't fix me just yet. I have laughed when they look so clever and talk about being on the right track.*" He pauses and leans back in his chair. "Don't they all sound the same, eh, Neil?"

"*That joke about Leather Apron gave me real fits,*" Shelley continues reading. "*I am down on whores and I shan't quit ripping them till I do get buckled. Grand work the last job was. I gave the lady no time to squeal.*" His voice slows as he reads on. Without pausing in the reading, both men lean forward.

"*How can they catch me now. I love my work and want to start again. You will soon hear of me with my funny little games. I saved some of the proper red stuff in a ginger beer bottle over the last job to write with but it went thick like glue and I can't use it. Red ink is fit enough I hope ha ha. The next job I do I shall clip the lady's ears off and send to the police officers just for jolly wouldn't you. Keep this letter back till I do a bit more work, then give it out straight. My knife's so nice and sharp I want to get to work right away if I get a chance.*" Shelley stops reading and looks up at Neil. "It's signed—*Good Luck. Yours truly, Jack the Ripper.*"

"Let me see." Neil reaches for the page and scans it. "One page, proper hand, decent spelling. There's a postscript here." He reads aloud. "*Don't mind me giving the trade name. Wasn't good enough to post this before I got all the red ink off my hands, curse it. No luck yet. They say I'm a doctor now. Ha ha.*"

Shelley shakes his head. "Not like the others, is it? Jack the Ripper? Gives me the creeps that name does. And those ha ha's at the end…"

Neil studies the paper in his hand, frowning. "Agree. This wrong 'un knows the crimes, reads the papers at least. He could be a gent pretending to be a regular mate— or just a loony. Let's show this to Anderson."

He stands slowly, knees protesting from the hours at his desk. The two men walk without comment over to the head detective's desk at the back of the large open crowded room. Since the second murder, Anderson has been keeping long hours, too. They all have.

Neil feels again the bit of pride that puffs his chest when he puts on his uniform in the morning and walks his beat at night. He had done well at that inquest, telling about finding Polly Nichols's body. He wishes he were back out on the streets now, dark as they are. He's had no more nightmares since that first night. Just uneasy dreams of the miss with the hair that reminds him of County Wicklow, though he hasn't been back in years now. The witchy one who draws his gaze more than she should. *Lucy.*

The two men wait as Anderson scans the letter impatiently. "Hoax," he declares, dropping it on his desk. He picks up the envelope and studies it. "But go to Central News Agency and find out who got it. You hear this part?"

Anderson picks up the letter again. "*Keep this letter back till I do a bit more work, then give it out straight.* This nutter wants us to release the letter. He has a *trade name*, the bounder! I wouldn't put it past those journalists to float this boat themselves. Go check them out."

Anderson removes his reading glasses and pinches the bridge of his nose. "Go on then!"

## EVENING STANDARD (LONDON)
### September 29, 1888

Because they have not yet been able to lay their hands upon this fiendish criminal, it does not at all follow that Scotland Yard is utterly incapable and corrupt. The unprecedented difficulties which the police have had to encounter in their search for this wretch ought not to be forgotten. He has, so far, left them nothing to go upon.

There is not a weapon, not a button, not a fragment of clothing, not a footprint, to help them.

The slayer of these poor women has been seen by no one. His sanguinary work is done almost in a moment and he vanishes without leaving a trace.

# Chapter Twenty-Seven

WHITECHAPEL, SEPTEMBER 29

The pelting raindrops don't bother Elizabeth Stride as she walks towards Queen's Head Pub. It's just after 6:00 p.m. when the heavens open up and sheets of rain lash the dirty cobblestoned streets of Whitechapel.

Elizabeth, Liz she calls herself now, has six pennies in her pocket and is eager to spend it. She earned the money cleaning rooms at 32 Flower and Dean Street, a large lodging house with over a hundred beds crammed in it. Hard work, but Liz was used to it. She has worked as many things: servant, coffeehouse proprietor, charwoman, and prostitute, though she never considered the last a profession of choice.

Liz has neither an umbrella nor coat to protect her from the elements. She does have a cheap, black crepe bonnet which nicely covers her brown hair, now threaded with streaks of gray. The bonnet was a castoff from the woman she calls her sister, though she is no blood relation. In reality, the bonnet is too big for Liz's head, so she stuffed it with folded newspaper in the back to keep it secure.

Liz looks up at the darkening sky and lifts her face to feel the fat, cool drops of rainwater run down her cheeks. Most of the men and women are scurrying along the East End streets, cursing the rain, eager to find shelter. Not Liz. To her, the rain is a blessing.

That's what her father always said. Rain was a welcome sight on her father's farm in Torslanda, Sweden. A gift from the heavens, he said.

An image of her girlhood flashes through Elizabeth's mind. Even at forty-five years old, she still vividly remembers her childhood as a happy time. She can almost see the golden fields of grain, hear the cows lowing in the distance, and smell the hay stacked high in the barn.

The bucolic vision vanishes as quickly as it came. Elizabeth curses loudly as she steps into a deep puddle, soaking her old leather, spring-sided boots and splashing filthy rainwater on her stockings and petticoats. A string of profanity erupts from her mouth that she's powerless to control.

Liz is powerless over much of her body lately. She has trouble seeing clearly. She can't get her legs to move the way she wants them to. The right side of her body is often numb. And she has fits that later she doesn't remember. Though this last problem proved helpful the last time she was arrested for drunk and disorderly conduct.

She peers around in the rain and hopes not to see that Constable Neil who arrested her the last time. He'd taken pity on her, though, and suggested she see a doctor.

"Let this be the last I see of you," Constable Neil had said. "You get yourself to a hospital and find something that cures you. Not the drink."

Liz carries on walking towards Commercial Street in her wet boots, muttering to herself. She squints to try to ascertain the deeper puddles, but to no avail. Her eyesight is blurry and getting blurrier, and there's a pain behind her eyes that never abates. A few drinks will help.

Then she'll return to Flower and Dean Street and the dilapidated lodging house she calls home. It is one of the better doss houses in a street that some think of as the worst in all of Whitechapel. Liz has stayed at far worse places overrun with bed bugs and rats, often running over her very body, and her nostrils filled with the stench of human excrement, urine, and unwashed bodies. Flower and Dean Street is not pleasant —but at least number 32 is clean, or cleaner, thanks to her, and the rooms are better ventilated than most.

Liz has known many other homes in her lifetime. Her family's cozy farmhouse in Sweden, grand homes where she'd worked as a servant, others more modest where the mistress of the house was not much older than she.

She'd lived with her husband, John Stride, above the coffeehouse they were trying to run on Upper North Street until they'd had to give up the business with nothing to show but debt.

Liz has done stints in the workhouse. When she was younger and prettier—when men would often comment on her blue eyes, wide forehead, and shiny brown hair—she worked in small rooms owned by a madam who rented out the beds.

She doesn't think of that now. She thinks only of the gin she will drink to soothe her ailing body and mind. Then she'll have dinner at the doss house—a bit of potato, bread, and cheese, if she's lucky.

Liz tightens her checkered neck scarf to keep out the blowing rain and wind, and puts her head down as she walks. She knows the way, even if her feet sometimes feel wooden and don't cooperate. She doesn't know why her body is failing her. She is older, yes, and has worked hard her entire life, scrubbing, cooking, cleaning. Is it the syphilis she had when she was younger?

Never mind that, Liz, she tells herself. That is yesterday's news.

When she returns to 32 Flower and Dean Street after her time at the pub, Liz is pleased to find people she knows gathered in the kitchen of the doss house. A long wooden table and bench hold several men and women. There's a coal fire burning in an open fireplace with a grate where a few potatoes are roasting. The air is warm and smoky, but Liz doesn't mind. It's a welcome change from the elements.

She takes off her bonnet and black cloth jacket, both now soaked from the rain and smelling slightly. She places them near the open fireplace, warms her hands, and listens to the talk of the doss lodgers who are on about their favorite subject.

"At least the rain might keep away that Leather Apron murderer," says one woman.

"The police ain't doing nothing to capture him, neither," says another.

"Ay. They don't care about women like us," Liz joins in. What follows next is a string of profanity about the police, whom Liz has no fondness for nor faith in. She cannot help her outbursts. She wonders if she is going mad.

But no. She has good cause to loathe the police. Any police. She remembers what it was like in Sweden to be hounded by them. She was considered a "public woman" and put on their register of shame. She was subjected to examinations, her body roughly inspected for signs of disease. And then she was incarcerated even though the disease was not her fault. She never gave up the name of the man who put her in the family way. The baby didn't live. But she lived and has suffered ever since.

"Liz," says Catherine, one of the few women she is friendly with, "we agree with you. If the police had cared about poor women they'd have caught Leather Apron by now. But there's no need for that kind of language. Why don't you rest a bit and sit here on the bench?"

Liz doesn't sit down. Though she cannot read, she hears

the newsboys' shouts about how ineffective the Metropolitan Police are. And once her mind is on a certain track, she can't give it up. What are the police doing to catch Leather Apron? Why do they harass poor women like her trying to lay down their heads rather than nabbing the killer? She is shaking with rage as she shouts these questions to the group in the kitchen, who've mostly fallen silent.

"We'd be better off trying to catch that killer by ourselves," Catherine finally agrees. That seems to calm Liz down, and she asks to borrow Catherine's clothes brush.

"You cannot be thinking of going out in this weather again? And what of Leather Apron?"

Liz scoffs. "I will be back for my bed later tonight. I need a bit of fun and, don't worry, I shan't be alone. That murderer won't be coming near me."

Her clothes mostly dry and brushed clean of mud and debris, her belly full of potato and bread, Liz leaves 32 Dean and Flower Street without wishing her fellow lodgers a good night.

As she walks towards Commercial Street again, she spots something red on the ground. She bends over to pick it up. It's a single red rose with a bit of maidenhair fern attached. Who could have dropped it?

Liz shakes the water and dirt off the rose and pins it to her black cloth jacket. She smiles. She looks smart, she thinks. She never wears jewelry or ribbons. She has neither money nor time for that. But maybe with her rose some man will find her gay and buy her a pint or two.

On the way, she meets a man she's seen before, an army fellow, who takes her into a doorway and presses against her. Liz allows herself to be taken and pockets the two pennies afterwards. It is going to be a good night.

She makes her way to the Lion's Pub and sits alone while the storm rages outside the warm pub. She will wait until it lets up a bit and then make her way home. But the storm lasts longer than expected, and Liz grows sleepy after a few pints. She must leave.

When she walks home, alone, her bonnet askew, she is approached by another man on Berner Street. Liz is too tired to resist his advances, though he is rough when he pushes her into an alleyway and tries to take her against a blackened, grimy archway in Duffield's Yard.

"Stop it!"

"You're not made of glass," the man says, his fetid breath in her ear.

The transaction complete, the man pulls up his trousers and rushes off. Liz shouts after him to pay her. He tells her mockingly, "You ain't worth a penny for that."

She shakes her head. Her feet have that wooden feeling again, as if they don't belong to her body and she cannot get them to obey her mind. Her head is aching. She must see a doctor. Constable Neil is right about that—the only thing he's right about. She hasn't been well in a long time.

Liz has heard of a doctor. What's his name? He runs a hospital, an asylum, for women. No. She can't go there. She shudders at the thought. She has heard rumors of what happens to the women there. And she herself has spent time in a hospital for women with the pox. She won't subject herself to that poking and prodding again.

No. Better to get some rest and hope that she is stronger in the morning.

Liz adjusts her two thin petticoats and straightens out her stockings as best she can. Then she takes out some cachous she bought earlier to sweeten her breath. She unwraps one to put in her mouth. But before she has a chance to, there's a rustling sound and a cold blast of air chills her.

Liz turns her head, but her vision is too poor to separate the shadow from the larger shape that suddenly moves. When she sees the knife, it's too late. The cachous scatter on the ground next to the still body of Liz herself.

# Chapter Twenty-Eight

"I've been a roaming! I've been a roaming!
Where the meadow dew is sweet,
And like a queen I'm a coming
With its pearls upon my feet."

Kate Eddowes sways unsteadily on her feet in the narrow jail cell but her strong voice carries all the way to the desk where George Henry Hutt, the jailer at Bishopsgate station, sits.

"Will you pipe down in there," he shouts at Kate. It's a command not a question.

"I will not! Don't you like my voice? I've made my living singing ballads and songs. I've been told I have a lovely voice. Everyone says so. How about another tune then, if ya don't fancy that one?"

Kate sings even louder, her tune echoing off the hard brick walls.

"Hark everyone, gather round. Hear my murderous tale of Leather Apron, who moves without a sound. The police, they cannot find him. They dunna look in haste. He murders poor women. It is us he hates. 'Twas on a dark and moonless night, he killed first in Buck's Row place—"

"I said that's enough singing and carrying on outta you!" George Hutt is angry. He gets up and pushes back his chair and stands before the tiny jail cell where Kate has been for the last several hours.

"Then let me go," Kate says.

"I'll let you go when you're sober and capable of looking after yourself."

"I am now. Very capable. Very sober. Who wouldn't be in this place?" Kate juts out her chin. She'd fallen asleep after being arrested for drunk and disorderly conduct. And though she's not quite sober, there's no reason to let her jailer know that.

Her entreaties are eventually effective. Kate steadies herself as Hutt reaches for his keys to unlock her cell.

"Mind you go straight home," Hutt tells her. "It's too late for a drink now. And next time you get arrested it's fourteen days in Southgate prison, not a few hours in Bishopsgate."

"I've no intention of letting you lot arrest me again," Kate says defiantly.

Kate walks through to the station office, fastening the strings of her black straw bonnet, trimmed in green and black velvet, as she does so.

"Don't you go and get drunk again," Hutt warns her again.

Kate stands by the desk and waits for the discharge officer to hand back her possessions. He asks again for her name and address. Kate had given her name as "Nothing" when she was first arrested and refuses to give her real name again. But she's good at making up an alias. She's done so many times in her life. Kate has no fixed address but gives a false one as well. If she had money, she'd stay at the doss house at 55 Dean and Flower Street. But she has not a penny to her name.

"It's your fault my husband's going to give me a right hiding when I get home," Kate says, pretending she has a home to go to.

Though she's gotten many hidings over the years, particularly from Tom Conway, the man she truly loved and called her husband, the man whose children she bore, two of whom died in her arms, Kate is now with another man, John Kelly, and he has not beaten her. It's his boots she'd pawned earlier for food and drink.

Kate holds out her hands impatiently for her belongings. She's handed all of her worldly possessions—a piece of red silk gauze that she ties around her neck to keep out the chill, a large pocket handkerchief in need of washing, a tin box containing tea and another with sugar that she and Tom had bought just yesterday morning when they had money, two black clay pipes without anything to smoke, one empty tin matchbox that reminds of her of the tin factory where she worked as a young woman and the long line of tin workers in her family, a metal teaspoon, a small comb, a thimble, and several buttons. She stuffs these in the pockets of her dark green chintz skirt, filling them out.

The officer seems to blush when he hands Kate her menstrual rags, one still stained with blood that hadn't come clean. Kate smirks at his discomfort as she puts the several rags in her pockets. Then the man quickly gives her a small mustard tin containing two pawn tickets. Finally, Kate takes a broken pair of spectacles and one red mitten, the mate lost years ago, from the jailer and stuffs these in as well.

Pockets bulging, Kate turns to leave, but not without insulting her jailers, calling them right cocks for locking her up.

Then she heads out into the night, wondering where she will lay her head. At least it's not raining as hard as it was before. Soft drizzle doesn't so much fall from the sky as surround her, hanging on the heavy and ubiquitous sulfurous fog.

Kate is wearing man's boots and all her clothing on her person—a cloth jacket; man's white vest, a castoff from John; a bodice; and several other skirts under her green chintz. The rain won't bother her at all. But it's black as tar tonight and the few gas lamps in this part of the East End don't give off much light.

Her head still fuzzy from the drink, Kate thinks of John and wonders where he could be. Neither of them had money for a bed. Kate had told him she thought to approach her grown daughter, Harriet, begging for money. But it had been years since she'd seen her own flesh and blood and she isn't even sure of the street where Harriet lives. Like Kate's sisters, Harriet had turned her back on her long ago, wanting nothing to do with Kate.

Better to head for Houndsditch, where she and Kelly had last been drinking, and see if she could find him there.

But she is tired, oh, so tired, and she hasn't had anything to eat in a long while. The beer has turned her stomach sour. The smell from the jailhouse mixed with her own unwashed scent and now the fetid stink of rotting garbage bothers her nose as she walks.

All Kate wants now is to lay her head somewhere. If only that constable hadn't found her drunk and singing on the street corner. She wasn't harming anyone. Now she's lost track of time and of John. Two heads are always better than one when it comes to surviving on the streets of Whitechapel.

Kate turns down Duke Street. Maybe she'll run into someone she knows who would stand her for a drink, as she had done countless times for others when she had the money.

But her feet don't want to carry her any further. No sense looking for John now. It is late, after 1:00 a.m. at least. She'll find him in the morning.

Kate knows she needs to find a quiet corner or risk the

beat policeman coming along and waking her up. She knows most of the sheltered nooks and dark alleys where she won't be disturbed. The brass of those police! She has no fondness for them, always bothering women like her.

When she gets to Mitre Square, just off Whitechapel Road, Kate turns into a somewhat secluded spot. She's in luck. Perhaps it's the rain or the fact that other rough sleepers have found softer corners to lay their heads, but the southern-most corner is vacant. Indeed, the square seems uninhabited.

Kate sits up against a brick wall and brings her knees up to her chest. She begins to hum a tune to herself. She wasn't lying to the policeman when she said that she'd made her living with her voice. That was long ago and far away when she was with Thomas Conway, the enchanting Irishman who'd stolen her heart as a girl. Tom, the only man she's ever truly loved. The two of them traveled from town to town, peddling whatever they could sell, singing ballads, and loving as well as fighting.

The tune Kate hums is from a happier time, before the fights and drinking and babies, before the starvation and the workhouse. From when she was young and pretty, not forty-six years old, her bones old, her beauty gone. Kate drifts off to sleep.

Kate Conway, née Eddowes, is not woken up by a policeman this time, but by a flash of silver, a sharp knife held by the devil himself with glowing, evil eyes.

# Chapter Twenty-Nine

**EAST LONDON ADVERTISER**
October 1, 1888

## A THIRST FOR BLOOD

The two fresh murders which have been committed in Whitechapel have aroused the indignation and excited the imagination of London to a degree without parallel. Men feel that they are face to face with some awful and extraordinary freak of nature. So inexplicable and ghastly are the circumstances surrounding the crimes that people are affected by them in the same way as children are by the recital of a weird and terrible story of the supernatural.

It is so impossible to account, on any ordinary hypothesis, for these revolting acts of blood that the mind turns as it were instinctively to some theory of occult force, and the myths of the Dark Ages rise before the imagination.

Ghouls, vampires, bloodsuckers, and all the ghastly array of fables which have been accumulated throughout the course of centuries take form, and seize hold of the excited fancy. Yet the most morbid imagination can conceive nothing worse than this terrible reality; for what can be more appalling than the thought that there is a being in human shape stealthily moving about a great city, burning with the thirst for human blood, and endowed with such diabolical astuteness, as to enable him to gratify his fiendish lust with absolute impunity?

MAYFAIR, OCTOBER 1, 1:00 A.M.

The booming sound of thunder shakes Lucy's bed, causing her to wake with a jolt. Her heart beats fast. Her breath comes quickly. Shallowly. She shakes her head, and her long, red curls fan out along her shoulders. Lucy had been dreaming. No, not dreaming. She'd had another nightmare. But though she tries to remember it, the particulars fade fast like the sugar on her tongue when she snuck cubes as a child. She cannot hold on to images she saw in her dream. The only thing left is a feeling of dread that fills her entire being. Is it the storm?

Lucy is not one to be afraid of the elements. In fact, she's often loved the drama of storms—when the heavens unleash fury in a way she wishes she herself could.

The rain pounds against the windows as if trying to get in. Lucy approaches the window. Over the sound of the storm, she hears a voice.

"Listen. Lucy. Listen to me. Come now."

The next instant something is upon her, around her. A man, a dark shape with cold hands that grip her tightly. Lucy wants to scream, but the sound is stuck in her throat. She tries to free herself but he is too powerful.

"No!" she thinks. The demon laughs.

And then he bends towards her until his face is inches away. His eyes lock onto hers until Lucy feels herself softening, giving in.

"You, Lucy Rutherford, are mine."

A pain. A sharp, piercing, jab that brings with it a burst of intense pleasure. Then Lucy collapses into the arms of this strange man and is carried outside into the night, far from her father's house and all she has known.

Whitechapel, October 1, 2:00 a.m.

Constable Neil leaves Leman Street Police Station with his bull's-eye lamp. He'd been pulled from his usual beat to watch over Miss Rutherford, but tonight he wants to check back on his nightly rounds.

That letter from "Jack the Ripper" has unnerved him. There have been no killings in recent weeks, and though the investigation is still floundering, things are beginning to calm down a bit—both at the station and with the public. That is, until this Ripper fellow.

Neil doesn't know what to make of the last letter. Right mad, whoever wrote it. He doesn't really believe it's from the killer. Probably some maniac or someone wanting attention. He cringes at what the press will make of it.

"It's not fit for man or beast out here," Neil thinks, pulling his tall custodian helmet lower to shield himself from the downpour.

He's no sooner left H Division than his woolen trousers are sodden. His long tunic will protect him from the cold and the rain somewhat, but what of the poor sots who are sleeping rough tonight? Nooks and covered doorways are few and far between, and though it is his job to tell people to "move along" when they're sleeping on benches or obstructing the pavement, he doesn't always comply with the letter of the law.

Truth be told, Neil pities the poor inhabitants of Whitechapel. It's the children, especially, who get to him. He's seen them picking pieces of orange rinds or blackened apple cores off the pavement and stuffing them in their mouths to stave off hunger. Outside the market, men, women, and children elbow each other out of the way to scrounge scraps of rotting vegetables or fruit from garbage bins.

How, in a country as great as his, is this poverty possible?

Neil shakes his head and hurries with his lantern to make his first checkpoint in time. Tonight, after the fury of the storm, he expects fewer people on the streets, fewer arrests for drunk and disorderly or petty thievery. Who wants to fight in a downpour?

Though he's been made part of the special force of the criminal investigation unit, Neil is glad to be back on his beat, despite the weather.

Outside, casting the light of his lantern against the brick walls of the cramped houses and into the dark alleys and doorways, he feels as if he at least is protecting the inhabitants of Whitechapel from this demon who cuts women's throats.

It's more misting now than raining, the air thick with moisture and fog, the storm having almost washed itself out but done nothing to clear the air.

Tonight he hears only his own footsteps on the pavement, slick with rain, garbage, and sewage, which seems to run through the streets at all times, even more so tonight with the deluge.

But then he hears something else. Human? Animal? Neil thinks the latter. A lone howl, the kind that sends a chill up his spine. Not a dog. Not like Barnaby. A wolf? *Impossible!* he tells himself. There are no wolves in Britain. Certainly not in London's East End. The howling abruptly stops.

Then a figure emerges out of the shadows ahead of him. He feels a gust of cold air and sees a flash of white clothing.

"Who's there?"

Neil holds out his lantern in front of him. He expects to hear footsteps on the pavement. But he hears nothing. He sees nothing. The figure has vanished.

He walks on to meet his sergeant. He must be tired. He's hearing animals howling, seeing shadows where there are none.

Neil has just turned the corner onto Whitbourne Street when he sees two figures entwined against a shop window. Can't they find a less public place for their lover's tryst? This is his first thought. His second is that there is something very familiar about the woman.

Could it be? Or is he hallucinating? The woman is slight of build. Her long red hair is unconstrained by any head covering.

"Lucy!" Neil shouts and rushes to cross the street.

In that instant, the male figure vanishes. Neil looks both ways down the road but sees nothing. No one in either direction. The woman lies crumpled next to a shop.

Neil crouches down next to her. It is Lucy—and her face is deathly pale. Her thin nightdress is soaked, revealing the curves of her body underneath. Neil feels for a pulse. It is weak. Then he notices her neck. Two bright spots of blood, like red berries, bloom on her neck.

"Please, God, no!" Neil prays. It can't be the Ripper. Not Lucy.

A soft moan comes from Lucy's bluish lips. Neil quickly picks her up. He must get her somewhere safe and revive her. Not the station. A hospital? No. For some reason, he thinks that is not the correct option either.

He will take her home. She stirs in his arms. Neil gingerly

puts her down, then takes off his police tunic and covers her with it. He must find a hansom cab.

A mixture of emotions rages through him. He should have been watching her! The next is fear and wonder. How did she get here? What is she doing in Whitechapel?

Neil hears clopping horse hooves and carriage wheels on the cobblestones and looks up. It's not a cab but a market cart, with an open top and single driver.

He calls to the driver to stop, saying he's a police constable in need of assistance. The driver immediately complies; fortunately, the cart is not full of produce. It is not luxurious but it will have to do.

He commands the driver to assist him in getting Lucy into the back. She moans as the men lift her into the cart. There is nothing soft in the back of the cart, so Neil covers Lucy with his overcoat and holds her head in his lap. Then he gives the driver Rutherford's address in Mayfair, holding her hand the entire way.

It is Sally who answers the bell when they arrive. The maid practically faints when she sees Lucy. Sally summons another maidservant and Neil carries Lucy upstairs to her bedroom. He has never been in a woman's private chambers before, a thought that briefly enters his mind as he lays her on the satin coverlet.

Lucy's eyes flutter open. The color is returning to her cheeks.

"You're safe now," Neil tells her. She nods.

"Ahem," Sally says behind him.

Neil steps away and asks if Lord Rutherford is home.

"Nay. He's at work somewhere," Sally says. "Now, if you'll beg my pardon…"

"Of course."

Neil knows that Lucy will be well tended to in the capable hands of her maid. He is glad he's asked the driver and market cart to wait. He needs to get back to Whitechapel as quickly as possible and scour the streets for the man who did this to Lucy. Fury runs through his veins.

**EVENING NEWS (LONDON)**
October 1, 1888

EXTRAORDINARY LETTERS THROUGH THE POST: A BLOOD-SMEARED POSTCARD FROM "JACK THE RIPPER"

The Central News says: A postcard bearing the stamp "London, E., October 1," was received this morning, addressed to the Central News Office, the address and subject matter being written in red, and undoubtedly by the same person from whom the sensational letter already published, was received on Thursday last. Like the previous missive, this also has reference to the horrible tragedies in East London, forming, indeed, a sequel to the first letter. It runs as follows:

*I was not codding, dear old Boss, when I gave you the tip. You'll hear about saucy Jacky's work tomorrow. Double event this time. Number one squealed a bit. Couldn't finish straight off. Had not time to get ears for police. Thanks for keeping last letter back till I got to work again.*
*"JACK THE RIPPER."*

The card is smeared on both sides with blood, which has evidently been impressed thereon by the thumb or finger of the writer, the corrugated surface of the skin being plainly shown. Upon the back of the card some words are nearly obliterated by a bloody smear. It is not necessarily assumed that this has been the work of the murderer, the idea that naturally occurs being that the whole thing is a practical joke.

# Chapter Thirty

The delicate bone china saucer cracks in two when Lord Rutherford forcefully returns his coffee cup to its place. Dark, black coffee seeps out onto the white silk tablecloth set for breakfast.

"Burn this paper and all the morning papers," the Home Secretary says, throwing the newspaper on top of the broken shards and stained tablecloth. Without looking at his butler, he storms out of the dining room, cursing under his breath.

Two more murders in Whitechapel the same night by this Ripper fellow, as the press were calling him. And what was Warren doing about it? He'd appointed Sir Charles Warren Chief Commissioner of the Metropolitan Police over two years ago and thought Scotland Yard could be in no more capable hands. Warren was a military man and an archeologist. "A man of science and of action," the press called him then. They are not calling him that now.

Warren also has a reputation for ruling with an iron fist— without the velvet glove. He's blunt and determined and men fear him. Not Rutherford, of course. While Warren was no marionette, Rutherford could count on him to keep his confidences.

Now Rutherford has to nip this latest mess in the bud. No more Ripper letters and hysteria stirred up by the press. Rutherford has too much to lose—he doesn't want anyone looking too closely at his mining operations, or at the club he has leased out nor at any of his businesses. He has too many secrets to keep.

He will summon Warren to his chambers this morning and talk through what must be done. He'd trusted the commissioner with the dock fire and see how that turned out.

As he collects his hat and walking stick in the front hallway, Lord Rutherford's thoughts turn towards his daughter, Lucy. She has been looking very pale. He heard there was some commotion last night. Has she been stricken by more of those nocturnal wanderings? Could that infernal fiend he'd inadvertently unearthed be the cause of it? No, God forbid. Maybe he should get that doctor to look at her again.

Then he hesitates. No. Lucy is fine. Mere hysteria, that's what has caused her ramblings. At least he's got that constable looking after her as well. Even if Warren is incompetent, that younger fellow seemed responsible enough.

He really must see about marrying Lucy into a good family sometime soon. She is of age, and she needs a strong man to look after her.

He'd meant to be on top of this marriage situation before now. He'd received several discreet inquiries about his daughter, but none that he considered suitable. Perhaps he ought to install a governess again? Lucy was so distraught when her beloved governess left two years ago that he gave in to her entreaties to be without one. Yet there must be someone he can hire for this sort of thing.

As if his thoughts had summoned her, he sees Lucy at the top of the stairs. She slowly descends to say goodbye to him just as his butler is helping him into his overcoat. At a glance, she seems worse this morning, woefully pale and thin. He must get that doctor to come see her again.

"Mind you stay inside today, Lucy," Lord Rutherford tells her. "I do not want you going anywhere. Not until…"

"The Ripper murderer is caught?" she says flatly.

That she knows the name of this fiend surprises him but he does not let it show. "I forbid you to read the newspapers. There is too much filth and hysteria written by these journalists, and you need not get corrupted by any of it."

He expects Lucy to agree, but she is silent. "Do you understand me?"

"Yes, father," she says at last. "Completely."

"Good. Good. You may have Mrs. Hepworth for tea here if you desire, but under no circumstances are you to go wandering today." He pats her cheek, which feels cool beneath his hand. Lucy steps away, covering herself with her shawl. She really must be coming down with something.

He feels better as he exits the house, having made his thoughts clear to Lucy. He does not need to spell out his fears —and they are not contained in the pages of the *Pall Mall Gazette* or any other paper—for her safety. What could he say to her that would be believable?

He steps into the open door of his carriage and a hand closes it after him. If anything happened to her…! No, he mustn't go down that path. How was he to know what was on his ship with the diamonds from Kimberley? How was he to guard against something so evil, so sinister, that he dare not name it? The carriage jolts into motion with the clip clopping of horses' hooves.

And then these Ripper murders. Well, they have to stop. Warren had better capture this murderer and bring him to justice.

He is not particularly concerned about the murder victims themselves. Prostitutes, he thinks. What other kind of woman would be on the streets in Whitechapel alone that late at night?

While Rutherford feels for the fallen women of the city in the abstract—has supported shipping them off to Australia or housing them in Magdalene homes—he does not feel anything in particular for the murdered women. Yes, their deaths were brutal. But so were their lives. Once they get a taste of alcohol and vice of all kinds, there is no one who can truly save them.

He stares idly out the window as his carriage takes him through Green Park toward the Palace of Westminster. Still, he must put a stop to the murders and then there will be no more hysterical press covering these events. Who knows what else these journalists—many of them no doubt trying to make a name for themselves—might uncover?

Lord Rutherford has not risen to his position by being cautious in his business and personal life, and he's not about to start now. He needs that fiend apprehended and destroyed— out of the public eye.

Why haven't Warren's men caught that unholy fiend? He is not a patient man, and he's already used up his store. Maybe it's time to take matters into his own hands?

# Chapter Thirty-One

KENSINGTON, OCTOBER 3

"Mr. Hinton, have you been ill?" Lucy asks the journalist when he is led into Maude's sitting room. She didn't mean her question to sound quite so alarming, but the man looks a fright. His eyes are sunken, his skin pale white, and his clothes hang off his thinner frame. He wears a scarf around his neck, quite tightly, Lucy thinks, and does not remove it. Nor his coat. The man is positively skeletal.

"Nothing serious," the journalist replies. "Just a tad under the weather. But I'm fine now."

Though he tries to sound reassuring, Lucy thinks she detects an undercurrent of fear in his response. For the first time, she wonders if he has someone at home to look after him. A mother or sister perhaps? He wears no wedding ring.

"Do take a seat, Mr. Hinton." Maude motions to a chair near the window, but Lucy sees the journalist hesitate before sitting down.

"Do you mind if I draw the curtain?" he asks, then he

proceeds to pull the curtain closed at a nod from Maude. Most peculiar, Lucy thinks.

"I'm so very glad you contacted us," Maude says. She doesn't seem as startled by her guest's appearance or behavior as Lucy is. Due to her husband's profession, Maude must be used to being in the presence of sick people, Lucy speculates.

"We were going to write to you. We understand how very busy you must be, and we will waste no time in getting down to business and let you get back to your work," Maude says. She pours tea and hands her guest a cup.

Lucy notices that the journalist's hands shake slightly. What could be the matter with him? Lucy has a sisterly urge to bring him a rug for his lap and feed him something more substantial than tea. The poor man. It must be the murders in Whitechapel and his work that has affected him so very much. He would have to be a monster to write about such horrific things and not be the worse for it.

"We're hoping you can enlighten us—confidentially, if you don't mind," Maude adds. Lucy nods in agreement. Her friend pauses and Lucy notices Maude's agitation.

"I've found…these." For the first time, Maude falters. She holds out a few of the cartes de visite she'd found in her husband's office. Lucy sees her friend blush as she does so.

Mr. Hinton scans the cards. He frowns. "I don't understand. Where did you get these?"

"They were found in my husband's office." Maude raises her head and looks at the journalist. Lucy admires how forthright she is.

"I see."

"Do you recognize them?"

"I recognize these kinds of cards. They are passed around at a club I've heard of, though I've never been there myself." This time, it is the journalist who seems to blush.

"What do you mean?" Lucy asks. "Been where?"

"To the gentlemen's club near Whitechapel. I've heard

about it, but have never seen it with my own eyes. The cards, I would suspect, are from that club."

"And what type of club is it?" Maude's question is pointed.

Mr. Hinton looks down at the ground rather than meet Maude's eyes.

Lucy, who sits nearest to him, puts her hand on his forearm. "We are not so very delicate that you cannot tell us. Please."

"It is a secret club," he starts, then stops. "There are rumors—mind you that these are things I've heard, not seen or confirmed—of a trade in women."

Maude gasps. "A trade in women?" She blushes and appears to be on the verge of asking another question, but does not.

"Thank you for telling us, Mr. Hinton."

"Jonathan, please," he interrupts.

Maude nods. "Jonathan then. We trust that everything that we've discussed in this room today will remain amongst us."

Jonathan and Lucy both nod.

Maude's expression turns pleading. "Will you look into this club for us, Mr. Hinton? I mean, Jonathan. Will you use your investigative skills to uncover any connection to my husband?"

Jonathan nods slowly. "May I borrow one of these cards?"

Maude wrinkles her nose and thrusts a pile at him. "I'd give you them all but I must return them in case my husband notices them missing. Take any you choose."

Jonathan picks one at random and tucks it in a pocket. "And now, if I may ask you something, Miss Rutherford?"

Lucy looks at him in surprise "Of course."

"I wonder if your sleepwalking has persisted?"

Jonathan's hands seem to shake even more when he asks this, Lucy notices. She cannot recall telling him about her nocturnal wandering, but perhaps she or Maude had mentioned it.

"My wanderings are back," Lucy says. She glances at the journalist to be sure he understands this was also to be kept secret. Her father must not find out that she has left the house against his orders. And he must never find out about last night.

"Of course, I do not remember them," Lucy continues. But I've been plagued by horrible dreams. And something else…" Lucy stops.

She remembers very little of her strange dream and sleep-walking though Sally said she was brought home by a police-man. Lucy blushes at the thought and shakes her head to dislodge the picture of Constable Neil finding her wandering at night. She has revealed too much of herself already. Jonathan Hinton is really a stranger, and she should not be sharing what happened to her with any man.

"Why do you ask?" Maude said.

Mr. Hinton hesitates. He seems at a loss for words. "I, too, have been plagued by horrific nightmares," he begins. "And though I know that men are less suggestible than women…" He pauses as Lucy and Maude exchange a glance. "Men are considered less suggestible than women," he corrects himself. "I was hoping that you had a cure for your nighttime ailment that may work for me."

"Tell me about your nightmares," Lucy demands.

Jonathan shakes his head. Lucy can see that his face has reddened. "It is not something I can truly put words to," he says. "And I'm afraid I've already taken up enough of your time." He stands up to go. "Thank you so much for the tea, Mrs. Hepworth. Miss Rutherford."

When Emily shows Mr. Hinton out Lucy and Maude are left alone. For a few moments they sit in relative silence as the clock ticks steadily.

"What is wrong, Lucy?" Maude's voice is soft and gentle, but Lucy feels her friend's probing. She thought she had hidden her agitation. She fingers the high collar at her throat.

Maybe she too appears as pale and sickly as Jonathan. Maybe her nightmares are somehow linked to his, as he implied. Maybe…she shivers. And then she tells her friend what she recalls from last night. Her strange dream of flying through the night air and how, when she awoke, Sally told her she had been found far from Mayfair, by Constable Neil, with two bite marks on her neck.

Bethlem Royal Hospital, October 4

"Hold her down!"

Edward glares at his assistants; they should know the routine by now. The young woman on the bed squirms and shrieks, which hurts his eardrums. He tries again to pin her arm in place for the syringe.

"Where's the restraining jacket?" he barks.

He keeps his eyes on the lunatic as a guard leaves to find bindings. Proper equipment should be ever at the ready! There should be straps attached to the bed! He wonders if he will ever succeed at making this a model asylum. Not if he has to depend on these buffoons to get the job done. The fiends can be uncannily strong. His head jerks back to avoid her clawing fingers.

"Dark, dark, the fog—and the hands. Cold! Slithery hands on my skin. Oh, save me! Mercy on my poor soul." The ravings descend into sobs as the woman continues to thrash and struggle on the bed. The pale skin of her arms is marked with scratches and her long dark hair is a tangle. They have to be more careful.

"Same as before, sir. Doctor. Same as the others," the guard mutters as he bustles back to the bed. He pushes one of her thin arms through a hole in the leather vest. "Says she were taken away. Says she were hooded in the dark. Says there were rumblings under herself, hands on her." He grunts and shakes his head, his voice lowering. "Even the private parts. Mind's gone."

Edward shoves the syringe into the girl's shoulder and she lets out a whimper, her wild eyes locking on his for a moment. Insanity of the manic type, with occasional delusions.

He grabs for her file and scribbles a quick note of the time and dose. He is quite out of breath now from the struggle. And his waistcoat is wrinkled. He glares at the woman as she subsides onto the bed with a low moan. How unnecessary this all is. If they would only cooperate! This could be much easier for him, and for society too—because these women serve no useful purpose.

Personally, he believes madness once inherited is incurable. He has colleagues in Italy and France who disagree. They believe insanity is an acquired condition, due to a brain injury —or even a damaged upbringing.

That charlatan Bernheim is one of those soft-headed thinkers. But medical men know that brain injuries result in a quite different pattern of symptoms, like subcranial swelling. And the influence of nurture on young minds is too various to measure, so where is the science in that?

Why, his own childhood had a full share of the rod, birch, and "demon cleansings" in the basement. He was none the worse for it. Deprivation and fear had made him all the stronger. Those "psychologists" are deeply misguided. The best that can be done for those doomed to lunacy is to keep them under lock and key.

Insanity is in the blood at birth, he is sure of it. That's why he had taken such pains to investigate Maude's family line and interview her doctors about her health before making his offer. She was prime stock—and dowered too. It took funds to advance in London—and save madwomen from themselves.

He straightens his coat as he stands up from the bed. The

girl is quiet now, at least. Sometimes that is the best one can hope for. He would keep them all sedated all the time, if he could, though there were do-gooders who objected. Science must be advanced—by photographing women in the throes of their hysteria or documenting the physiognomy of mental diseases. And there was money to be made.

Lost in his thoughts, Edward has forgotten about the guard in the room, who is saying something.

"...those women in Whitechapel?"

"What?" He snaps to attention. "No, under no circumstances are the patients to have newspapers! Those are my orders!"

"Of course, yes, yes." The man wrings his hands and shifts from foot to foot, his ring of keys jangling at his waist.

"She's settled." He gestures at the woman slumped over on the iron bed frame. Some nurse would probably come along and cover her. "Show me the new ones," he says.

Every Thursday, he looks over the new females, evaluates their condition and suitability, and sorts them into categories. They need fresh blood. Ha ha! He smiles grimly at his own joke as he checks his pocket watch. He likes to be home before Maude expects him. He does not quite trust her. Nor any woman. He is going to have to put a stop to these visits with Lucy Rutherford, and to hell with her father's patronage. The thought gives him a little rush of pleasure. He would enjoy thwarting that arrogant lord. And he enjoys denying his wife. He likes to watch her struggle to obey him, as she must.

# Chapter Thirty-Two

WHITECHAPEL, OCTOBER 7

The mood in Whitechapel has become even more volatile, Jonathan finds. Inhabitants are still terrorized, but they're also becoming more vocal and taking matters into their own hands. Now that the killer has a name—Jack the Ripper—and is not just described by an article of clothing, he's become that much more real.

Jonathan attends a meeting of a vigilante group at the Working Lad's Institute, where the talk is of nothing but tracking this murderer down and how the police seem incapable of doing so.

"The slayer of these poor women has been seen by no one," exclaims one man with a long, reddish beard and hair to match. "You yourself wrote that he vanishes without a trace." He points to Jonathan and all eyes turn towards him. He feels himself growing hot. His cheeks flush.

Jonathan recalls the last time he was in the building and how he nearly fainted. Tonight, he doesn't feel nearly as weak, but he's not well. That much is clear to him—and to his land-lady, Mrs. Cavendish, who frets every time she sees him.

He's exhausted, both from work and from the nightmares that beset him when he lays his head down on his pillow. He dreams of unspeakable things, of the piercing pleasure and pain of being bitten. And then, horribly, he himself has the urge to bite, to suck blood to satisfy a lust he's never felt before.

Jonathan wakes each morning feeling feebler and more exhausted than when he went to bed. And ashamed of himself for his dreams that seem so real. He's buried the cross Mrs. Cavendish insisted he keep with him in the very back of his closet.

"The police—well, they cannot be everywhere at once," the red-haired man continues. "We need to take matters into our own hands." There are loud cheers and agreements on all sides.

Only Jonathan remains quiet and doesn't join in the fracas. He is too busy writing the beginning of his article, scribbling the words hot and fast in his notebook.

When the vote is called to form a Vigilante Committee, with the red-headed man, Mr. Heath, as the committee chair, Jonathan abstains. He has absorbed enough of the tenor of the meeting—and of the men's words—to finish his article for the newspaper.

He is thinking about the murderer's stealthy methods, how he comes upon the women so suddenly and noiselessly, a dark shadow in the night, unseen by everyone but the victim, presumably when it is too late. Jonathan shudders. His words capture the feeling of his dreams. He is consumed by a presence that lurks just out of sight.

*The outrages have, in all cases, been perpetrated upon women, and they have been effected in each instance with a swiftness, a dexterity, a noiselessness, and, we might almost say, a scientific skill, which are, surely, very rare accomplishments in the class from which murderers are commonly drawn.*

Jonathan pauses to write down the words that come into his fevered brain. Yes, he has not slept and his body is so very weary, but his mind is sharp. The words flow almost as if he is channeling them from an outside source.

*At present it is said that every spot in this quarter of the town is visited by the police patrols once in twelve minutes; but, short as are these "beats," it is clear that they allow margin sufficient for the commission of the most revolting crimes. A policeman cannot be everywhere at once; and if the instant he turns his back it is possible for a woman to be killed and cut to pieces on the spot from which the echoes of his footsteps have hardly died away, it must be admitted that both prevention and detection present difficulties of no ordinary character.*

In a rush himself, Jonathan describes the extraordinary speed with which the last two murders took place, and just how audacious the Ripper is to murder another woman not even half a mile away, right under the nose of two watchmen in Mitre Square, who heard nothing and saw nothing. How does the murderer do it?

It's as if the fiend appears out of thin air and vanishes the way he came—so like his dreams, he thinks again. No. He must focus. He scribbles the last paragraph of his article, urging the public to assist the authorities by declining to be led into a frenzy of fear or an epidemic of unfounded suspicion.

He must get to the news agency quickly and file his story.

Later, when his article makes the evening papers, he's quite pleased.

October 8, note from Frances Cobbe on plain stock, no envelope.

*I send this by the usual route, in haste. Pls respond in the usual way.*

*Two more murders! We must redouble our efforts. The women of Whitechapel need us. This murderer slinks about and strikes at will while our so-called police force does nothing. I will not have it. What is Warren doing? The Home Secretary? Nothing. Are they deliberately letting this madman run loose?*

*Investigate Lord R. Miss P. has him under watch herself.*

*To wit:*

*—Look into Lord R's inventory arriving from Cape Town since murders began. Send itemized report, with valuations.*

*—Send someone to the WLI. Make sure she reports back on all meetings and spreads the word—quietly!—about the Women and Weapons class. Look out for any promising candidates. Remember, they need to be firecrackers! And also cool-headed. A paradox, to be sure.*

*—For G—'s sake, organize more escorts! We can't have women wandering the streets alone.*

*One last thought, a puzzle piece that fits nowhere. Jarvis looked into Metropolitan Police reports of missing women this year and found one anomaly. Besides the East End neighborhoods, there is a steady trickle of women disappearing from Bethlem Hospital. All deemed insane, but we know that can be flubdub. Get Lil in there to poke her nose about. That's the Nasty Doctor's place, cuss him!*

*To the ramparts!*

*—F*

*Chapter Thirty-Three*

Jonathan Hinton does not want to investigate the gentleman's club at 19 Whitbourne Street. He has his hands full with the Whitechapel murders and "Jack the Ripper." He doesn't want to be outside shivering in a hired coach he can barely afford—just as dawn is breaking on this unlovely street. If only he hadn't promised Mrs. Hepworth and Miss Rutherford... He has already put off this errand for as long as he possibly could, and now he is doing as little as he possibly can.

He should have come at night and gained entrance, using the card borrowed from Mrs. Hepworth, to observe the proceedings. He grimaces, imagining rouged women with paunchy, mutton-chopped men from the City.

He could have struck up a conversation with a barman or found his way to a servant's hall and befriended one of the boys who hung around public houses, hoping to earn a few pennies delivering messages. Those boys know everything about everyone.

But Jonathan had felt an instinctive aversion to this nighttime excursion. The very thought of it made his body shake and his muscles slacken. So instead he has come at the crack of dawn, when he is least likely to learn anything. Posing as a hansom cab driver, he idles in a coach at the corner, wondering how long to linger. He feels utterly ridiculous. He is not a detective! Hasn't he discharged his obligation just by coming here? Belying its notorious reputation, the house seems buttoned down and prim in the early morning fog.

With a gentle tap of the reins, Jonathan nudges the scrawny horse into a slow trot past the front door, which maintains its stoic imperturbability. The entire house is silent as a tomb. He pauses at the alleyway leading to the back entrance and cranes his neck to see down the narrow close. Here there is still evidence of the night's revelries—a torn stocking lying on a cobblestone, shards of broken glass catching the bits of light that pierce the fog, the smell of sweat and sex lingering in the air... Jonathan wrinkles his nose and turns to leave. He will tell the women that he tried.

As he glances back at the club, his eyes are drawn to a first-floor window where a couple embrace, half hidden by velvet curtains. A tall wiry figure bends a smaller figure over one arm, pressing their bodies close together. It is a man, a strong man who easily bends a woman's body to his desire, burying his face in her neck. Her hair is a long tangle of braid against a white chemise. Jonathan is riveted.

As he watches, a roar starts up in his brain. He can feel the man's ravenous mouth on the woman's throat—so pale and soft. He can hear the sound of lips smacking, smell the tangy scent of her skin, and taste the sharpness of her... Dear God! Jonathan leans forward despite the recoil that races through him as he realizes what is happening. He feels it as if he is there in the room with them, enthralled by a stabbing rush of pleasure. His own body is swooning, he feels dizzy...but he cannot look away.

Just then, the man raises his head and looks directly

through the window at Jonathan. Ice-blue eyes meet his and the jolt is electric. Jonathan starts trembling and closes his eyes in terror. When he opens them, the figures in the window have disappeared. He clutches the reins as he struggles to catch his breath.

A sharp whistle cuts through the quiet and through Jonathan's confusion.

"You!"

A figure in white stumbles out of the back door of the club, held up by two men, one on either side. Footsteps advance hurriedly.

Before Jonathan can react, the men are opening his carriage door and pushing the figure inside. He can see now that she is slight, very pale, and barely conscious. One man jumps into the coach with her and the vehicle shakes as his weight settles. The other slams the door and bangs on it as a signal to go.

Sick with fear, Jonathan looks back down the alley and sees the man—the man from his dreams he is sure of it—standing in the doorway, arms crossed, eyes burning with a malicious glee, smirking at him. He is ruddy with health and vigor. Slowly, he licks his lips.

The trap door of the cab opens and a man shouts. "Get along then! We're in a hurry, man. Bethlem Hospital, quick as you can!"

With a start, Jonathan breaks out of his reverie and automatically snaps the reins. The horse bolts into action and the coach carries Jonathan away.

# Chapter Thirty-Four

Sir Charles Warren has brought together the best police inspectors and constables from several different beats in the Whitehall division of the Metropolitan Police Force, including Constable Neil, and assembled them for a secret meeting at Scotland Yard.

Warren glances around the room, noting the puzzled looks on these men's faces. They're wondering, no doubt, why they've been summoned. Such a secret force has never been assembled in the history of the police. And yet, they've never faced a killer as diabolical and as elusive as this Ripper fellow, though Warren, like Lord Rutherford, despises the name.

Warren must be discreet. After all, detecting is the work of the head of the Criminal Investigation Department, Robert Anderson. Warren can't stand the man, but at least he's been out of the country since the first murder. He's only recently returned from his month's holiday in Switzerland. The press has had a field day with Anderson's absence, broadcasting that the head of the CID has been on holiday while a murderer has been terrorizing East London.

"Gentleman," Warren begins. He stands before the men. All eyes are on him. "You who are sitting here have been called together for one purpose and one purpose only. To apprehend the Whitechapel murderer. So far this killer has outwitted our best efforts. That is why we must do better. We will do better. We will apprehend this sadistic murderer of women and bring him to justice."

The men nod in agreement. A few murmur their consent.

"But we must be very discreet. No one can know about our special force, especially the press. Understood?"

Every man nods.

"And how are we going to bring this murderer to justice, you may well ask?" Warren pauses for dramatic effect. The men in the room look back at him, solemn and attentive.

"You have each been highly recommended for your skills at police work, and where one or two might have failed, many together will not. We will work in pairs. We will start at the beginning, and go through the evidence again. We will go door-to-door talking to witnesses. You will devote your time to this and nothing else."

Warren describes how the special force will work. Since theirs is a secret mission, no information is to leave the room. They must be as stealthy as the killer they are pursuing. They will begin by pooling information into one central location— this office at Scotland Yard. Any further details, eyewitness statements, or inquests, will be centralized and only accessed by anyone on this team.

"This is the very latest in modern detective work, gentle-men," Warren tells them. "A covert operation, if you will, the first of its kind here in Scotland Yard."

He assigns the men to work in pairs. Then he asks if there are any questions.

Constable Neil has one. "What are we to make of the supernatural element?"

Several men's heads turn to face him.

"Kindly explain yourself, Constable Neil." Warren's brow puckers with sweat. His waistcoat suddenly feels too tight, too hot.

The chief examines his constable. Neil is tall, nearly six feet, with a thick mustache and intelligent brown eyes. He has thought of him as an ally, but if he's asking about something supernatural perhaps he needs to keep him at arm's length?

"As you know, sir," Neil begins again, "we receive hundreds of letters, telegrams, even visits from people who claim they've received spiritual information about the murderer."

"Spiritual information?" Warren narrows his eyes at Neil, his voice deliberately skeptical.

"Yes."

Warren scans the table where the men are seated, many of them nodding in agreement.

"Just last week a clergyman in Newmarket came in to tell us he had a dream that revealed the names of not one but two murderers," Constable Neil continues.

"There are two of them now?" Warren tries to make light of this news but inwardly he is curious. In his travels, he's seen soothsayers who could predict the future, who knew more than could logically be explained, but he keeps that information to himself. He won't be ridiculed in the press for listening to a spiritualist.

Besides, what he's seen of table-rapping sessions and seances have made them all seem like hoaxes to him. There is no shortage of charlatans, so-called spiritualists, even clergymen reporting dreams or visions of the killer.

"And what are the names of these two murderers, according to this esteemed clergyman?" Warren does not try to keep the sarcasm out of his voice.

"Pat Murphy and Jim Slaney, sir." Constable Neil looks at the Commissioner. The blood rises to the man's face. Warren almost takes pity on him.

"Do you have more information on where to find these ruthless killers?"

Neil swallows. "According to the clergyman, they will be walking past 22 Gresham Street at precisely 4:10 p.m. on Wednesday 28th November 1888."

"Ah, then we shall be sure to keep an eye out on that exact location when that day arrives in what—just a few weeks? I'll assign you, Constable Neil, to personally apprehend the killers when they reveal themselves on that date."

There are a few guffaws from the other men on the team. But Warren silences them immediately.

"There is another one, a Mrs. Bright, a spiritualist," Constable Neil continues. "Says the police are barking up the wrong tree. Says they'll be more murders…"

"Every police station has been inundated by these so-called spiritualists, table rappers or whatever they call themselves," Sir Charles interrupts the constable. He needs to quell these rumors.

"Now we see even clergymen are not immune from the hysteria. We have a special file where we keep these accounts." Warren points to a round trash bin near the door.

Many of the men laugh again. Good, Warren thinks, he has discounted the fake spiritualists and his men suspect nothing supernatural at work. He is joking about the rubbish bin, and the men know it. Every letter and telegram received is carefully kept in a file with letters they've received from the public.

"In addition to catching this killer—and I don't for a minute believe there is more than one—we must bring order and reason to the populace of Whitechapel and beyond. We must dispel these rumors that the killer is a supernatural being or can be apprehended, in any way, through these so-called spiritualists. Good detective work, gentlemen. That is what I need from you. Not more hysteria and speculation."

There are nods all around, including from Neil. In truth, Warren admires the man's bravery for bringing up a topic that is no doubt on everyone's mind.

When Warren is satisfied that the men know the seriousness of their mission, and that they will be discreet, he dismisses them. He has a meeting with Anderson, the Chief of the Criminal Investigation Department, later that day, and he vows to reveal nothing of his secret task force. The man is incompetent, and he has a sworn duty to Rutherford.

"These wretched victims belong to a very small class of degraded women who frequent the East End streets after midnight, in hope of inveigling belated drunkards, or men as degraded as themselves." Robert Anderson stands firmly before Sir Charles Warren, outrage in his face and words.

"I've spent the entire day of my return to London and half the night reinvestigating the entire case, and I've come to the conclusion that the police are to blame." Anderson's Irish accent is stronger when he is angry.

He had been on holiday for his health—as prescribed by his Harley Street physician—and was not happy about being hounded by journalists and summoned back to London. Warren can see that in the very twitch of the man's mustache. He has never warmed to Anderson, whom he considers unsuited to his role and a spy for city government.

"In what way?" Warren is equally angry. His voice is clipped. He has worked hard to gain the trust of the force and he is not going to see his police blamed.

"These wretched women are plying their trade under definite police protection—your constables, sir. I advise that we let the police of that district…"

Warren notes that Anderson can hardly bring himself to say "Whitechapel" or "East End," such disdain he has for the poor inhabitants in that part of the city. Had the murderer been loose on the West End, well, Warren wonders what Anderson would have to say then?

"In my opinion, we should let the police of that district receive orders to arrest every known 'street woman' found on the prowl after midnight, or else let us warn them that the police will not protect them."

"You do know it is illegal to arrest women simply for being out on the streets after midnight?" Warren's face flushes under his beard. Anderson is insufferable. "And you might further recall, my order in July of last year concerning those you label street women?"

Anderson's expression doesn't change.

"Let me quote it for you." Warren feels his anger rising further. "A police constable should not assume that any particular woman is a common prostitute unless she so describes herself as such or has been convicted as such."

Anderson grimaces. "Why else would they be out at night? You know as well as I do that not every unfortunate woman on the streets at a late hour is plying her trade."

Warren thinks of all the women he's crossed paths with from Gibraltar to Jerusalem and wonders that the chief inspector has not noticed their vast variety. Every British citizen, he thinks, should be mandated to live abroad and see something of how other peoples live.

"That is neither here nor there. If you protect the right of these loose women to be on the street, then you allow the maniac to have access to them whenever he pleases."

"And locking them up would prevent the Ripper from striking again?" Warren can barely contain his fury.

"Precisely. It would be doing a favor to these unfortunates, who cannot help themselves, and who lure men to be as degraded as they are."

"Outrageous!" Warren has had enough. He pounds his fist on his leather desk, harder than he'd intended. "We do not arrest our citizens for no reason, other than the lateness of the hour. Sir."

Warren is shaking with anger. He curses the press in his mind for relentlessly harassing Anderson, which summoned the man home. "And how do *you* propose to capture the maniac?"

"It's simple. I could reveal his name now."

Warren pauses. What exactly does Anderson know? "Then you will save us all a lot of time if you do so."

"He's obviously living in the immediate vicinity of the murders. If he's not living alone, then the people he's living with are aware of his comings and goings and refuse to give him up. They must be aware of him disposing of his bloody clothing and aware of his butchery. And yet, they do nothing. They protect him, instead."

"And his name, sir?" Warren unconsciously clenches his hands. His lips are tight.

"He's obviously an immigrant from the Jewish quarter, and that is where the police should be looking."

Ah. Warren understands now. Anderson wants to find a scapegoat among the Jews. "So you don't have Ripper's name then?"

"That letter calling himself Jack the Ripper is a hoax from a journalist. Anyone can see that. But if the police force here had half the powers that the French police possess, an arrest would have been made by now."

"We cannot arrest people for going about their business, whether you approve of that business or not. And we cannot arrest women for being poor. Nor can we arrest people because they fit a certain type that you think is the killer."

"We are done, sir." Anderson picks up his hat. "I have

given my opinion on how to stop the murders and I can see that we are not in agreement on this point. Or any other."

After Anderson has left his office, Warren finds he cannot sit still. Everyone, it seems, has a theory about who Ripper is. Some, like Anderson, blame the Jews who live in the East End. Others blame anyone foreign or different in some way. Warren has even heard that some blame the police themselves—or a conspiracy among the elite.

The chief isn't convinced that Lord Rutherford's unholy transport is solely to blame. Though he had poked fun at Constable Neil's clergyman, he, too, wonders if there are two murderers. One of this world. A maniac. A lunatic. A human butcher. But the other? An undead, unholy being from another world.

In his travels, Warren has seen many things he could not explain. It wouldn't be the first time man has unintentionally unleashed something evil with unforeseen and horrific consequences.

### "PHANTOMS"

(Letter to the KURIER CODZIENNY, translated from the Polish)
London, October 23, 1888

London today is a horrible city, full of terror.
The events of the last few weeks are more character-
istic of phantoms and vampires than of human
beings… Twelve thousand armed and educated
constables are helpless…

The phantom, vampire or ghost comes and disappears, not seen and not heard by anybody, except his
victim, to whom he was coming…

One of these hypotheses is worthy of mention owing
to its originality and probability. There are outstanding

and experienced people who say that the perpetrator of these bloody murders is mad, and the cause of his madness is the "thriller literature" which has been very popular in England for many years—crime stories and plays.

# Chapter Thirty-Five

The mist is dense when Lucy Rutherford leaves her father's house for the last time. A wet, icy shroud wraps around her. Beads of water condense on her pale face and neck. She doesn't feel the cool moisture. Though her eyes are open, Lucy does not see. Nor does she start when a dog howls a mournful call. Her mind is focused on other sounds, a strong voice beckoning her onward.

Lucy has managed to evade the sleeping Sally and not rouse any of the other servants. She rose and dressed in darkness, the force inside her directing her movements.

"Lucy. Listen to me." Her mother's voice is in the wind, surrounding Lucy. Calling her. Insistent.

Lucy has no fear. No urge to escape. This is her fate. And she must go.

Out front, a black carriage is waiting in the clammy fog. Two horses, darker than the night itself, are poised like statues waiting for a command from the coachman. The carriage door swings open. Lucy walks towards it.

The carriage is empty. Lucy slides inside.

When the carriage door shuts and Lucy is entombed, she feels a slight bubble of panic well up. Her mother's voice has gotten fainter. It's a distant melody now—but is there a note of warning?

Lucy strains to hear. As the horses bound away from her father's townhouse, Lucy is jolted, and for a moment the spell abates. She wants to get out of the carriage. Now. She opens her mouth to yell to the driver. No words escape her lips. She tries to bang on the window but finds she cannot raise her hand to the glass. Her limbs are like weights.

The horses pick up their speed.

Onward they gallop over cobblestone streets, the carriage tossing Lucy this way and that.

She must fight the lethargy, she tells herself. She must not continue this journey. If not for her own sake, then for her father's. Surely he would miss her?

"Stop," Lucy tries to scream at the coachman. He neither hears nor slows down.

"Lucy. You are mine." She hears it then. A cackling laugh, a voice she has heard before.

Where is it coming from? She is alone in the carriage.

Is she dreaming? No. The tear that rolls down Lucy's cheek is real. She has been taken against her will. And there is no one to help her. No Constable Neil. Not her friend Maude. No one knows that she is in danger.

Lucy shivers in her thin dress. A deep sense of foreboding fills her.

And then the rocking of the carriage stops.

∼

Bethnal Green, November 6, noon

.  .  .

The wheels of the hansom cab rattle loudly over the cobblestone pavement, wreaking havoc with Maude's already frayed nerves. Yet again she draws aside the closed curtain to peer outside. Where is she? She doesn't recognize these narrow streets, these public houses. They had turned away from the river some time ago and the fog cloaks the street lamps in blurry haloes. Rain pelts the windows of the carriage. Surely she should have arrived by now. She fingers the calling card in the pocket of her cloak.

The vehicle lurches to a stop, and Maude hastily replaces the thick veil that covers her face completely. She pays the driver and, before she can ask him to wait, he wheels away. She is committed now. With a deep breath, she turns to the door behind her and raps with the brass knocker. There are lights on upstairs at least, a soft glow that fails to illuminate her surroundings. She is here, that is all that matters.

The door opens and the landlady must have made some sense from Maude's garbled explanation, apologizing for the early hour of her visit, because she leads her to a cozy sitting room warmed with a crackling fire.

"You'll want some tea on a day like this." The woman bustles about. "I'll pour and then fetch Mr. Hinton for you. It must be serious business to bring you here."

She introduces herself as Mrs. Cavendish. The woman has a faint burr, not from Edinburgh like Edward. Highlands perhaps? The thought of Edward makes Maude shiver and move closer to the fire.

She accepts the landlady's cup of tea without comment and waits, staring into the flames, as the sounds of footsteps recede. Eventually they return again, and Maude imagines she can hear the anxiety in Jonathan's step.

"Mrs. Hepworth! My goodness, I..." The journalist's gaze flies from Maude's heavily cloaked figure to his landlady's curious face. "Please, have a seat."

Mrs. Cavendish settles into the armchair she had clearly

been roused from and picks up a portable desk as if returning to her correspondence. They will not be left alone then. Of course not. Maude leans forward and places her teacup on the end table between her and Jonathan.

"Miss Rutherford–Lucy–is missing." She tries to keep her voice steady. She must not sound hysterical.

"How do you know? When was she last seen?" Jonathan jumps up and gets a tattered notebook from his desk. Then he flips the pages until he finds a blank one. "Time? Location? Any witnesses?"

"Her maid Sally alerted my Emily. She thought Lucy might have paid me an early morning visit. But it was I who was meant to visit Lucy this afternoon at her home–she is no longer allowed to visit me," Maude falters. Edward has forbidden the visits but there is no need to reveal that information.

"I have just come from Mayfair, and the servants could not find her. Lord Rutherford is away on business. According to the servants, he left alone early this morning, and has not yet been informed about Lucy's…disappearance." Maude can think of no other word.

"Do you believe Miss Rutherford had another sleep-walking incident?" Jonathan pauses.

Maude shakes her head. "I do not know. Sally was sleeping in the same room with Lucy yet saw and heard nothing."

Maude is proud of herself for the clear and steady way she answers the journalist's questions, though her pulse is galloping. She eyes the captain's clock on the mantel. Time is ticking. She must do something before Edward returns and finds her absent. She stands abruptly and pulls on her gloves.

"We must look for Lucy," Maude says. "We must find her."

"Where?" Jonathan asks.

"At the gentlemen's club. We know Lucy's father and my

husband have some connection there. If Lucy has been taken, that is the first place to look." Somehow, the words sound worse out loud than they did in her head.

"Taken?" Jonathan looks around the room almost wildly. His cheeks are flushed against the pallor of his face. Has he slept at all since she saw him last? He hasn't touched his tea. "By whom? Why on earth…? Who do you…?" He sweeps a hand over his forehead and struggles to speak.

Mrs. Cavendish sits up straighter and opens her mouth. Maude senses that she has been paying full attention to the drama unfolding in her parlor.

"You do not remember me," Mrs. Cavendish says. "But I made your acquaintance—and Miss Rutherford's— at Miss Cobbe's lecture."

Maude looks at the landlady and blushes. She does not remember. There were so many women there. She remembers how nervous she was that Edward might find out and how she looked over her shoulder but not always in front of her.

"I apologize," Maude begins.

"It is no matter," Mrs. Cavendish says. "But I want to warn you that I have heard about this club through my association with Miss Cobbe. It is not safe for you to go there."

Jonathan looks at his landlady in surprise, then he turns to Maude:

"I have been investigating the gentleman's club, since you showed me those…" He clears his throat. "You know. And I've looked into your husband as well. There does seem to be a connection… Women have been reported missing from the asylum and I found a driver who picks up passengers there— only at night. It's certainly suspicious and we could alert the police—."

"I do not think we have time for that," Maude interrupts. "And have the police caught the Ripper murderer? My faith in Scotland Yard does not equal yours. Lucy could be…"

"I agree with Mrs. Hepworth," Jonathan's landlady says.

"The police are ineffectual at best in protecting women in Whitechapel and its environs. What hope do we have of them finding Lucy?"

"Do you have an alternative suggestion, Jonathan?" Maude asks.

"I will go by myself and investigate. Mrs. Cavendish is correct. The club is not the place for…," he stops. Maude sees that Jonathan probably wanted to say "women," and yet that would include the women at the club as well, the nude ones on display for men to do as they wish.

"You," he continues. "I will report back on what I find."

"You must be very careful," Mrs. Cavendish says. "There is evil there."

Jonathan nods. Maude looks up again at the clock. She must return home. She never knows exactly what time Edward will return, and if he should catch her out? She shudders at the thought.

"Then it is a plan," Maude says. "I trust you will communicate to me immediately if you find Lucy."

"It is probably best you wait at home," Mrs. Cavendish says to Maude. "Lucy may yet come to you there. And I will see if Miss Cobbe can offer any assistance." Maude nods her goodbyes and takes her leave.

She feels more hopeful now, or at least less afraid.

# Chapter Thirty-Six

The little fool! Edward presses his lips together and dismisses the man with a brusque wave. With a slight bow, the man pockets Edward's sovereign and leaves as silently as he had arrived. A blast of cold air enters the hallway, chilling him further. Edward makes his way back to the parlor, thinking. Who has she seen? What does she know? He pours himself a brandy out of habit. He never drinks, but a glass in the hand helps him think.

His fury rises and crests under his ribs. How he hates her at this moment. Her wide eyes and downturned mouth. Her cringing ways. For all his care and concern, this is how he is repaid! She has failed at everything he asked of her: obedience, loyalty, discretion. All he wants is for her to make no impression at all. And produce a child, though the act itself sickens him. There would be no child now. He would never have to go through with that disgusting procedure again.

He throws himself into his chair and rehearses his next steps. He has another plan, of course. There is always another plan. He lingers over it, turning each step this way and that, looking for holes or weaknesses. There are none. He puts down the untouched glass carefully and rubs his hands together. He will be prepared for her when she gets home. Oh yes. He will be ready.

Mayfair, November 6, late afternoon

Lord Rutherford sits at his desk, a glass of whiskey untouched beside him. He stares at the *Evening News* spread out before him and glances at a headline, "The Work of the Police." He has half a mind not to read it. And he has half a mind to ask for Sir Charles Warren's resignation. As Home Secretary, that is his right.

He had planned to be away all day on business, another mining operation he is thinking of acquiring up north, but the terms were not favorable, and he's angry he's wasted his time. He waved away his butler saying he was under no circumstances to be disturbed. He needs to sit and think. It's a mess. All of it. And he is not used to feeling he has no control.

He'll give Warren until the end of the week, and then cut him loose if there are no developments. Does Warren take him for a fool?

He takes a large sip of the scotch, enjoying the burn down his throat, and reads the newspaper.

*Since the murders in Berner Street, St. George's, and Mitre Square, Aldgate, Detective Inspectors Reid, Moore, and Nairn, and Sergeants Thicke, Godley, M'Carthy, and Pearce have been constantly engaged under the direction of Inspector Abberline (Scotland Yard), in prosecuting inquiries, but, unfortunately, up to the present time without any practical result.*

"Without any practical result. What do these men do all

day?" Lord Rutherford throws the paper down in disgust. Special force, indeed, he thinks. Warren is incompetent. He knows the danger out there. What is he doing with his police force, never mind his so-called special, secret force?

Rutherford picks up the newspaper again, scanning for any information that the journalists are on to Warren's secret force.

*As an instance of the magnitude of their labours, each officer has had, on average, during the last six weeks to make some 30 separate inquiries weekly. Since the last two murders in Whitechapel, no fewer than 1400 letters relating to the tragedies have been received by the police. The Times says that the detective officers, who are now subjected to a great amount of harassing work, complain that the authorities do not allow them sufficient means with which to carry on their investigations.*

"Bloody hell." Rutherford tosses the newspaper aside. The implied criticism of the lack of manpower falls first on Warren, but it ends with him.

Lord Rutherford pushes his chair back and paces his office. He had asked Warren to find the stowaway fiend and the Ripper maniac. And he has not been able to apprehend either. They can't be one and the same, can they? No. Impossible. Warren is incompetent, that's all there is to it.

Rutherford exhales loudly and walks to the window. He pushes aside the heavy damask drapes and looks out. The moon will be bright and nearly full later. That will bring out all the lunatics, he thinks.

First thing tomorrow morning, he'll send for Warren. He needs an arrest. He needs results.

Suddenly, there's a knock on the study door. It is Sally, his daughter's maid, who comes in trembling before him.

"Your Lordship." She bows before him.

"Yes, what is it? I asked not to be disturbed." He hates being interrupted when he's deep in thought.

"Your Lordship, I…"

"Get on with it," he shouts, and it feels good to take out some of his frustrations on the trembling servant before him.

"It's Miss Lucy. She is…"

"Is she sleepwalking again? I told you to watch her. Incompetence, all the way around. Send for Dr. Hepworth immediately. We must put a stop to this nonsense."

"I do not think the doctor can help," she says.

Rutherford slams his hand on his desk. "Are you disobeying an order?"

"Lucy is missing my lord." Sally bursts into tears before him.

"What do you mean missing? Where is she? What have you done with her?"

Rutherford stands up to his full height and Sally cowers before him, practically bending double as if he might strike her. He has never struck any of the help and is pulled up short at the thought of it. "Nothing, sir. Miss Lucy is not in her bedroom. She went out this morning. Or we think she did. None of the servants saw her go. When I woke, she was already gone. I knew she was to meet with Mrs. Hepworth but then Mrs. Hepworth came but Lucy was not here. I waited, thinking Miss Lucy would return home soon, that maybe she was with Miss Cobbe… Oh, it is all my fault." The maid starts to cry. "I don't know where she could be."

"Cobbe? Who? What? This is utter nonsense." Rutherford strides past Sally and calls out for his manservant. But he can't shake a feeling of dread in his bones. He had forbidden Lucy to leave the house. He'd left strict instructions for the servants to keep her under surveillance. And that constable as well. What's-his-name?

Can no one do their damned job?

"Sanders," Rutherford says to his manservant. "I understand my daughter is not in this house at this moment and that no one has seen her today. I want you to organize a search and find her. Immediately." Rutherford turns back to face Sally.

"Is she with that doctor's wife? Have you inquired there?"

Sally nods. "I sent one of the girls to Kensington. Both the doctor and Mrs. Hepworth are not at home, and Miss Lucy has not been there."

"She must be somewhere." Rutherford is not in the habit of shouting at servants, but he does so now. "I need you to find her. Find my daughter!"

# Chapter Thirty-Seven

Maude removes her gloves and unpins her hat, handing them to Emily at the door. She murmurs the usual words and listens to the usual report on the supper menu and table settings. In their modest home, Emily does a bit of everything. But Maude's mind is leagues away, whirling over the plans she has made with Mr. Hinton and Mrs. Cavendish.

She had wanted to go to the gentlemen's club, but they insisted she return home and wait. Maude has been waiting her entire life, she has realized. But for what? She does not entirely know and cannot put it into words.

Mrs. Cavendish had proved surprisingly resourceful—and quite adamant in her insistence that they not rush off to the gentlemen's club. Jonathan will investigate first. Mrs. Cavendish will alert Miss Cobbe and get her advice. Surely that is a better—and safer—plan.

"There you are. Where have you been?" It is Edward, blocking the door to the parlor as she moves toward it. Maude suppresses a gasp. Shouldn't he be at his office? When had he arrived home?

"Why, at Miss Rutherford's for tea. Remember?" She draws her composure over her like a cloak, holding very still as she meets his eyes. It always paid to be calm with Edward. Very calm.

"I don't think so."

Maude blinks. "What…what do you mean?" She isn't even sure how to respond. Suddenly, her heart starts racing ahead of her thoughts. Edward glances into the room behind him, then back at her, his expression grim.

"Facial tics. Stammering. Typical signs of lying. Unexplained absences. Time that cannot be accounted for. I told you, it is a sad case. I fear it will come to a crisis if I don't intervene with the proper treatment." He is speaking to someone behind him, but Maude cannot see over his shoulder. She starts to edge away from him.

"Edward—" There is no way he is joking. Edward never jokes. Maude takes another step backward and almost stumbles over a coat rack. "I don't understand." Her husband looks like a stranger, his face emotionless. With a quick darting motion, he reaches out and clamps a hand around her wrist, dragging her back toward him.

Maude hears herself gasp. She sees her arms pushing him away, all without fully comprehending what is happening. She is in her own home. This is her hallway. Surely there are servants who would… Where has Emily gone?

Two burly men emerge from behind Edward and hold her arms while Edward clamps a damp handkerchief over her mouth and nose. She has seen men like that before—when she had once met Edward at his hospital. These men are orderlies. She twists her head away from the foul smell against her face.

"I know you did not see Miss Rutherford today. I know that you are conspiring with her against me." His voice is very quiet at her ear.

Maude continues to thrash against the arms that hold her captive. The effort makes her inhale more of the horrible odor. Already her vision is dimming. "Help!" she mouths against the cloth. She shouldn't breathe. She won't.

"See the animal strength she has!" Edward sounds almost impressed. He leans in again. "I. Won't. Have. It." Each word stabs her in the throat.

How does he know? Maude scrambles to hold onto something steady as her vision tilts. *Lucy.* She was—

Her limbs give out, and she slumps against the two men who hold her.

"Gentleman, you know what to do. A husband is responsible for his wife's well-being, and this must be done. I consign her to your care." Edward hands over a folded set of papers.

"It is surely a mercy and a blessing that I have my very own hospital to ensure she is safe from any more delusions." The words seem to arrive from a great distance, and make no sense. And then Maude is senseless.

# Chapter Thirty-Eight

BETHNAL GREEN, NOVEMBER 7

With a shaking hand, Jonathan pours himself a glass of water. He gulps it down, spilling some of it on his chin and his neck. There is a slight burn where the water drips on his neck. The two tiny wounds have yet to heal.

He is so insatiably thirsty. But the water does not quench his thirst.

Jonathan takes out a handkerchief from his trousers' pocket and wipes his brow. The cloth comes away wet with perspiration. He must have a fever. He has felt so ill as of late. Though Mrs. Cavendish has prepared him supper almost every night, mostly warm soups with a bit of mutton, he hasn't been able to stomach any of it. The thought of food makes him violently ill, and he pushes away the plates, always claiming he has no appetite.

What is the matter with him? He's exhausted, that is the long and short of it, he thinks. It is his work. He can't write quickly enough to satisfy the public appetite for news about Jack the Ripper.

The other favorite topic is the sheer incompetence of Scotland Yard and Sir Charles Warren. Jonathan himself was at Whitechapel most evenings on the hunt for fresh news to satisfy the reading public's voracious demands.

He is overworked. And now Lucy is missing and he must go back to the gentlemen's club. But something is holding him back. He is unwell. Feverish. He collapsed shortly after Mrs. Hepworth left. He should not have promised her to help find Lucy.

Jonathan's nightmares have also gotten worse. A seductive voice calls his name, softly, as if it comes in on the fog. It is a man's voice, low and deep. And Jonathan melts and gives in to the siren song. He will go anywhere to follow the voice. White hot desire spreads through his body and his loins. He wants to give himself over, to be consumed, to be ravished.

Jonathan gnashes his teeth and hangs his head in shame. Then he unconsciously touches his hand to his throat. No. He cannot admit it to himself. Those bites, the attack that he suffered outside the cemetery, and here in his own bedroom.

This is the stuff of tall tales. He does not believe Mrs. Cavendish's stories about her husband and the men on the ship. And yet, how can he account for the bites and his nightmares and his burning desire for… He dares not name it.

Jonathan has to keep his wits about him. He has work to do.

He puts on his coat. The black wool hangs on his too slight frame. He has lost weight, one or two stone. He has long ago stopped looking in the mirror. He no longer shaves and has let a beard grow in.

"Why, you're a skeleton." He hears his mother and sisters chastise him. They would insist on fattening him up. They would fuss over him, make him broths, ply him with choice meats, and cover his legs with a blanket like an invalid. The thought is comforting.

He vows that when this is all over, when Jack the Ripper is

caught, after he has helped Mrs. Hepworth find Miss Rutherford, he will make a proper visit to Bath. He will be restored to
health in the bosom of his family. Maybe he will even take the
waters.

Jonathan buttons up his coat. Despite the heavy wool coat,
he is always cold. Indoors as well as out. He can never get
warm. He needs to see a doctor. Perhaps there is medicine he
can take.

When he opens the door to his rooms, he nearly falls
down. Mrs. Cavendish is standing there. In her hand is a clear
glass bottle filled with liquid of some kind. Instinctively,
Jonathan raises his arms to shield his face. His eyes burn as if
she's thrown acid in his face. But when he looks, Mrs.
Cavendish has not moved. She hasn't assaulted him. The
bottle remains capped.

"It is as I feared," she says. "This is holy water." She holds
out the bottle, and he recoils as if he has been stung by a scor-
pion. Jonathan slams his door shut.

"Mr. Hinton. Jonathan." His landlady bangs on the door.
"It is not too late. Let me help you."

Jonathan doesn't need help. He needs to find Miss Rutherford. And he must go to the gentlemen's club discreetly. Dr.
Hepworth is a very dangerous man to corner. Then there is
the Ripper on the loose.

His thoughts swirl in his heavy head. On an impulse he
scribbles a note to his colleague Smith and tucks it into his
notebook, leaving it on the desk for Mrs. Cavendish to find.
Later. He needs to go. Now. Without thinking, Jonathan goes
to the window. To his surprise, it is already open. His room is
on the third floor, but moments later he finds himself on the
sidewalk below. How has he gotten there? He simply thought
that he needed to get out, and there he was.

How strange. He hadn't jumped. It was as if he'd flown
from the window. He gathers his coat more closely around

him. He isn't injured in the slightest. In fact, he feels stronger, certainly stronger than he was when facing Mrs. Cavendish.

The voice is back. It beckons Jonathan. This time he thinks he hears a female voice too. Is it Miss Rutherford? His feet take him in the direction of Whitbourne Street.

November 7. Page torn from bound journal, scribbled in pencil

*Dear Miss Cobbe,*

*Forgive me. I write in haste—our fears confirmed. The worst has befallen JH. Escaped LR still missing. No word from M. We must help. I will collect reinforcements and meet you at 10 Bells. Do not tarry! AC*

# Chapter Thirty-Nine

His stomach rumbles, though there weren't two bites in there to knock together. Constable Neil pats his hand on his middle. There, there, I'll get you some grub soon. Maybe.

When his watch is over.

Neil huddles a little closer to the gas lamp post and goes back to staring up at the front windows of the townhouse across the street. Nice digs, that doctor has. And still young. He scratches one foot against the other, trying to stem the tingles that are starting. He's getting too old for this, he thinks. He likes a nice bed now. A soft pillow. A full plate of bangers and mash. A pretty little thing to squeeze is too much to hope for. A girl with red hair.

A shadow crosses the top story window. Neil knows from a brief conversation at the servants' door that this was the doctor's private domain. His office, they said. Kept locked. What was he doing up there, well past the work day? The street lamp above him flickers.

It was a circuitous route that had brought him here

tonight. He had spent many nights watching over Miss Rutherford—Lucy, inside his thoughts. And then there was the night he'd found her in Whitechapel, of all places. Thank goodness he was on his beat because otherwise? No. It's unimaginable.

And he'd searched high and low looking for the man who'd accosted her. He thought he'd recognize the bloke. Though when Neil returned to scour the streets of Whitechapel the man had vanished—and no one he'd asked had seen him. Much like the Ripper himself who seems to come and go as silently as the fog.

Since that night, he'd often followed Lucy during the day as well on her visits with Mrs. Hepworth. They were up to something, those two, but he couldn't figure out what. They attended a lecture together, which would be respectable if they weren't the radical bluestocking kind. They disappeared indoors for teas and luncheons, occasionally reappearing to saunter through the Rutherford's well-tended garden. Mostly innocent, but the way they whispered together set his copper's nerves jangling.

So he watched them. Miss Rutherford in her fur-lined cape, sweeping into a carriage, as regal as any princess from a fairy tale. Miss Rutherford, head thrown back to laugh exuberantly at something Miss Hepworth had murmured too low for him to hear. What brought that flush to her cheeks? Too often he found himself wondering about her when he had no business but to watch and wait.

Then, two days ago, Mrs. Hepworth had shown up at the Rutherfords' home as usual and, after a brief disappearance inside, she had re-emerged, alone. Neil had straightened up from his slouch behind a broken and abandoned cart. He had not been able to be on duty that night, but came to Mayfair in the early morning. He saw Lord Rutherford leave.

Then he'd watched as Mrs. Hepworth had retraced her steps slowly, twisting her gloves and frowning at the ground. A servant hailed her a hansom cab, then he turned his attention back to the house. He knew something was wrong. He has not seen Lucy, and the servants are all a flutter. Lucy is missing. And he had not been there to protect her.

Neil clenches his fist as he stands, stationed outside Doctor Hepworth's home. He is waiting to speak to Mrs. Hepworth. Alone.

But she is nowhere to be seen neither. The servants are too scared to speak to him, which was no good sign itself. Neil shifts again on his aching feet, wondering for the thousandth time if he should notify his superiors, who would notify the Lord Devil… And take the case out of his hands. And what if there was a chance Miss Lucy didn't want to be found? What if she has gone to some relative's house? He'd look a right fool. His gut tells him this isn't the case.

No, he'll wait a little longer, just to keep an eye on the doctor at the window.

As he watches, the light goes out upstairs. After a few moments, the front door opens and Dr. Hepworth stalks out the front door, dressed all in black and carrying a medical bag. An unmarked carriage draws up to the house and barely stops before the doctor leaps into it with a murmured command. The driver cracks a whip, and the vehicle disappears into the dark.

Neil snaps open his pocket watch and makes out the time under the uncertain light. Past midnight. What kind of duty calls the doctor out so late? Neil doesn't like the suspicions that are forming at the edges of his mind, nor how close they are coming to Lucy.

With grim determination, he decides to make one more attempt at the servants' quarters. He crosses the street in several long strides and lets out some of his frustration on the back door.

"Stop yer banging!"

The door opens just a crack, but Neil pushes one scuffed leather boot inside.

"Hey!" The young maid glowers at him, arms crossed over her chest. "What's your business here? I've done nothing wrong."

Neil leans close to her red face. "I am Constable Neil. And who might you be?"

The maid stiffens further and takes a step back, scanning his figure in the doorway. "Em…Emily. Why do you need to know? What do you want?" She looks about the darkened kitchen as if checking for a place to bolt.

Neil pushes past her into the room and pulls out a rough wooden chair, gesturing for her to sit, which she does warily, arms still tightly crossed. He ignores her questions. They are a waste of time.

"Your mistress. Mrs. Hepworth. Where is she?"

The maid's eyes fly to his, and she shakes her head briskly. "Can't say."

"Can't say or won't say?"

"Can't say!"

Neil studies the girl's flustered face. There's something here. He knows it and she knows it. He knows this maid was sister to Annie Chapman. A funny thing, that. A coincidence that makes Neil feel uneasy.

He lets her dangle for a minute as he scans the room. A heavy cast-iron pan hangs over the open fireplace, which fills one wall. A coal scuttle and larder squeeze into another corner. The rough-hewn table they sit at is scored by knife marks and old burns. A candle is lit on a shelf near an open doorway covered with a bit of faded gingham curtain. The pantry, he surmises, where she must roll out a bed pad at night to sleep on. Not like the fancy setup at Rutherford House, that's for sure.

Neil turns back to Emily and studies her face. "I think

she's missing. I've been watching her friend Miss Rutherford. She's missing too. What do you think of that?"

Emily says nothing, but her face goes pale.

"When did you last see your mistress?"

"Day before." The words come out in a whisper, but Neil feels the familiar satisfaction of information loosening, like the crack of a hard nut in his hands. He moves quickly to get all the details he can, though Emily balks at saying—or guessing—where Mrs. Hepworth might be. He can't tell if she doesn't know or is too fearful to tell him. She keeps glancing at the door and windows nervously, as if someone might find him there. Finally, she whispers. "It were two men as took her away. I saw." Her voice lowers. "From the hospital."

Neil absorbs this in silence, watching as the maid starts to sob. "And Annie… I should have. I didn't know. I didn't know. She wanted to tell me something and I thought it was just the drink again." She wipes her eyes with her apron. "Lord have mercy on her lost soul."

They sit for a moment at the bare table, in the candlelight.

"You better leave, sir." Emily's voice is still quiet, but her tone is firm. "The bobbies done nothing for my poor sister, and you can't do nothing now for my poor mistress." She bites her lip as she looks at him, as if hoping he could read her mind so she needn't say another word.

What on earth is keeping this household so nervous-like? He rises and wonders how to proceed. "Thank you. I'll be on my way. I can tell you are a decent girl and a good maid. Mrs. Hepworth is lucky to have you."

He puts his hat on his head, looking at the floor as he adds. "Too bad it is she left no clue you could pass along to me, quiet-like. No one would know because no word was spoken." He lets that notion settle in her brain as he shuffles closer to the door. "If you think of anything useful, I'm at Leman Street Station. I won't tell no one."

He is moving as slow as he can, but still he has reached the doorway when she puts a hand on his arm to stop him. With a fierce expression on her face, she disappears behind the curtain, and reappears breathing fast. "Here. Now go on!" Her voice starts rising as her panic takes over. "Go!"

Neil knows when to cut his losses. He folds his hand over the object she thrust at him and leaves as quietly as he can. No need to get that brave girl in any soup. He feels the object in his hand, but it isn't until he gets back to the flickering gas lamp across the street that he can see what it is.

It's a cheap carte de visite, the edges worn down by handling and the subject common enough. A woman on a bed, clothing askew, her limbs managed for best viewing angles. There is no knowing smirk on this lady's face, though. She seems—quite asleep, in fact. He squints closer at it.

My God, he thinks, it's Annie Chapman, younger by several years. And are those restraints on her wrists? Neil swallows his recoil and flips the card over for the studio stamp. But there is none. The carefully printed label reads "MANIA— FEMALE TYPE. BETHLEM ROYAL HOSPITAL."

*Chapter Forty*

Someone is stroking her hair. And singing softly, though Maude can't make out the words. She draws in a deep breath through her mouth and swallows. Her mouth is dry and tastes strange. Eyes closed, she tries to assemble some pieces of memory, slowly shifting from her side to her back on a thin mattress. The bed frame creaks and the stroking and singing stops. She opens her eyes.

A face leans over hers, eyes staring, the skin stretched taut to form deep hollows under the cheeks. Maude scrambles backwards on the bed, heart pounding.

The other woman nods solemnly and moves away. Maude takes in the bare room at a glance. Whitewashed walls. A high window, barred. The smell of…bleach. And urine. A row of iron bedsteads march down the length of a rectangular room.

"Wait! Where am I?" Her voice comes out as a whisper.

"Bedlam." The other woman nods again, her gaze steady. Clutching her hospital gown in one hand, she moves away, limping.

With an effort, Maude sits up and takes this in. She has been stripped of her day gown and left in chemise and petticoat. She raises her hands to her hair, which is coming loose. No pins. She rubs her aching limbs and shivers in the drafty room.

She can explain. She would explain. Gingerly, she places one foot on the concrete floor, then the other. She is standing, that is something. She shuffles toward the middle of the room, where a metal door clangs open and closed.

"Sir!" Her voice sounds small and feeble to her own ears, but the man in the orderly uniform turns and looks at her. Before she can say a word, he turns away and resumes carrying a bucket to one of the beds, water slopping on the floor.

Maude pauses, pressing a hand against her forehead, and wills her fear and uncertainty away. A matron bustles past, arms full of dirty linens. Instinctively, Maude reaches out and grabs her sleeve. "Ma'am!"

The nurse halts in place, and peers at her face, disengaging her sleeve. "Now there. None of that." She has a red face and her eyes disappear between the rough patches of her cheeks. A wisp of gray hair has fallen out of her mobcap.

Maude draws herself up as best she can. "My name is Maude Hepworth. I am Dr. Hepworth's wife. There has been a terrible mistake—"

The matron lets out a guffaw. "You're the one, then! We was warned about you. You do look a mite toffish, with them pearly whites. You better get back to bed, *Mrs. Hepworth.*"

The matron chuckles some more as she heads toward the metal door. She bangs on it with one fist, and it opens from the other side with a loud creaking sound. She disappears through the gap and the door shuts with another bang.

Maude stands stock still, absorbing the overlapping shrieks and moans, the flurries of motion, and the unnerving stillness from different corners of the echoing room. Slowly, she returns to her bed. No, not her bed! She doesn't belong here. She knows that with a cold, hard certainty, despite the lingering fuzziness in her brain. Edward can leave her here; his authority is absolute. Her sister would never know. Lucy is missing. Mr. Hinton and Mrs. Cavendish would have no idea where to find either of them. Maude accepts these facts with a calm that surprises herself. Yes, these things are true. Her situation is real. She is not insane. She needs a plan.

~

Bloomsbury, November 8

Amelia Cavendish holds a lantern up over her head and peers down the narrow alleyway. Nothing. She has checked five times already, and it is hardly worth doing, the fog is so thick. Sounds of scurrying makes her tuck her heavy cloak closer. She doesn't want rats brushing against her ankles. The smell is almost as bad as the shadows. Below her, a few steps lead to cobblestones slick with urine and ale. But then, they don't want any stray visitors wandering down this way.

They chose this location behind Euston Station specifically to be invisible in plain sight. Amelia listens intently for the sound of any rattling wheels, but hears only the rise and fall of shouting from the pub around the corner. Even on a cold, dank night like this, the drinkers spill over onto the sidewalk.

With a sigh, Amelia heaves the back door open and returns to work. For a moment, she stands with her back against the door and marvels, again, at all they have accomplished.

The large chamber is two stories high, the windows blacked out with cloth. But a massive electric bulb, swaying gently from a hook in the ceiling, illuminates the whole cavernous space with a metallic light. One wall is lined with wooden shelving that stretches horizontally from corner to corner. These shelves hold enough artillery for a Prussian battalion—heavy-handled muskets stack up against American rifles and bursting boxes of ammunition, long gleaming swords and pointed daggers heap together, polished to a high shine.

In another corner, a pile of bows is matched with quivers full of sharp-tipped arrows. Elsewhere there are iron manacles, heavy chains coiled into circles, leather whips, and cudgels. It is a fearsome armory, and it makes Amelia proud.

Across the room, some twenty or thirty bodies silently work to prepare for the campaign ahead, Amelia notes approvingly. They have had many a dress rehearsal, and now they are ready.

"Ladies!" Her voice echoes through the room and everyone snaps to attention, primed for action. "Our leader has not yet arrived but we may leave at a moment's notice. We suspect that Miss Rutherford is at the gentlemen's club on Whitmore Street. Our inside source saw her there. I suspect that Mr. Hinton has been drawn there as well. I fear they are both under the control of some powerful, insidious being. I await news of Mrs. Hepworth, but we know where to look. Her husband may have prevented her from meeting me this morning, but he will not prevail against us!"

From all corners come the muffled sounds of cheers and hisses, as if escaping from every mouth. Amelia bites back a smile. These are her girls. She trained them all herself. Frances Power Cobbe might be the head of their force, but Amelia is the strong arm. She has never told her tenant where she spends most of her waking hours. Jonathan has never suspected a thing.

"New recruits! Over here—line up to introduce yourselves and pair off with your mentors."

There is a jostling of bodies and Amelia observes the women with satisfaction. Five new girls, just in time!

Mrs. Josephine Ferro, Imogen Lock, Ludmilla Czerny, Rita Blume, Miss Emily Mackie. The women nod and shuffle off. The last gives a little curtsy, like she's used to service. "No need for that here, Miss Mackie!"

Just then the entry door flies open and a curl of yellow fog sweeps in. Ah, just in time, Amelia thinks, turning to greet her comrade. A round figure in a heavy black cape pushes into the room, stomping her boots against the cold. Frances Power Cobbe, known to her vigilante female crew as Fan, fills the open doorway, arms akimbo on her wide hips. The room grows quiet in anticipation and her voice rings out like a bell.

"So, my biddies, what have I missed?"

# *Chapter Forty-One*

Mary Jane Kelly feels a strange foreboding in her chest. She's due at the gentlemen's club in less than an hour. A cold shiver runs down her spine when she thinks of going. Why tonight of all nights does she have a sudden aversion? Nay, it's more than that. It's fear.

But what is she afraid of? She's survived far worse in her twenty-five years. Indeed, she escaped being sold into slavery in France. She had foolishly believed she was going to be married in Paris, only to arrive there and find her supposed gentleman suitor had instead inducted her into a brothel.

The first tip-off? The trunk she'd sent on ahead of time, filled with expensive gowns, jewelry, and leather gloves—gifts from wealthy gentlemen clients—had mysteriously gone missing. The second was the strong instinct to run when she met the French woman who'd offered to house her until the wedding.

Mary Jane spoke fluent French. She knew the woman was

a madam, her house a brothel, and that once she took shelter there, she'd never be allowed to leave.

Still, Mary Jane managed to outsmart her captors. For in addition to her beauty—she was buxom and pretty, with cornflower blue eyes and long wavy chestnut hair—Mary Jane had been gifted with intelligence, both book knowledge and cunning. By keeping her wits about her and following her instincts, she had engineered her escape and returned to London.

But she couldn't go back to her life in the West End, to the gay parties in St. John's Wood. She became a fugitive. The man who had sold her was looking for her. He would send her back—or worse.

She had to go somewhere more discreet, somewhere the long reach of the French madam and her English pimp couldn't reach.

Mary Jane finds this in the anonymity and crowds of Whitechapel. There are many gay women like herself. The streets are crowded at all hours of the night. She can blend in here and make a new life for herself.

Mary Jane is no fool. She knows her beauty won't last. She is determined to make the most of it while she can. And though she'd left Paris far behind, she'd kept her Parisian name, Marie Jeanette, when it suited her to use it with clients.

She would promenade with two or three girlfriends, other gay women like herself, along Commercial Street or Whitechapel Road. Despite the fact that the gown she wears now is frayed and not nearly as fine as the ones that she used to wear, Mary Jane takes pride in her appearance and is always neatly turned out. Like her two friends, Mary Jane wears no bonnet or hat on her head. She needs to advertise that though she may look like a lady, she is not of that class.

After her near imprisonment in Paris, Mary Jane vowed never to depend on or trust a man again. She hasn't. She has lived with two other men. She shared a room with one in

Bethnal Green, but he had a terrible temper, particularly when drunk, and she left him before he could permanently scar her face.

At the moment, she has a room in Miller's Court, a small dark room, partitioned from a decrepit worker's cottage. She shares the ten-by-twelve-foot room with her new "husband," Joseph. But since the Ripper murders, Mary Jane has made space for at least two other women to spend the night at 13 Miller's Court as well.

"It's not safe to be sleeping rough, Julia," she told her friend, an older woman who hadn't enough money for a bed. "Not with Jack the Ripper still on the loose. Sleep here with us."

Unlike many of her women companions, Mary Jane is literate. She eagerly reads the newspapers aloud to her friends every day. They live in fear, though that doesn't stop them from making a living. They just hope the police will soon catch the killer terrorizing the East End.

When she offered to share her room with her friend Lizzie, another streetwalker, Joseph moved out.

"No matter," Mary Jane told Lizzie. "Joseph cannot support me, and I must earn my living as I know how."

Still, Mary Jane feels more anxious now that Joseph is gone. The walk to her room at 13 Miller's Court is full of dark corners. She picks up her pace when she goes out at night and turns repeatedly to look over her shoulder to make sure she isn't being followed.

Not that she is exactly safe in her room. During one of her frequent fights with Joseph, usually when they'd both been out drinking at the pub, Mary Jane had put her hand through a glass window next to the door and broken it. Though she'd stuffed it with rags to keep out the cold, it would hardly keep an intruder out.

Tonight, Mary Jane is home with Lizzie, but she plans on going to the gentlemen's club.

"Don't expect me back tonight," Mary Jane tells her friend. "So if you need to make use of the room, know that I will see you in the morning."

Mary Jane has been invited to a party at the gentleman's club by one of her wealthier clients. The older man, Mr. O'Shea, is Irish like herself, and he reminds her of her homeland.

She'd met him at the club a couple of times before. It is safer there, in some ways, yet more dangerous in others. For behind the closed doors, and cloaked in gentility, men could do whatever they chose with women more freely, without consequence.

"Can I go with you?" Lizzie asks her, as Mary Jane wraps her only shawl around her.

"No, dear. It is not the place for you. Not even for me. The things that go on there…" She stops and looks at her friend. Lizzie is so young, younger than she. And she's had a difficult life. She's been a gay woman since she was fifteen.

"Maybe another time. I will ask my friend for a recommendation. A nice man that you can meet there."

Not every gay woman can get into the club. What's more, Mary Jane has received high praise from several gentlemen, some of whom she is sure were founding members, and she does not want to lose her opportunity. Her youth is fleeting, she knows.

The drinks will flow like a stream there, and she's looking forward to it. She can almost taste the champagne on her tongue; she has such a fondness for it. She should be grateful for a good night's wages, she tells herself. Lizzie would be out on the foggy streets where it was far more dangerous.

With a shake of her head, Mary Jane closes the door at 13 Miller's Court and makes her way towards Whitbourne Street. Though she can't see more than a few feet in front of her because of the fog and the dim glow of streetlights, she scours the darkness to make sure she isn't being followed. She will not fall prey to the Ripper. She hasn't escaped from so much peril in her young life for it to be cut short.

Whitbourne Street, November 8, 11:00 p.m.

The sharp, pungent scent of cigar and pipe smoke threatens to engulf Mary Jane when she steps into the gentleman's club. The air is so thick with it that the fog is denser inside than outside. Mary Jane instinctively raises her hand to cover her nose and mouth, but then drops it. There's no escaping the fumes.

Music is playing loudly. The striking sound of a piano rises above the laughter and noise of so many women and men packed into the main hall. Mary Jane doesn't like this type of music. The tune is quick and frenzied, meant not to soothe but to stir the blood of those who hear it.

She can already see men and women together rubbing against each other on the dance floor of the large first-floor room. They still have their clothes on, which won't be the case as the night wears on.

This is a gentlemen's club in name only. There are similar ones in Haymarket, where Mary Ann used to live and work, but this one has a more dangerous air, as if anything could happen.

And anything did. Mary Jane has often seen men and women fornicating in corners. Or naked women dancing with several men who were fondling them. The air is close and hot. The smell of smoke, bodies, drink, and sex fills the air.

Mary Jane does not like it here. But Mr. O'Shea frequents the club and asks for her specifically. He pays her well. Tonight, she definitely needs the money. She is fourteen shillings behind on her rent. She must pay her landlord or he'll put her out on the street and bar the entrance to her room in Miller's Court. And then what would happen to her? She can't take the chance of sleeping rough. Not until the police catch the Ripper. She shivers when she thinks of the silent murderer who has evaded capture.

Mary Jane accepts a glass of cheap champagne and downs it quickly. She will limit herself tonight. Three at most. Maybe four. She can't afford to let her guard down here. She's heard the stories—nay, she's heard the cries of women, tied and beaten by sadistic men who take their pleasure that way. There have been rumors, too, of bestiality, though she herself has neither seen nor heard such things.

Mary Jane scans the crowd. It's difficult to see through the smoke and the wall-to-wall thrum of bodies. Even the women are smoking, something that she finds particularly unladylike.

Mary Jane skirts the wall along the dance floor. She hasn't yet spotted Mr. O'Shea, an older gentleman, with more white than black in his beard, though he has the libido of a much younger man.

O'Shea is not sitting at one of the stools at the bar. Nor is he at the billiard table, which is being used as a makeshift bed for several couples.

Mary Jane then searches the dining hall with its heavy, round wooden tables and chairs. The tables are stacked with uncleared plates, thick with gravy, and the remains of congealed fat, meat, and vegetables. More couples are fornicating here as well.

Mary Jane turns her head away. Has her client forsaken her? Did he feel he'd waited long enough and chosen someone else? There are dozens of women to choose from. No. She is only a few minutes late. Perhaps he's waiting for her in one of the quieter rooms upstairs?

It would be more like him. Mr. O'Shea doesn't condone making a public spectacle, but rather prefers to bring Mary Jane to a more discreet location where they can be alone.

As she begins to ascend the carpeted stairs, Mary Jane is thankful she can't hear the jarring notes of the music quite as loudly. The air is cooler as well.

When she gets to the second floor, the noise is quieter still. She looks down the long hallway. Every bedroom door is closed. There's no sense in knocking. Her client wouldn't have shut the door if he were still waiting for her.

Mary Jane climbs to the third floor, where the air is even clearer and the music much more faint. Only a few couples have ascended this far. She is about to walk down the hall when a chill washes over her, like a cold breeze, as if someone has left a window open.

She finds her limbs are like dead weights. She tries to take a step forward but cannot even lift her foot. It's as if an invisible force is holding her back.

Then she sees something truly remarkable. A young woman with long, flowing red hair stands before an open doorway. Yellow mist spills from the doorway, where a strange-looking man is waiting.

The woman is not part of this club, Mary Jane can tell immediately. No, she is from the upper classes. Her thick, plum-colored cloak, the shiny tresses of her red hair, speak of money. What is a woman of her class and beauty doing here?

*Chapter Forty-Two*

Jonathan feels as if he's gliding rather than walking through the dark streets of Whitechapel. His mind and limbs are not his own. It's almost as if he is two people now. The former Jonathan—the faithful son, dutiful brother, and budding journalist—and the new one, weary and languid, who feels inhabited by something other than himself. Something he cannot name. The sensation is very strange.

He must hurry now. Lucy is in danger. He can feel it, as if they share the same blood in their veins.

He no sooner has this thought than he finds himself standing before the large wooden door of the gentlemen's club at Whitbourne Street. How did he get here so quickly? It's as if he's been transported.

His forehead is clammy, and he wipes his brow with his handkerchief. He must be on the verge of hallucinating from exhaustion. Still, he has a job to do and he can't give in to speculation about his health.

He raps on the door. He's been here once before—to

investigate Mrs. Hepworth's photographs. That was another life. Another Jonathan. The door is answered immediately by a manservant in a black-and-white uniform. The man is a burly fellow whose waistcoat strains to hold his girth. His beefiness is the point, Jonathan surmises. The man serves as a guard as well, only letting those in who've been invited or whose faces he recognizes.

Jonathan holds out a carte de visite that he finds in his pocket. How strange. The beefy man takes it, then looks at Jonathan.

For a moment, the journalist feels he will be turned away. Then the manservant moves aside to let Jonathan enter.

Immediately, through the din of men and women laughing, the harsh-sounding notes of a piano, he hears a voice calling him. It's the same one in his dreams—seductive, sibilant, and irresistible.

The voice calls his name, telling him to come. His limbs obey. Jonathan is barely aware of the vast numbers of men and women, the smell of smoke, alcohol, and human sweat, as he instinctively heads for the stairs. His gaze is fixed straight ahead, though his eyes are unfocused and unseeing.

The voice is louder on the third floor, and Jonathan pauses at the top of the stairs. He begins to walk down the hallway and almost trips over a young woman crumpled on the floor in front of him.

A wave of fear washes over him. Jonathan bends down to help the woman. She has long chestnut hair and pale skin. She is young, beautiful, and reminds him of his oldest sister. For a brief moment, the spell is broken.

He reaches for the woman's hand. He must help her. Her skin is frigid, yet he thinks he feels a pulse. He must find a doctor. He must…

Then he sees something that makes him pull back in horror. Two bite marks with tiny drops of blood bloom on the woman's long, slender neck.

His hand goes instinctively to his own neck. And just as suddenly as he pulled away, he reverses course and grabs the woman to him. Savagely, he bites her on the other side of the neck and drinks. Laughter echoes in his head as blood pours down his throat.

Jonathan abruptly stands up. He wants to gag. He pulls at his hair. What has he done? What has he become? He is vile. Filthy. Inhuman.

And yet, there's an energy in him that he's never felt before. It's electric. He's positively buzzing with some new force in his veins. He almost wants to laugh at himself. He's strong and powerful and—

A scream cuts through his thoughts.

One part of Jonathan's brain registers that it's Lucy. He quickly wipes his mouth, drawing blood onto his fingers. Then he wipes his bloody hand on his trousers and rushes down the hallway.

And there in a bedroom at the end of the hall is Lucy with the man he recognizes from his dreams. Lucy is bound to a chair, her arms and legs tied, and the man is towering over her.

Jonathan cannot look away from the man's face. His eyes are the darkest blue yet glow with a light unlike anything he's seen. He is tall, aristocratic looking, and when he smiles, he reveals sharp white teeth. Jonathan has felt those teeth on his neck, felt them penetrate his skin, and for a brief, horrific moment he wants to feel that again.

The man laughs, a throaty roar that echoes in Jonathan's skull.

"Welcome, my dear boy, draw closer." The voice is deeply seductive.

"Don't! Jonathan. No!" Lucy tries to warn him but is silenced with a wave of the man's hand.

Despite part of his brain telling him to listen to Lucy and

run, Jonathan moves one step closer. Then another. And another.

"We've never been formally introduced. Allow me to officially make your acquaintance. Count Vloeken of the House of Valur." The Count nods his head in Jonathan's direction, and to his horror, Jonathan mirrors the act.

"You have come of your own free will, have you not?"

Jonathan finds himself nodding in agreement.

Lucy is shaking her head no and looking at Jonathan, pleading with her eyes for him to help.

Jonathan cannot look at Lucy. He cannot move. His legs seem to have grown roots into the floor.

"And now, dear boy," the Count says, "I have a very special treat for you. I've been waiting for this moment to bring us all together. To finish what Lucy's father, Lord Rutherford, started."

Jonathan's face must register surprise, as the Count continues.

"Yes, Lord Rutherford drew me here on his ship. I saw you the night of the dock fire. You were so brave, Jonathan. I would have perished if not for your help in quenching the fire. And now I'm here to repay the favor to you, and to exact revenge on the man who brought me to this country. Lucy Rutherford, you will join us. Your father will curse the day his greed resurrected me."

Lucy struggles against the restraints. "Jonathan. Don't listen to him. It's me, Lucy. It's not too late."

This time, the Count does not silence Lucy with his hand. Swiftly, he bends over her, loosens her restraints, then raises her up to draw the sweetness from her neck.

Jonathan watches. He can taste the blood in his own mouth. It is sweet and salty and pure, and he thirsts for more, though he has not moved from his spot.

With a flash of his coat, the Count makes way, summoning Jonathan to move closer towards Lucy.

# Chapter Forty-Three

BETHLEM ROYAL HOSPITAL, NOVEMBER 8, MIDNIGHT

Maude lies perfectly still on the thin mattress of her cot. She bites her lip to keep from shivering, whether from fear or cold. After long hours in this dreadful place, she knows its chill drafts and eerie noises. Now the room is silent except for the snoring of her nearest bedmate. From further away comes the muffled sounds of crying.

She had seen a poor soul bound and gagged earlier this afternoon, then carried away. What has Edward done? And who would know what had happened to her? Who would dare to ask Edward her whereabouts? Only Cordelia, and that could take weeks. Her sister wouldn't even miss her regular letter for another fortnight, then she would certainly try writing before traveling to London.

As these thoughts circle yet again in her restless mind, Maude hears a soft footfall at the farther end of the room. Carefully, with barely perceptible motions, she turns her head to peer through the darkness. A sliver of moonlight from a barred window sheds a weak light on the concrete floor near the door. As Maude stares—unblinking—she sees a shadow cross it.

Her heartbeat picks up, and she thinks frantically of her plans. She had so carefully conspired to avoid the medications that kept the rest of the room subdued. They all sleep like the dead around her, whereas she had mimed chewing the tablet under the attendants' watchful eyes, then held it under her tongue until she could spit it out under the water pump when they lined up for their ablutions before bed.

She and twenty other women had splashed cold water over their faces and hands, shivering as their plain chemises got soaked and stuck to their skin. Maude can think of little else to do except stay awake and observe, be vigilant and watchful for any opportunity.

Who is this person creeping into the room with such stealth?

Maude has to focus to hear any noise at all, but gradually she discerns that the steps are coming closer, pausing at each bed, then moving on. Are they searching for someone? Is it Edward, come to finish her off? Edward wouldn't dirty his hands himself, Maude realizes, but he was not above sending an associate…

She almost gasps as the iron bed nearest her creaks. He is close! She fights against the impulse to spring from her bed and run away. There is nowhere to run in this ghastly place. She will pretend to be asleep. But just in case, she curls her hand into a fist and waits, tense as a board, for the person to reach her next. Closer…closer!

Maude feels the shift of air over her face but keeps her eyes tightly shut. All her senses are alert to the threat above but she focuses on staying still, breathing steadily.

A hand claps over her mouth!

"Do not stir! Wake up—now. It is I."

Instinctively Maude starts to squirm against the hand covering her mouth. Her eyes snap open with fear and she blinks to see the face above hers. It is wrinkled and sallow, with a long scar across one cheek; one eye is covered by a patch. For an eternity the two women stare at each other.

"Mrs. Cavendish," the woman hisses. The voice is barely a whisper.

Though her mind can hardly comprehend, Maude's body relaxes. She nods slightly and Mrs. Cavendish slowly takes her hand away. With one more stern look, she grips Maude by an elbow and pulls her out of the bed. Looking her over, she gives another quick nod and tilts her head toward the metal door.

Wordlessly, Maude follows, the concrete cold against her stockinged feet. What is the plan? Can they possibly escape here unnoticed? She doesn't dare ask. Silence is paramount.

At the door, Mrs. Cavendish collects a bucket and mop, pulling an attendant's uniform out of it and shoving it at Maude. "Hurry!" she says under her breath, but Maude has already grabbed it and pulled it over her head, making her way with her hands on the wall as she follows Mrs. Cavendish through the door and down a dark corridor. Ahead of them, an electric light hovers over the intersection with another hallway.

"Follow my lead!" Suddenly Mrs. Cavendish starts singing quietly, knocking the bucket against the wall and floors as she weaves her way toward the light. In the pocket of her uniform, Maude finds a kerchief and hastily ties it over her hair. She keeps her head down and grabs the mop. A stench rises around her and she almost gags.

"...Men must work and women must weep!" Mrs. Cavendish sings out.

Her pulse racing, Maude bends over and grunts, putting a hand to the wall as if to steady herself. She can't see the man at the desk, just four wooden legs and two stout ones squeezed into an orderly's uniform. Maude hears the jangle of keys as the man shifts in his chair to look at them.

"Yer cleaning in the middle of the night, what? Whass yer name?" the man grumbles.

Mrs. Cavendish points at the bucket. "We're here special. Someone got the sicks." She gives a theatrical shudder. "Got all over you, hey Bets? Clumsy cow!" Mrs. Cavendish cackles, pulling Maude toward the man. "See?"

The man recoils, stumbling back from his desk as Maude nears him. With a start, Maude realizes that her uniform reeks. She tenses with disgust and makes herself laugh as hard as she can, though it sounds more like snorting. She doesn't trust herself to speak in front of this man without giving herself away.

"Drunk as lords youse two. Shameful!" the guard says, waving a hand over his nose. "Get out!" He gets slowly to his feet and unlocks the door behind him.

Mrs. Cavendish gives a shaky bow and passes through the door into the night, still weaving and singing a little. Maude follows, still on high alert.

As soon as they turn the corner of the stone building, Mrs. Cavendish whirls around on Maude, pulling off the smelly garment.

"We'll have to wait to clean you up. Come along now. We must meet the others."

Still in a daze, Maude stumbles along behind toward the waiting cab.

≈

Whitbourne Street, November 8, midnight

When Jonathan approaches Lucy, he's drawn to the bright red droplets of blood that bloom on her slender white neck. How enticing she looks. How he wants her. No, not her exactly. This is not personal. He longs to bite into her neck, to feel the

warm coppery blood fill his mouth, and then to have her ener-
gizing life force surge through his body.

He doesn't think these thoughts. The feeling is beyond
words. He simply knows that he needs to drain the quickness
of her life, the beating heart and soul, and have it flow
through him, lighting him from within.

He bends his face towards her.

"That's my boy," says the Count. "She is yours."

Jonathan opens his mouth. His teeth are sharp. Warm
saliva fills his mouth as he bends closer to Lucy. His face is
inches above her neck. His hand rests on her slender shoulder.
He can feel her soft breath on his face.

The urge is stronger now. He feels as if the desire is
coming not only from him but also from the Count beside
him, urging him on, though he hasn't spoken again.

Jonathan is about to bite down. He has no thought of
anything else but of what he must do.

Lucy's eyelids flutter open. Jonathan pulls back slightly and
looks up at her. Her gaze is unfocused at first. Then she turns
and her green eyes find his brown ones. He reads a question in
her glance.

What has he become?

He's suddenly overcome with intense desire. He cannot
help it. The lust rages inside him. And yet, at the same time,
as he stares into Lucy's eyes, he sees the faces of the women
he's most loved. His sisters and his mother. They've sacrificed
so much for him. What would they think of him now?

In the deep recesses of his very soul, he can still feel the
love and care of these most dear to him. And he loves and
cares for them in return.

Is he a monster?

No. Jonathan shakes his head.

No.

He cannot. He will not destroy her.

He must save Lucy.

With almost superhuman will, Jonathan closes his mouth. And steps away.

The Count hisses behind him.

"You cannot escape what you are, Jonathan, what you've become." The sibilant voice winds its way into his ear.

Jonathan turns to face the Count. The man is taller than he is and looms even larger before him somehow, as if he is floating above the floor.

"I am not you. I will not be you." Jonathan's words are strong, though his body is suddenly weak. He wills himself not to give in to the languor that envelopes him. His legs want to crumble but he wills himself to stand tall.

From the corner of his eye, Jonathan senses movement. Lucy.

Jonathan steps closer to the Count, trying to shield Lucy behind him.

"You cannot protect her." The Count laughs, a sound like screeching vultures that chills Jonathan to his core.

He wants the sound to stop. Jonathan covers his ears.

In an instant, the Count hauls Lucy up from the chair, then suspends her in the air, pinning both arms behind her back. Vloeken laughs as he dangles Lucy before Jonathan, then shoves her back just out of his reach.

"Let me go, you vile monster!" Lucy struggles against the Count's hold, kicking furiously against him.

Jonathan reaches to free Lucy from the Count's grasp. But the vampire only laughs, a screeching sound that is no laugh at all.

In an instant, Vloeken moves Lucy away from Jonathan, as if she is as light as air. Then with Lucy in his grasp he suddenly rises in the air before Jonathan, who is powerless to stop them.

Jonathan hurls himself at the Count. Instead of running

into the cold body of the fiend, he's met with the sharp corner of a sideboard.

The Count laughs again. He's somehow behind Jonathan, gripping Lucy's arms even tighter, so that she writhes in pain.

Jonathan lunges again. When his hands meet nothing but air, this time he stumbles over a chair that snaps as he lands on it. He crashes to the hardwood floor.

Sharp pain radiates from his face. He sits up. Dazed. Blood gushes from his nose.

"Jonathan!"

Through his hazy vision, Jonathan sees Lucy struggling to free herself from the Count's grasp. He is too much for her. He holds her like a fish on a line, dangling her above the floor.

Jonathan stumbles to his feet and reaches for Lucy. Though he is dizzy and weak, he is more himself. He is not a fiend. He has one overriding thought. Lucy is in trouble. He must save her.

"Release her!" Jonathan commands the Count, gathering his strength as he stands.

"As you wish."

With speed and force, the Count hurls Lucy across the room. She hits the far wall and crumbles to the floor, unmoving.

"What have you done?"

"I did what you asked, dear boy."

Jonathan rushes to Lucy. He bends down and puts his face next to hers. She's breathing. Then Lucy moans softly. She's alive, thank heavens. But she needs a doctor.

Jonathan must get her out of this room—away from the Count, away from this awful club—and take her somewhere safe.

"You are not going anywhere," the Count says as if reading his mind.

Without moving from his spot, the Count looks towards

the bedroom door. It slams shut, and Jonathan hears the metallic snap of a lock. They are trapped.

The Count moves closer. "You cannot save her. You are both mine."

# Chapter Forty-Four

Mary Jane hears music. Someone is playing the fiddle. Is it her father? Her heart suddenly fills with warmth. She thinks of her home in Limerick. Is she at the pub with her father and brothers? She hears people laughing. The floorboards are vibrating beneath her. They must be dancing. She wants to join in the fun. But she can't move. Why is she lying down? Has she fainted?

Her eyelids are like lead weights. She struggles to lift them. The music sounds sharper than before. Not like fiddle music at all. This is no Irish jig. No. It's a piano playing loudly and fast, the pianist crashing the keys frenetically. She doesn't like this jarring tune. And the laughter isn't coming from familiar voices. It's higher pitched. It's the fake laughter of women. Then someone is shouting. Glass is breaking. The piano player stops. More noise. Then cheers and laughter. The music starts up again. Where is she?

Mary Jane's first thought is that she's had too much to drink. Her head is heavy. Her limbs feel distant, as if they belong to someone else. With great effort, she sits up and pulls her dress around her. She looks around in a daze. Why is she sitting at the top of a stairway?

Then the night starts to come back to her. Leaving her room in Miller's Court. Walking hurriedly to the gentlemen's club. She was to meet Mr. O'Shea. And then what happened? She recalls seeing a woman with long red hair. Mary Jane looks around. Where is she and the strange man she was with?

She's heard of horrible things happening to women at the club. Part of her wants to find out where the young woman has gone and see if she is in need of assistance. Another part feels a huge wave of revulsion. She must leave this club and never come back.

Mary Jane pushes herself to stand up and almost faints. Her vision narrows. The floor sways up to meet her. *Steady on,* she tells herself. She closes her eyes and wills her legs to support her. What was in her drink?

She has no more thoughts of meeting her client. She vows never to come back to this club again, no matter how far behind on the rent she is. She won't let Lizzie come either. This is no place for either of them. Nor for any woman.

Mary Jane descends the first two stairs. The thick smell of tobacco stings her nose. She feels a sudden wave of nausea and grabs the banister. She must gather her strength before she goes downstairs. The last thing she needs is to draw attention to herself in any way as she tries to leave. She prays that no man will grab her and ask her to dance before she can get to the front door, and then to the clean, cold air outside. The asking, she knows, is a euphemism. There's no such thing as asking in this club, only taking. She vows she will not be taken.

But as she slowly starts to descend again, she hears a voice crying out for help. Mary Jane stops and turns in the direction of the plea. It must be coming from one of the bedrooms in the upper floor hallway.

"Help me, please!" It's a woman, a young woman, and well-bred by the sounds of her cry.

The woman screams, "Help me." Again. And again.

Mary Jane shakes her head. No. She cannot afford to help this woman. She needs to get out of the club immediately. Though her body is weak, Mary Jane's determination is strong. She must save herself first.

Mary Jane takes another step. Despite the music and laughter floating upward from the lower floors, she can still hear the young woman. And another voice. A man's. His laugh is unlike anything she's heard before. It makes every hair on the back of her neck stand up. Mary Jane needs to get out of there as quickly as she can. She has a strong instinct for survival, and her instincts are telling her there is evil here.

Yet Mary Jane pauses. Her hand grips the banister. Two more sets of stairs, then a quick walk through the large dance hall, and she will be free of this place. *Go, go,* one part of her brain tells her.

Mary Jane hesitates. She is sure the woman is in trouble. She knows what it's like to be taken against your will. Mary Jane was just a young girl when it happened to her. It's not something she has ever forgotten, even when she turns herself into gay Marie Jeanette.

Perhaps this is why Mary Jane has such a soft spot for her fellow gay women. How could she not offer her friends a safe floor to sleep on when otherwise they would be sleeping rough? Even if it led to more rows with Joseph, this was better than allowing her friends to be easy prey for a maniacal killer roaming the streets of Whitechapel. Until the police caught this Jack the Ripper, there was no safe place to sleep outdoors. If Joseph could not be generous, then it was best he left.

Mary Jane listens again. She cannot hear the young woman any longer. The fast-paced piano music is too loud. She is at the front door now. The burly servant in black and white does not move to open the door for her. Will she be trapped? Is he going to refuse her an exit?

But no. The manservant opens the door, and Mary Jane rushes through it.

The first thing she does outside is gulp the cold, night air. After hours of breathing in the thick cigar and pipe smoke indoors, her lungs demand a purer substance. She exhales and vows never to go back to the club again.

She pulls her thin shawl tighter around her shoulders. In the distance, church bells strike one. She normally wouldn't leave the club at this hour, not with the Ripper still at large and a long walk back to her lodging at Miller's Court—and not when she could have spent the night in a warm bed with a warm body. But the things she has seen at the club, the horror and repulsion that overwhelmed her, have proven too much. Better to risk the walk home than to stay in the club for one more minute.

Mary Jane begins walking briskly towards home. Then she stops, suddenly.

Is she mistaken or is there a slight rustling noise behind her? There's no wind on this moonless night, so it can't be the elements. She turns around and peers into the darkness. Her eyes look for a figure, even as her heart beats a tambourine in her chest.

She doesn't see anything. Perhaps it was a bit of stray newspaper or a cat searching for food? She picks up her pace and keeps her focus on getting home as quickly as possible.

*Chapter Forty-Five*

"You stink to high heaven, madam." The coachman holds his nose with one hand as he helps Maude out of the coach with the other. Mrs. Cavendish follows without a word, ignoring the hand the coachmen offers her next. Maude has a newfound respect for the mild-mannered landlady. She has skills—and courage.

And she owes the woman her life.

With an effort, Maude ignores the sour smell from her clothing. If she thinks too much—about anything—she will be lost.

During the carriage ride, Mrs. Cavendish tells her a hair-raising story about creatures rising from the dead and feeding on the blood of both men and women. It is incomprehensible to her, but Mrs. Cavendish seems to think that Lucy and Jonathan are victims of such a monster.

Maude clutches a carriage blanket around her shoulders and tries to get her bearings. In a building across the street, glimmers of light edge heavily curtained windows on every floor. When a curtain parts, Maude can see shadows passing back and forth, their evening garb silhouetted by the lights. Figures merge together, entwine, then separate to stumble, laughing, out of sight again. Music blares whenever the street door opens, and sounds of revelry spill onto the sidewalk.

"There!" Mrs. Cavendish had frozen in place and now points toward the sky at a rooftop. The moon hangs low and yellow, hazy with the fog still rolling on the streets. Maude stares at the point where the black roof meets the black sky and thinks she sees something move.

"What...?" Suddenly there are black masses swarming over the roof, descending on ropes to the narrow balconies lining the top floor, clinging to drainpipes, and climbing down the ornamental facade. Maude watches as the figures land and straighten to their full height. They unpack files and crowbars from bulging bags tied to their hips and begin forcing open windows. They wear black uniforms that allow for great freedom of motion and light slippers, Maude notices. One of them shifts a handhold and Maude suddenly realizes the figure is female.

"There's a woman up there!" she says, astonished. She counts ten figures. One by one, silent as death, the figures infiltrate the house.

"They are all women," Mrs. Cavendish says, her voice filled with pride. "Aha. Here we go. I would have left you in the coach but Miss Rutherford may have need of you." She sets off toward the front door of the house, just as another figure nears it.

"Lucy? Lucy is here?!" Maude hurries to keep up with the older woman. They all converge on the front door and the other figure raps on it with a stags-head walking stick. Maude has seen that walking stick somewhere—somewhere very different.

"Miss Cobbe?" she whispers. The sconce over the front door flickers briefly and the figure turns, revealing Miss Cobbe's florid face. She winks broadly at Maude, just as the door opens.

"My good man, let us pass!" Miss Cobbe raises her voice, the walking stick held high. She is dressed in a voluminous black cape, with a high-brimmed hat covering her gray curls. Maude sees her twirl the cape around her shoulder, revealing a holster at one hip and a whip coiled at the other. Maude gasps.

The butler looks like no butler Maude has ever seen. He fills the entire door frame with his towering bulk. He lowers his shaved head to smirk at them. "I don't think so, ladies. This ain't your kind of place, you know." His smile is cruel and filled with crooked teeth.

"How tiresome," Miss Cobbe says. With a sudden motion, the walking stick thumps hard on the ground and the butler yelps in pain as he loses balance on one foot. He lunges for Miss Cobbe, but she is quicker, drawing her pistol and holding it steady at his chest.

"Out of my way." The words ring with power and authority. The butler backs away, his face contorted with fury. His eyes dart this way and that, seeking someone to warn.

"Bind him."

Mrs. Cavendish unspools a long length of rope and expertly trusses and gags the man as if he were a chicken to roast. She kicks him with one pointy boot as she passes him, lying on the carpet by the door.

"Hurry!" With surprising speed, Miss Cobbe heads toward the staircase. Around her, the patrons gawk and stare, seemingly confused by the hubbub.

"*Police!*" Miss Cobbe yells out in her stentorian voice. And with that, there is a stampede toward the exit.

Struggling against the flood of bodies moving toward

them, Maude and Mrs. Cavendish hasten to follow Miss Cobbe. Is this Edward's club? Maude thinks with a shiver of revulsion. How on earth has Lucy ended up here, and what has happened to her?

# *Chapter Forty-Six*

Jonathan has two beings inside him now, but room for only one. When he looks at Lucy motionless under the Count's spell, he sees not her but his sisters. He can even hear their laughter and gentle teasing. He's transported back to the cozy cottage in Bath, sitting with his three sisters and his mother by the fire. One of them is reading the latest Mary Elizabeth Braddon novel aloud. He wants stronger stuff. Dickens. Trollope. Not sensationalism. His sisters tell him he's being a snob. The image fades.

Jonathan stretches out one hand. He must save Lucy. His sisters, if they knew, would expect no less. This is his duty.

In an instant, he pulls back his arm. The urge is gone and with it the Jonathan who lived another lifetime ago. He's overtaken by a stronger, competing beast inside him. This Jonathan wants to ravish Lucy, to feel his teeth puncture the soft white skin of her neck. He can almost taste the smooth velvety blood filling his mouth, giving new life to his hollowed out body.

A sardonic laugh cuts through his reverie. The Count. Jonathan knows that his thoughts are being perceived by the Count, even without speaking them. They are bound together now.

A deep self-loathing fills him then. Aside from the devoted brother, where is the journalist, the seeker of the truth, who works so tirelessly to better his fellow citizens? That part of him rises to the surface. He needs to pen this story and warn others of the evil that has taken hold of Whitechapel. But another thought flashes through his brain: Isn't he part of the evil as well?

Jonathan wants to wrench his hair and pull at his skin, to tear off his human flesh as punishment for what he has become.

Suddenly, he hears a noise. It sounds like an angry mob, like the kind he has written about in Trafalgar Square. Shouts. Grumblings. Stamping of feet. It's getting louder. And closer.

The Count hears it too. In an instant, the looming figure of the Count swoops down on Lucy, enveloping her in his arms.

Jonathan looks towards the window. At the same time, the Count is suddenly there. He opens it. Jonathan intuits the Count's plan. He is taking Lucy. He will fly out into the night before the angry horde can stop him.

The Count glances at Jonathan. The edges of his lips curl into a thin smile, revealing two sharp teeth. He has won. Who can stop the Count now?

Lucy moans. She's waking, roused from her spell by the sudden movement. She's calling for someone. Her father?

The Count snarls.

The mob is getting closer. There are shouts—"Step aside. Out of my way!" Someone is pounding at the door. There's no time to wait.

Whether from the noise or because some spell has been broken, Lucy is fully awake now. Her deep green eyes are full of terror. She struggles against the Count, who holds her as if she is a doll, light as air.

He must act. Now.

Just as the Count is ready to escape with Lucy, Jonathan flies at him. He's never had the ability to move so fast. He has only to think it, and before his legs can carry him there, he's leapt several feet across the room.

"Release her!" Jonathan stands before the Count, blocking the window. He may be a shell of a man, hollowed out and filled with evil, but there is still something human left.

"Out of my way, you fool!" The Count barely touches Jonathan, yet he's thrown backwards with the strength of ten men.

Jonathan doubles over, gasping for breath. He's too weak to stand.

The banging at the door grows more fierce.

"We will break down this door!" a loud female voice shouts.

Jonathan raises his head.

The Count, with Lucy in his arms, is about to vanish into the night.

Summoning all his strength, Jonathan lunges once again at the Count, seeking to grab Lucy from his arms and pull her free.

There is a tussle of bodies. His. The Count's. Lucy. She is awake and fighting back. The Count loosens his grip on Lucy as she struggles against him.

"Run, Lucy," Jonathan says, pushing her away.

The Count's eyes glow like fire as he lifts Jonathan off the ground and throws him against the far wall as if he were no more than a pesky insect.

Jonathan's head thumps against a heavy wooden sideboard. He crumples to the floor.

Where is Lucy? Has she escaped?

"Jonathan!" The sweet voice of his sister Beth is calling him. "Jonathan!" the voice says again, louder this time.

Jonathan wills his eyes to open. He wants to respond to his sister and tell her he is alright, but the air has left his body. He is too weak to speak or move.

There is a loud commotion around him. The crack of wood. A chair breaking. Shouting. Feet stomping. Where is Lucy? Has the Count got her? He must wake up and help her.

Then he feels a gentle hand on his shoulder and hears the sweet voice again. Only it's not his sister.

Jonathan opens his eyes and sees Lucy kneeling next to him. He feels the vicious pull of the count battling inside his mind and soul, rising up to claw at his throat. He wants to rip into her flesh. His face stiffens into a snarl and for a moment he sees Lucy draw back in fear.

His teeth are sharp under his tongue and his fingers are curving into weapons. He fights against the tide within him, but his strength ebbs. He is losing this battle. Lucy's pale face seems to waver before his eyes, then he sees the ominous shape of the Count swoop down to grab his prey. He is too late to save her.

# Chapter Forty-Seven

"Where is Lucy?" Maude looks around the room wildly as she finally reaches the door. Cobbe had rushed up the stairs, and Maude had followed, gasping for breath and battling the flood of men hurrying down the stairs, fastening their shirt studs and cufflinks as best they could. It would have been laughable if Maude weren't so terrified for her friend.

She clutches the blanket she still wears around her shoulders and tries to understand the mayhem in front of her eyes.

Two women in form-fitting black uniforms stand at the window, half leaning out. They whisper to each other and point into the black night beyond. A ray of moonlight pierces the room, where furniture is overturned and broken and an ornate mirror has shattered. Shards of silver lie on the thick pile rug, and a broken chair lists to one side.

A cold wind blows in from the open window, framed by red velvet curtains. Two more women huddle near a figure on the floor, but Maude can't see it clearly. Her heart jumps with fear.

"Gone." Cobbe stands with her back to Maude in the center of the room, hands on her hips. For a moment her head hangs in defeat, but then she whirls around to face Maude. "We must pursue them immediately—or he will run to ground again. If he has Lucy, he has his revenge."

With a few snaps of her fingers and sharp looks, Cobbe directs the four other women in some mysterious undertaking. They sweep through the room, restoring order and pocketing a few loose objects.

"Wh—at? Lucy is gone? Where? Who took her?" A sob rises in her throat. Suddenly Maude feels her legs give out, and she slumps in the door frame. As the room clears, she notices the still body on the floor. With a moan, she stumbles closer and falls beside it. It is Jonathan.

"Lu...cy..." His voice is a mere whisper. His lids flutter open. Maude stares into an abyss. What has happened to this poor man? "Mrs..." His vision clears as he seems to recognize her face.

Maude thinks she sees the faintest relaxation of the tormented expression, a shadow of relief. She presses one of his pale hands in her own and feels its warmth fading. His mouth moves again, and she leans closer.

"What is it, Jonathan? Don't try to speak. Save your breath and your strength. We will find a doctor." The word reminds her of her husband and Maude shrinks involuntarily, then recovers. "We will get help for you."

He shakes his head slightly, then winces. He closes his eyes again. "I can see them—in my mind. I can feel that creature's resolve..." He trembles and draws a shallow breath. "The docks," he whispers. "Go there. Now."

Maude watches as Jonathan's body shimmers briefly then dissolves into mist. She feels a cold shift of air brush past her, then nothing. When she looks up, astonished, she sees Miss Cobbe standing before her. The room seems to spin as she gulps back more sobs. "No, no." She shakes her head.

"Did he know where Lucy went?" Cobbe asks.

Maude blinks.

Cobbe leans in close to Maude's teary face as she hauls her up by her elbow.

"Listen to me. We have no time for feelings. Later I will explain to you the true evil that is now swarming London, leaving death and despair in its wake. Now you must *move*. We must find Lucy and you must come with me. Your husband has committed you to an asylum, Mrs. Hepworth. What do you suppose he will do if he finds you again?"

Miss Cobbe is right. She is not safe. Maude looks down to where Jonathan's broken body had lain. It is gone.

"Jonathan said to go to the docks," Maude says. She takes a deep breath and focuses on the task ahead. She must save herself and her friend.

*Chapter Forty-Eight*

Lucy had struggled against the Count in vain. He had held her tightly as he'd leapt from the window. She had squeezed her eyes shut, certain they were going to fall to their deaths. They hadn't. Somehow, when she opens her eyes again, she finds herself in a dark carriage, sitting across from the Count.

"Where are you taking me?"

The Count doesn't respond at first. Lucy feels a cold chill that starts at the tip of her head and goes to the soles of her feet. She shivers involuntarily. The man sitting across from her—nay, he is no man but a beast, an evil thing—notices her shivering and points to a blanket next to her on the seat. Lucy ignores him.

"Where are we going?" she asks again, firmer this time. She will not show fear.

"We are going home."

"To my father's house?" Lucy's spirits rise. Though she'd recently been dreaming of her mother, it was her father who would know just how to dispose of this demon.

The Count gives a short laugh that reminds Lucy of the sharp bark of a dog or a wolf.

"I insist that you release me! Now."

"That's not possible. Your father has taken something from me, and now I will return the favor."

"What did he take from you?"

"Peace. Death."

"I don't understand. You're here now. Undead, or whatever it is you are."

"What I am…"

Lucy waits for the Count to continue, but instead he pulls the curtain on the window aside and looks out. Lucy can see only blackness.

"Are you the Ripper?" she asks. She holds her breath. It would make sense. This demon who attacks women—though she'd seen him attack Jonathan as well—could be the maniac who has been terrorizing Whitechapel and the poor souls there.

The Count gives a short bark again, then turns to look at Lucy. His ice-blue eyes glow like fiery metal. His gaze bores into her. Though she tries to turn her head away, some force holds her so that she cannot look away.

"You would not be here if I were."

Lucy clutches her hands together. All of the Ripper's victims were women of the lower classes, poor unfortunates whose lives Lucy couldn't imagine. And yet, maybe the Count is toying with her. Maybe she would wind up just as the others, her throat slit, or worse. But first she would be forced to pay for something the Count believed her father had done to him.

The carriage seems to be flying over the cobblestone streets, though Lucy has seen no driver and no outriders. The horses' hooves clatter noisily. The vehicle rocks back and forth and shakes with a preternatural force.

She wants to look out the window and get her bearings. She wants to rescue herself, and bolt out the door. But instead she is caught in the stern mental grip of this creature, whose eyes hold her captive. If he isn't the Ripper, then who is?

Suddenly, a cold blast of air brings the thick scent of salt to her face. The Count smiles thinly, exposing sharp teeth. "We are near, we are near," he murmurs. "Soon this wind will take us far from these ugly and crowded shores, this land of corrupt and benighted souls. Ah yes, you think I brought evil here but know that I found it instead—more blood and strife than I've seen on battlefields. I had already wearied of human suffering ages ago, when my mate and I entombed ourselves. But I had never imagined the wickedness I found here in your modern 'civilization.'" His tone holds an audible sneer. "It is time to return to my serene and silent haven under the mountain. And for Rutherford's sins, I shall take you from him— and with me."

With a new surge of panic, Lucy starts to struggle against the Count's mental hold when the coach stops with a jolt.

"We have arrived. My dear, your barque awaits you."

# Chapter Forty-Nine

As she walks through the dark streets of London, the fog around her thick as pea soup, Mary Jane longs for her bed in Miller's Court at the end of Dorset Street. While her room isn't much to speak of—she has just a small bed and a table— at least she doesn't have to sleep rough like so many other women.

There it is again. A noise. She's sure of it this time. Soft footfalls behind her. Holding her breath, she turns around again. Then she hears it. A man's laughter rings out in the night. Then a woman giggling. It is only a liaison. She must have walked right by without realizing she was close to the couple.

Mary Jane's heart grows lighter as she nears Dorset Street. She has just about made it safely home. She wonders if Lizzie will be in her bed tonight. Then she thinks not. Her friend was in the mood for a drink and some company. No doubt she is still getting both at this hour. Mary Jane does not judge. Her head is a little fuzzy from the champagne she drank tonight, though she has sobered up on the chilly walk home.

Mary Jane thinks of the lady she spotted at the gentleman's club, with her long red hair and fine dress. She herself was well-dressed once. Now the hems of her only dress are tattered and dirty, as much as she tries to pick up her skirts as she walks around Whitechapel. Its streets are filthy, and there isn't much to be done.

The room at 13 Miller's Court is empty when Mary Jane steps inside. She lights the nub of a candle on the table. Then she undresses and lays her clothing neatly on a chair. She has always tried to look her best, and respecting her clothing by caring for it helps preserve a neat appearance.

Mary Jane sings a song softly as she gets ready for bed. She will have better luck tomorrow, she is certain. She will stave off her greedy landlord and cut down on the gin. She'll save money for a beautiful dress again, like those she lost, like the one that young woman was wearing tonight.

She can almost smell the clean muslin fabric and feel the tug of the gown cinched a few inches above her waist. How pretty she will look in a fresh white color. Or maybe pale pink. Yes, that will suit her better. Hers will be in the latest fashion —short, puffed sleeves, and a small train down the back. Rather than the ratty hem of the dress she has now, her new gown will be embroidered and tucked at the bottom, the better to hang down delicately while she walks.

She smiles as she thinks what a fine figure she may still cut in a new frock. Men will turn their heads to admire her. As she starts to drift off, dreaming of a brighter day, Mary Jane hears a noise again. She is so very tired and rather than sit up, she pulls the thin sheet closer to her chin. She tries to get warm, but it is cold and drafty in her room. The rags she stuffed in the broken window don't really keep the breeze out.

Her eyelids are heavy. There's that noise again. She's sure she hears something. A cat maybe? Or another inhabitant of

Dorset Street? For a moment, she has a vision of Joseph. Is he coming back to her?

Tonight, she would welcome him back in her bed—if only to keep her warm as she snuggles up to him, as they used to. Mary Jane no sooner has this thought than flashes of drunken arguments also come back to her unbidden. She pushes them away. Joseph is gone. Good riddance to him. What she needs now is sleep.

The candle has burnt itself out. Another expense to think about in the morning. Her breathing slows. Her limbs grow heavy. Mary Jane turns over when she hears the click of the door, but doesn't open her eyes.

She does not scream because she doesn't see what's before her. In an instant, she feels searing, unearthly pain. Then blackness.

### PALL MALL GAZETTE
November 9, 1888

### NUMBER FIVE

FIVE undetected murders in one small district at the East End, and more to follow. One ghastly murder and mutilation in the West End to which there is no clue, and so far, while many innocent persons have been arrested, the murderers are still at large. There have been at least five women murdered in London within three months, under every circumstance of savage and fiendish atrocity, and the police are utterly at fault. Sir CHARLES WARREN'S policy of subordinating the detective department to the soldier's does not seem to be rewarded by the success which so brilliant and original a mode of strategy ought to command.

Of the latest, but not the last, of the murders in the East End we need say little. The murderer seems on this occasion to have selected a younger victim, and to have profited by the security of a locked room to indulge to a much greater extent than on any previous occasion in his mania for mutilation.

Sir CHARLES WARREN has abounded in the qualities which it was desirable that he should possess only in moderation, and he has been signally lacking in qualities of which it is impossible to have too much. The result is failure fraught with the gravest danger to the public. The position, it is fair to admit, does not wholly owe its disastrous aspect to the Chief Commissioner of Police. It has been made infinitely worse by what we have called the helpless and heedless ineptitude of the Home Secretary.

# Chapter Fifty

The sun has not yet risen on this cold November day, and Lord Rutherford has not yet been to bed.

Last night, the search for Lucy was fruitless. He thinks about his last meeting with Sir Charles Warren. He will ask for the man's immediate resignation—the public would demand no less—but that can wait until later. He must find Lucy first.

He sits in his study, staring at the morning newspapers he'd requested from his manservant. The ink is fresh. Lord Rutherford had been in too much of a hurry to have his servant iron them first.

*Yesterday a fifth murder, the most horrible of the series of atrocities attributed to the same hand, was committed in Whitechapel. As in all the previous instances, the victim was a woman of immoral character and humble circumstances, but she was not murdered in the open street, her throat having been cut and the subsequent mutilations having taken place in a room which the deceased rented at Miller's Court at No. 26, Dorset Street.*

He skims another paper, *The Daily Telegraph*, which

provides even more gruesome details. *"No reliable clue has been discovered as to the perpetrator of the crime,"* he reads.

How dare the press assert that there are no reliable clues? They can't possibly know what clues the police have, although he does give the journalist credit. They'd brought in police dogs. He's sure there is a leak from the special force, just as he's sure that the name Jack the Ripper is the invention of a journalist to drum up more stories and sell more papers.

Lord Rutherford exhales and gets up from his desk. He has read enough. A new chief commissioner is the first step. He needs someone competent at the helm to find his daughter and that fiend in that order.

Brooding at his desk this morning, he has been pushing away the unthinkable. What if the Count has his daughter?

Lord Rutherford recalls his first meeting with Count Vloeken. Not the disastrous conversation they'd had in London—no, this was in South Africa, when Lord Rutherford's miners had discovered an ancient crypt, partially destroyed by the blast in the diamond mine. Inside the crypt was an elaborately carved marble tomb. Another tomb lay shattered in pieces, destroyed by the blast.

Rutherford insisted the tomb be brought to him when he was in Johannesburg, and he had it unsealed.

No one could have been more shocked than Lord Rutherford to see a perfectly preserved corpse—for that's what he thought it was. The corpse of an aristocrat, judging from his clothing.

But this was no aristocrat, Lord Rutherford soon found out. This was a dark force let loose by colonial wars.

Once a Boer murdered by the English, Count Vloeken had sealed himself away, permanently, he thought. But Rutherford's mining operation had disturbed him.

"You have awakened me against my will," the Count had told him. "And you will come to regret it."

Rutherford had tried to destroy the Count in the Cape, but

the demon was wily and eluded him. Then months later he had heard stories of strange doings on one of his ships bound for England and realized the Count's master plan to pursue him to his own land for his vengeance.

At Warren's suggestion about how to destroy the fiend, Rutherford had ordered a fire set to welcome the villain when he landed. And it had almost been successful. He'd counted on Warren's expertise in archeology and ancient practices to help him. Indeed, it was Warren who confirmed that he'd heard and seen of such creatures that suck the blood of others, the never-dead who roamed the earth.

"It is bad luck that he was disturbed," Warren had warned.

"And we must turn his bad luck into my good fortune." Lord Rutherford had laughed. For the mine where the Count had been entombed was flush with diamonds. Rutherford hardly imagined how wealthy he'd become.

He shakes his head to rouse himself from this memory. How he wishes the fire had burned away this curse.

He shudders to think that Lucy could be in this demon's clutches. No. It's impossible. Unthinkable. And yet, Lord Rutherford has seen more unthinkable things than he could ever have imagined, and more anomalies than reason would have him believe.

# Chapter Fifty-One

"To the docks!"

"Onward and make haste!"

The voices swirl around Maude as she struggles to keep up with the women moving around her. They form an ever-increasing crowd before the gentleman's club, collecting supplies, calling for carriages—some whistling for hansoms like the lowest of street rats! And throughout the hubbub could be found the solid figure of Miss Cobbe, barking orders as she turns to speak to her lieutenants. Maude tries to stay as near her as possible.

They are a veritable army, she thinks with some wonderment. The black-garbed women seem to know exactly what they are doing as they leap into whatever conveyances they could corral and grab the reins. They move confidently through the world and speak loudly and…take action.

Maude absorbs it all with wide eyes and a newly-opened mind. This is how Lucy felt at Miss Cobbe's lecture, she realizes—like her world has cracked open with possibility. Lucy!

Dear God, where could she be and what does that fiend want with her?

Maude pulls up her still-smelly skirts and runs after Miss Cobbe, who is just heaving herself into a victoria, an open carriage drawn by one dark horse pawing angrily at the ground as a groom holds his lines.

"Be quick!" Cobbe says, making room for her on the single seat. To her astonishment, the groom tosses the reins to Cobbe, who cracks them as the carriage springs into action. "He's my very own. I call him Lucifer," Cobbe says, with a grin.

And then they are off, careening down the street with a crowd of women in carriages of all shapes and forms, and some pedestrians trotting alongside them.

Maude holds onto her seat and observes the first hint of dawn's light piercing the clouds above. The charcoal sky is getting paler, ever so subtly, but the yellow fog blankets out the sun's rays.

As they clatter along, Maude becomes aware of street sweepers and cart drivers hustling to get out of their way, but also of women calling out.

"What yer after? Where's the frolic?"

"Mind the grease!"

From doorways and stoops voices battle back and forth. "The Ripper! We got 'im" and "To the docks! To the docks!"

A few women carrying torches form a parade behind Cobbe's carriage, and other women join in, maids wearing serge and threadbare cloaks, shouting incoherently and shaking their fists in the air. Old women with bent backs and young mothers with babes in arms stand and watch the masses go by, then fall into line behind them.

"No more! Never more! We'll rip *him*, we will," the voices cry out as the torches cast shadows on the narrow tenements they pass.

The sky has shifted from slate to a pearly gray, and Maude

can feel the air changing as they near the river. Ahead she sees the thick, forbidding walls of the Tower of London and knows they must be close. The stink of fish and sewage grows stronger, and she starts to hear the low horns of barges that ferry goods from the many docks along the Thames to the channel ports like Gravesend.

How will they know the right dock? Miss Cobbe shows no signs of uncertainty, or slowing down, as she makes a sharp turn that sends Maude sliding half off her seat. She mutters something under her breath that Maude takes to be a curse.

With a yank on the reins, Miss Cobbe pulls up next to a dilapidated shack that looks to be half falling into the mud below. Wooden planks meet a few rusty nails at awkward angles, and a thatched roof seems to be more holes than straw. She puts two fingers in her mouth and lets out a piercing sound that brings a small girl scrambling out of the little hovel, barefoot.

Cobbe leans down from her tall seat and speaks to the girl in low tones, gesticulating with her hands. The girl nods eagerly and answers with her whole body, shifting from dirty foot to dirty foot and jabbing a finger down the river at the next set of wharves. Miss Cobbe tosses her a copper penny and launches back into motion.

"The girl's a treasure. What powers of observation! What acuity! She knows everything that happens on this side of the river, and she's never failed me yet. On we go now—hold tight!" And she speeds back to the front of the milling crowd of women heading toward the docks.

"St. Kate's! My lovelies. We'll catch him yet. Come along!" And, with one throbbing pulse, the mob moves with her as the sun peeks just above the horizon.

# *Chapter Fifty-Two*

THE THAMES, NOVEMBER 9, 5:00 A.M.

Lucy's heart is still hammering in her chest when the coach stops. Where are they? When she looks out the coach window, she can barely make out tall, hulking shapes. Masts crisscross against the gray sky. Long, low buildings and warehouses line the riverfront. They are at the Thames close to the docks.

Lucy does not want to leave the coach, but against her will she's lifted from her seat and set down roughly next to the carriage. Not two feet away, a rat scurries from behind a barrel and crosses in front of her.

"Come, we must hurry," the Count commands, grabbing her arm.

Lucy is powerless in his grip. The Count's hand is an icy claw. She tries to pull away and cannot. Her limbs are not under her own control. She wants to protest and finds her mouth is sealed shut. She cannot get the words to come out, though in her mind she is screaming, "No."

The air is pungent with the smell of rotting fish, salt from the Thames, and the industrial smells of coal and tar. It is quiet on the docks at this early hour of the morning. There are no human voices, only the mournful creaking of the wooden ships and the rhythmic lapping of the water.

In the distance, a whistle blows from a nearby factory, calling its workers. The gas lamps at the wharf are still lit, giving off an eerie, yellowish glow and illuminating the pale face of the Count, who holds Lucy captive next to him. His eyes bore into hers with an unearthly red glow behind the metallic darkness of his pupils.

When Lucy had sailed to France, the docks had been a bustling place of noise and activity, full of the calls of merchants and seamen. But if there is another soul present at this early hour, she cannot see or hear him. Surely there must be a night watchman—at least someone will come and turn off the gas street lights—but he is not here now.

An image of Constable Neil flashes into Lucy's mind. How she wishes to see him. She has felt safe in his presence, she realizes now. Only it is too late. There is no one here to save her.

The Count takes Lucy under her arm and half drags her into the dissipating fog and down a long wharf. Lucy is determined not to board a boat with the Count. She will not allow herself to be taken away from London, away from her home, her father, her dear friend Maude, and now Miss Cobbe's female detectives. Never before has Lucy felt herself a part of something as she does with the sisterhood she's recently found.

Though her limbs are imprisoned, her mind is not. She must find a way to save herself. If the Count is not the Ripper, then who is? And is her captor more or less deadly than the Whitechapel butcher?

She knows the fiend has supernatural powers. He's taken her prisoner, after all, invaded her dreams, and caused her nocturnal ramblings. This undead demon will not win, she vows. If the Count has a vendetta with her father, why can't it be settled without her? She has nothing to do with the business of men—or with this vampiric demon.

Lucy hears a voice above the lapping of the water. A woman's voice muffled in the fog. Someone is calling her name. No. She won't be fooled this time. It's another one of the monster's tricks. She's heard the Count mimic her mother's voice, summoning her whilst she slept. She will not be deceived again by this chameleon, this demon masquerading in human form. She shakes her head, wishing she could cover her ears to drown out the siren song.

Lucy peers into the dark, dank water of the Thames. If she could somehow free herself from the Count's vise grip and leap into its icy depths, it might swallow her whole. Then what? She cannot swim. Surely she would drown. Would that be preferable to the life that awaits her? No. She must not allow herself to think such impious thoughts.

She thinks of Jonathan and the look of sheer horror in his eyes.

Lucy looks not at the water this time, but at the dock, the barrels and crates stacked along its sides. If she could break free, could she fashion a weapon?

There is the calling again. It's getting louder. Then she hears other sounds. Footsteps on the docks, the squeaking of the wooden planks. There is more than one voice. There are voices.

"Lucy!" She recognizes the voice, the real human voice, of Miss Cobbe.

The Count hears it, too, and he loosens his grip ever so slightly on Lucy's arm. It is enough. She rips herself away from him and turns back in the direction of the calls.

In an instant, something catches Lucy's eye on the dock. A stack of metal bars that might have been used for a railing or to bar windows. They are covered with ash and dirt. Lucy lunges for one.

It is surprisingly heavy, and she needs both hands to hold it aloft, as she turns to face the Count.

He smiles. There is no fear in his visage, no concern in his glinting eyes. Rather, he seems to enjoy this new development.

"And what are you going to do with that?" he asks. "They have tried to destroy me once in the fire. Your father was behind it. Did you know that?"

What is he talking about? Lucy remembers reading about a fire at the warehouses on the London docks. That was months ago. She had puzzled over her father's involvement when she found the calling card in his office. The Count must be telling the truth. Her father was deeply implicated in these horrors. He had brought this evil here to London and into their home.

Lucy's anger grows.

The demon looks down at Lucy's feet, and she follows his gaze. Suddenly, rats come out of hiding, from behind barrels, under the docks. They circle Lucy, running this way and that. She wants to scream, but she will not give this demon the satisfaction of her fear. Instead, Lucy stands very still as a rat runs over her leather boot.

"Our ship awaits," the Count says. "Enough of this." He motions with his hand to the iron bar, and Lucy feels it begin to slide through her hands. She holds on with all her might.

"No," she says.

"Lucy!" She hears women calling her name, but this time the voices are fainter. She seems to be swallowed in yellow fog that makes it difficult for others to see her from the wharf.

"Over here!" she yells. Her voice is not as strong as she would have hoped. She can only hope it carries.

Lucy feels herself weakening in mind and body as the Count stands before her, boring into her eyes with his, holding his hand up to summon the metal bar from her.

"You are coming with me, Lucy Rutherford. You are to be with me for all eternity. Your father has taken from me what you will restore—my beloved Karlien. An eye for an eye is justice."

"Who is Karlien?"

"We have no time for that now. Away!" And with this command, Lucy finds herself walking closer to the count. The metal bar is still in her hand, but against her will it drops to her side.

The Count hisses. Lucy can feel his rage. He raises one hand, summoning her with a long, skinny finger. Lucy knows he intends to take her right here on the dock. The Count's lips draw back, revealing two sharp points.

Against every bone in her body, Lucy finds herself agreeing. She tilts her head to one side, her long, red curls falling over her shoulder, revealing the smooth, untouched skin of her neck. She feels a desire such as she has never known. She has no words for this feeling. She only knows it runs through her body like an electric force.

Lucy is inches away from the Count. She closes her eyes.

"Lucy!"

A sharp report. A stampede of feet. The boards of the wharf are shaking beneath her. And in that instant, the desire Lucy felt a moment ago is replaced by a wave of revulsion so strong that she gasps in horror and steps back.

What was she about to do? To give herself over to this fiend?

Lucy has only a moment to register this before the shouts of Miss Cobbe and other women get louder.

"Lucy!"

Summoning all her strength, and drawing on the strength of the women rushing down the pier, Lucy grabs the metal bar, raises it high, and brings it down on the Count.

He is too quick for her. He grabs the bar with his hand, and the two of them are locked together in an awkward embrace.

"There she is!" Lucy thinks she hears Maude's voice rising above the others.

The Count is hissing louder now. Lucy senses that he is about to change shape. No longer is the Count towering over her. He will be gone in an instant. *Quickly, quickly*, she thinks. She must stop him.

She has only one choice. The metal bar between them, Lucy pushes it forcefully, and, still locked together, she and the Count plunge into the dark, icy water of the Thames.

# Chapter Fifty-Three

The docks are thronging with women, shouting with anger and carrying torches to dissolve the dense fog hovering over the water. Constable Neil reins in his horse and leaps to the ground before it has quite come to a stop. He tosses the lines over an iron railing and prays it will still be there when he needs it. He had raced toward Whitechapel as soon as he heard about the latest murder in Miller's Court. For a moment his heart had stopped: God Almighty, could it be Lucy? She doesn't fit the Ripper's pattern, she shouldn't be in Whitechapel...but then, she is still missing!

Then, despite his relief that the victim wasn't Lucy, the scene at Miller's Court had been horrifying. As his fellow policemen swarmed the murder site, holding back angry residents and combing the streets for witnesses, he peeled away toward the river, following a gut instinct that strengthened as he saw the crowds heading that way.

He thought he saw Mrs. Hepworth race past in a cart and his suspicions were confirmed. Something was afoot. And the river, black and murky, is the obvious place to dispose of any bloody evidence of a crime. The Thames has been swallowing the city's castoffs for centuries.

As he pushes through the crowd, Neil catches a glimpse of a man's top hat rising above the sea of women and ducking between warehouses that line the riverfront.

In his mind's eye, he sees the tall figure of Dr. Hepworth, leaving his house that very night in an unmarked carriage, carrying a medical bag filled with surgical implements—or a long, sharp knife?. Could it be? He cranes his neck, but can't tell where the man has gone. He wants to follow the women who are chanting now, and see what the ruckus is. He *needs* to find Lucy. But reluctantly he turns toward the alleyway where the top hat has disappeared.

The early morning fog is lifting as Neil strains to keep the top hat in view. His boot slips on the damp cobblestones as he quickens his pace. The smell of dead fish and rank sewage overwhelms him. The man, whoever he is, seems to be heading closer and closer to the water's edge. Why? Neil thinks of all the missing evidence in the Ripper cases: the knife, the murderer's bloodied clothes... Whitechapel is not only the haunt of downtrodden women who make easy prey for villains, it is also only a mile from the river.

Neil clears a corner and sees the man ahead, moving quickly toward a red brick warehouse that seems to lean over the dark water below. The man pauses to glance quickly behind him and Neil flattens himself into a doorway. He hears a soft thud and peers out to find the street empty. He follows, heart racing, to the metal door that has closed behind his suspect. What if the door is locked? He'll have lost the man.

But no. Inside the gloomy entrance, a set of rickety stairs cling to the sidewall of a cavernous space.

Neil follows the sound of footsteps running upward. His own heavy steps echo through the space as he takes the stairs two at a time.

Light filters through barred windows high above his head as he climbs, mounting higher toward the roof. Another clang of a metal door and he knows his man has reached the top. Pigeons roost in the upper eaves and he hears the flapping of wings as the birds are disturbed.

Is there any other egress? What does he want up there? Again, he thinks of the river as a gaping maw, ready to swallow any evidence.

Neil bursts out onto the roof, breathing hard. A huge iron grappling hook swings out toward the water, ready to unload cargo from the furthest reaches of the empire. A tall figure leans over the low wall framing the roof's edge.

The wall runs around all four sides, with the nearest buildings on another dock. With Neil blocking the stairwell, there is no other way out. He has him!

"Halt!" Neil shouts. This is it. He knows that soon, the pieces of the Ripper crimes will fall together. He knows it deep in his bones.

The man whirls around, his black cape swirling open. His hat falls off and Neil sees the malevolent visage for the first time. It is a pale face, set in rigid lines of anger and hatred. A twisted smile forms as he looks back at Neil from across the roof.

It is Hepworth.

Neil eyes the bag in the doctor's hands and scans the distance between them. The crowds below have moved toward a commotion further east, but Neil can't spare a glance that way. He has to focus on his adversary. "I am the Metropolitan Police. You are cornered. Come away from the edge!"

"And have you arrest me? I think not." Hepworth's tone is mocking.

Neil studies the other man closely, committing the details to memory. Despite his calm tone, the doctor is disheveled. His chest heaves with agitation. His neckcloth lies loose and untied around his throat. He has been in some sort of scuffle, but Neil is too far away to see anything like bloodstains. Hepworth clutches at his medical bag with two hands. Had he been about to empty it into the Thames?

"Why would I arrest you?" Neil stalls. Keep them talking, that's what the articles say. At the same time, his hand creeps slowly into his pocket and feels for his weapon. He was one of the few given a weapon on Warren's task force. Now he is glad to have it.

Hepworth sneers. "I know you have me pegged for the Whitechapel murders. But you do not understand my work. I am a man of science, who studies the human mind, you ignoramus. Not a butcher."

Neil would like to pummel the man but thinks better of responding. He thinks the man may be in need of a doctor of the mind himself. Certainly Hepworth's mental state is one of distress—and something more. The man is hiding something.

Hepworth takes a step backward, balanced right at the crumbling barrier. Hepworth keeps his eyes on Neil with cool disdain. "Those deplorable women are my trade, my objects of study, my obsession. They cannot be saved, but their bodies have secrets to teach mankind. If only we can examine them.?" He smirks. Neil is almost impressed by the man's sangfroid.

"What are you doing up here then?" Neil calls out, edging closer himself.

"No further or I will leap into the Thames! I am a strong swimmer and I can easily make the other shore before you get around the bridge."

"It's three stories down. You won't want to risk it," Neil snaps. He takes a deep breath for patience. "So tell me then why you are here."

"I owe you no explanations, constable. I am a respected member of my profession. Out for an early morning stroll. Or a night on the town. It's no business of yours. Go your way before you make a fool of yourself with these accusations." Hepworth shifts his weight and glances down at the water below.

"I've made no accusations. Let's go to the station then. You can proclaim your innocence and off you'll go." Neil edges a little closer again and sees Hepworth's eyes narrow. He needs to rattle the man, get him off his game. He is cool enough to be old Jack, that's for sure.

"What did you do with your wife, doctor?"

Hepworth freezes. "My wife is even less of your business, you lout. Have you no respect for the sanctity of a man's home? Your vulgar Irish origins are on display, I'm afraid."

He is trying to provoke me, too, Neil thinks, but still he can't help the rise in his throat, the clenching of his fists. The weapon in his pocket draws him like a magnet. The wind picks up around them.

"She escaped," Neil calls out, louder now over the rising wind. He dares a glance at the streets below, but this part of the waterfront has emptied.

Everyone must be milling around the next dock, watching the drama unfold. Lucy might be there and in trouble. He has to end this impasse. "I saw her here in the crowd. Your scheme to imprison her in your asylum has failed."

For a moment, Neil thinks the doctor looks uncertain. His brow creases and his eyes dart to the side as if looking for his wife among the people on the ground. He is getting to the man. He presses on.

"I know about the women, too," Neil says, raising his voice over the wind. "The unfortunates from your asylum that you sell at the club. What would that do to your precious reputation if that got out, Doctor Hepworth? That you have a sideline in prostitution? Did Annie Chapman threaten to expose you?"

Hepworth says nothing, but bares his teeth in a snarl.

Neil holds aloft the carte de visite the maid had given him.

"Does this look familiar? It links one of the Ripper's victims to your own hospital. Is that why you killed her?" He prays all his instincts are correct. The pieces are falling into place.

*"Give me that!"*

With a roar of rage, Hepworth launches himself at Neil, leaping forward and barreling toward him like a steam engine. Without thinking, Neil pulls the weapon out of his pocket. He aims. The shot rings out like a clap of thunder, startling both of them. The revolver clatters from his hand onto the ground.

Hepworth's body jerks backward. Their gazes meet. Neil, still astonished and bewildered by his own reflexes. Hepworth, stunned and uncomprehending. Then, as if in slow motion, he stumbles, and pitches backwards over the low wall.

# *Chapter Fifty-Four*

Maude gasps from onshore, raising her hands to her mouth in horror. She sees thrashing in the water, but who or what it is she can't tell. Then Lucy's head rises for a moment. Her long hair fans out along the top of the river for a moment and then disappears underneath its surface.

Maude thinks of Shakespeare's Ophelia and prays that her friend does not meet a similar fate.

"Help her, someone!" Maude hears one of the women shouting. But no one dives in after Lucy.

Has the Count trapped her at the bottom? Or are Lucy's heavy garments dragging her down?

Maude peers into the dark water, hoping to spot another glimpse of her friend. She sees only the inky river holding on to whatever lurks beneath.

Maude senses movement behind her. Several women have gotten a hold of a rope coiled on the dock and are getting ready to throw a lifeline to Lucy. But where is her friend?

Maude hears Miss Cobbe bark orders to line up, and she

steps behind her, ready to do her part to save Lucy—if she's still alive.

There are nothing but small ripples across the surface of the black, foul-smelling Thames. Maude shudders as she stands behind Miss Cobbe waiting for a sign of life, praying that they're not too late.

~

Lucy has never felt the need for air more than she does now. Her lungs are about to burst. But she can neither exhale nor inhale. To do so would mean certain death.

The dark water sucks at her, pulling her down to its depths. The Count still has his icy grip on her as well. He refuses to let go. If she thought jumping into the water would cause him to drown, she was mistaken. The brackish water of the Thames has done nothing to loosen his power on her. And now, too late, she realizes her mistake.

Lucy tries to kick her legs. But her heavy dress wraps around her like a tourniquet, preventing her from kicking her way to the surface. How ridiculous it is to wear such impractical clothing, she thinks. But that thought is quickly replaced by another as the Count grabs her arm and pulls her away from the docks at a speed that surprises her.

He's taking her to the ship, after all. And if she doesn't drown first, she will soon be the Count's prisoner on a boat that will take her away from England and all that she loves. She can't let that happen.

Lucy struggles against the Count with all her might. Again she tries kicking her legs out, and, this time, she's able to free one leg from her waterlogged dress and make contact with the Count's body. But he doesn't register the blow.

Lucy decides to take another tack. If she can't fight him physically, she will have to outwit him. But how?

She lets her body go limp and closes her eyes. She will not resist. She will not fight back.

When she stops moving, Lucy notices that the Count does the opposite. He swims with her faster, at a superhuman speed. Surely, he doesn't want her dead? That is not quite as satisfying a revenge as entombing her for all eternity, making her a monster like him, and destroying her father in the process.

Lucy opens her eyes. They must be close to the surface of the river because she can see a lighter shade of gray just beyond the water.

She closes her eyes. With every fiber of her being, Lucy wants to open her mouth and gasp for air. Desperately. She doesn't care if she sucks in only water. She can't wait any longer.

Finally, her head breaks the surface of the water. She gasps and chokes.

When Lucy is able to breathe, she looks around and sees the Count has brought them next to a large, sleek vessel anchored in the river. He calls out to the sailors on board, and they are quickly hoisted up together, the Count grabbing hold of a line and pulling her up and out of the water with him. He is unfazed by the water and the exertion.

It is only when Lucy is on board, sitting in a heap on the polished floor of the wooden stern, that she realizes once again, she's trapped.

When it becomes clear that no rope can reach Lucy, that in fact, there is no one there any longer to throw the rope to, Maude wrings her hands and stands back from the dock, tears clouding her vision as she searches the spot where Lucy had been. They had been so close. And now Lucy is gone.

"We're not giving up that easily." Miss Cobbe's voice is firm in Maude's ear.

The women at the dock are still shouting Lucy's name, calling for her over and over. Their cries carry across the water, finally rousing other sailors, merchants, and dock workers. At this early hour of the new day, the wharf is coming alive. And not a moment too soon.

Maude turns her head as heavy footsteps pound the wooden planks. It is dawn, the sky a bruising shade of purple gray. The thick yellow fog still hangs like a shroud making it difficult to see.

Suddenly, through the mist, she sees a troop of men toward the dock. The first among them is Constable Neil, easily recognizable in his dark blue police uniform and tall custodian helmet.

"Where's Lucy?" he shouts.

Maude points toward the water.

Neil scans the horizon. Then he shakes his head and looks around the dock, searching for something. Maude follows his gaze.

Then she sees what Neil has spotted. A small wooden wherry boat is tied to the dock. Two sets of oars lie waiting in its unoccupied hull. There is no sign of a wherryman to row the boat across the Thames.

In an instant, Neil jumps into the boat. It rocks unsteadily, but the policeman rights it by holding on to the dock. Then he holds out his hand for Maude to follow.

Despite her age, it is Cobbe who clambers in the wherry first, with surprising agility, ignoring Neil's offer of assistance.

"Hurry, constable! That fiend has Lucy and he mustn't get away."

Then Cobbe calls for Maude and helps her down into the boat.

Neil unties the boat, while Cobbe hands Maude an oar. Maude has never rowed a boat in her life. She has never even been in one of these small wherry boats used for carrying people across the river, and she looks down at the object in her hands with dismay.

Impatiently, Cobbe grabs the oar from Maude, then takes up the other one. Neil grabs the other set of oars, and he and Cobbe begin rowing furiously away from the dock.

"You keep watch for Lucy," Cobbe commands.

Maude steadies herself on the wooden seat and peers into the distance, searching for her friend. Cobbe and Neil settle into the same rhythm. They soon propel the light boat into the fast current.

# Chapter Fifty-Five

THAMES, NOVEMBER 9, 5:25 A.M.

Lucy chokes and coughs up river water. Her soaked clothes are heavy and clinging. Her limbs frozen. The Count is unaffected by their swim in the frigid Thames. If anything, he seems invigorated by it. His pale skin glows with an unnatural tone as water drips down his face. He doesn't bother to wipe it away.

"Hoist anchor," he bellows.

Shadowy figures move on the deck, responding to the Count's commands. Lucy looks around, searching for someone—or something—to help her. She cannot let the ship leave with her on it.

The Count turns to her, his eyes like flint. "Well, Lucy. You've led me on quite the chase. But that is over now. You'll join me for my final act."

He holds out a long finger towards her, and, despite the weariness of her limbs and weight of her soaked gown, Lucy begins to obey. She stands.

Though he may control her limbs, the Count cannot

control her mind. Lucy shakes her head, and mouths the word "No" with defiance.

The Count takes a step towards her.

But just then, the loud clanking of the anchor chain stops. One of the seamen shouts, "It's caught. The anchor is snagged on something."

The Count snarls and turns around in anger to scream at his crew. "Free it, you fools. Now!"

Lucy's legs suddenly begin to buckle beneath her, and she stumbles backwards, hitting her back against the stern railing. As she grabs hold of the railing to steady herself, her fingers touch the cool brass of an oil lantern. It's secured to the ship's railing with a hook and clip.

With trembling fingers, she fumbles with the hook, trying to free the lantern. But her fingers are wet and slippery on the cold metal.

*Hurry!* She tells herself. She can't let the Count see what she's doing. Fortunately, his back is still turned away from her as he engages with the crew, who continue to struggle with the snagged anchor.

Lucy tries again to unhook the lantern. Exposure to the salt and sea air has made the metal hook stiff. Her fingers struggle to find the strength required to force the metal open. Finally, she's able to free the clasp from the railing.

Lucy holds the heavy lantern, its flame still flickering inside the glass chamber. She formulates her plan. If her father had tried to defeat the demon by fire once, maybe she can try it again.

She knows she only has moments before the anchor is released. If she hears the clanking of the anchor chain start again, her time will have run out.

With one quick motion, Lucy unscrews the lantern's base and spills the oil onto the polished deck. The pungent scent of the kerosene fills her nostrils, but she doesn't hesitate. Lucy spreads the oil in a thick trail, deliberately creating a line separating her from the Count.

"It's clear!" one of the crew shouts.

The loud clanking begins again. Lucy has mere seconds.

She takes a quick breath, and, in one swift motion, she smashes the lantern onto the oil-slicked deck. The glass shatters. The exposed flame meets the ready fuel.

Fire erupts instantly. Flames travel like lightning, greedily consuming the kerosene.

But Lucy does not stop there.

There are shouts from the men, "Fire!"

"You foolish girl!" screams the Count.

Through the growing inferno, Lucy sees the Count's furious face. He shields himself with his arms, backing away from the fire. Then he attempts to circle around it to get through to her. But his superhuman speed is blocked by the rapidly spreading fire. He howls and snarls.

Lucy, her fingers more practiced this time, quickly unlatches another lantern. She turns the base to release the oil and then smashes it onto the deck. It feeds the already growing fire.

Moving as fast as she can, she finds one more lantern, unhooks it, and this time does not bother spilling out the kerosene, but launches it directly into the flames.

There's a loud, eerie whooshing sound as a fresh breeze picks up the conflagration. And then red and orange flames shoot high into the sky, feeding on the varnished wood. They quickly spread up the sides of the ship.

Lucy, too, backs away from the growing fire, pressing herself as flat as she can against the stern railing. Her previously damp clothing has partially protected her from the blaze, but now she feels the full rage of the hot flames. Heat scorches her skin. Smoke stings her eyes and fills her lungs. She coughs violently.

While the fire has formed a barrier between her and the Count, it has also trapped her.

"Lucy! You cannot escape me!" The voice is in her head. Or is it coming from outside? She cannot tell. But she feels the Count's fury. Wherever he is, he has not released her yet.

Thick black smoke billows around her. She holds her breath because it sears her lungs, then erupts in a fit of coughing. Should she jump into the icy river again? Surely, this time she would drown.

Suddenly, a loud roar fills the air. One mast has caught fire. She hears splashing as some of the crew are jumping into the water. Is there a lifeboat?

The smoke is too much for Lucy. She coughs again violently. She has moments before the deck gives way beneath her feet. Moments before she is swallowed in the flames. She must make a decision. Die by fire or fling herself again into the murky waters of the Thames.

"Look, there!" Maude screams and points to a wooden ship down the river. Flames shoot up from the deck visible through the fog.

"That's where Lucy is. I know it." Maude feels the certainty in her bones. She only hopes they get there in time.

"Faster," Cobbe shouts to Constable Neil, though the two of them are rowing already as quickly as humanly possible.

The air is thick with black smoke that mingles with the yellow fog, but as they approach the burning ship, Maude shouts again. "I see her!"

Perched precariously on the railing is Lucy. The fire is fast encroaching behind her. Judging by the way she looks down at the water, it is clear she hasn't seen them yet.

"Pull the boat over there!" Neil shouts, and Cobbe begins turning the wherry around with an oar.

The sound of men shouting can be heard above the roar of the fire.

Where is the Count? Maude wonders. Has he escaped? But she doesn't have time to think about that now. They have to get to Lucy.

"Lucy. Jump!" Neil shouts up to her.

Lucy looks down and seems startled to see three people in the small wherry. But she smiles when she sees who they are.

"Lucy. We'll get to you," says Cobbe. "But you need to jump. Now!"

Maude watches as her friend looks behind her. Lucy hesitates for only a second. Then she steps off the railing and plunges into the cold water of the Thames.

At first, the cool water is a relief from the heat and force of the fire. But as she sinks down into the murky water, Lucy knows that she will die. She cannot swim, and she is sinking too fast.

At least her last view of life on earth was of her friends, three people who'd become dear to her in different ways. Constable Neil might never know how fond of him she is. But that is for the best. They could never be more than friendly acquaintances. Not in this life.

Maude, her closest and dearest friend.

Miss Cobbe, her fiercest inspiration.

Lucy takes comfort in knowing, too, that she chose this death. That she escaped the Count. She is no longer his prisoner. Did he perish in the fire? She cannot be certain. But she is certain that she will not spend eternity with him, entombed in a revenge plot against her father.

Lucy thinks of Lord Rutherford. Perhaps she has finished what her father has started. That thought makes her glad, though her father may never know what happened. There's so much about her he doesn't know at all. She's sorry that she's never revealed herself to him. But she loves him. She hopes he will know that.

As these thoughts go through Lucy's mind, she finds that she is not sinking after all. She is suspended–in water and time, hovering in darkness that both encircles and permeates her whole being. A jolt goes through her body and suddenly her limbs feel strong. Her legs kick out with newfound energy and power. She is rising towards the surface, propelled to survive. Lucy opens her eyes and sees four hands reaching for her through the water.

"I've got you, Lucy," Constable Neil says, pulling her up.

"I've got you as well, my dear." Cobbe's strong arms grab Lucy and help haul her into the wherry.

Lucy blinks against the morning light and Maude helps her to sit on the rocking boat, wrapping her arms around her to stop her from shivering.

"Row!" Neil says, picking up his oars. "We must get away from the ship."

"And that fiend," says Cobbe. "Before he aims to follow."

As they pull away from the burning ship, Lucy thinks she spots something above the roaring flames. Is it her imagination? Or has something flown into the sky? Whatever it is, it is quickly out of sight.

Lucy shivers and Maude draws her in tighter.

"You're safe now, Lucy."

## Chapter Fifty-Six

The morning light has finally driven away the last of the yellow fog over the river. The gawking crowds are dispersing now that the fire on the ship has fizzled out, leaving a broken hull half afloat in a field of charred wood. The air still reeks in the aftermath. Maude guides a freezing but very much alive Lucy, her sodden hem dragging behind her, back toward solid ground. Constable Neil follows them in silence.

Now that Lucy is safe, Miss Cobbe and her army of women have dispersed. There were cheers and talk of tea and celebration and future plans as the noisy band made their way down the docks.

What happens next? Maude wonders to herself. In the rush of the night's events, she hasn't thought beyond her own escape and Lucy's rescue. What was the fiend after?

"Vengeance," Lucy whispers, so Maude must have spoken aloud. "Against my father." She shakes her head and Maude understands she will not say more now. Maude pauses and turns toward the constable. He is commandeering a carriage for them.

"Was he the Ripper?" Maude asks, hesitantly.

Neil helps Lucy into the vehicle, carefully wrapping her in a horse blanket as she murmurs her thanks. He grasps Maude's elbow and guides her in next. Maude presses herself against Lucy in a vain effort to keep her friend warm.

"No," he answers finally, vaulting into the driver's seat. "He is another kind of monster."

Neil is silent again as he takes up the reins and leads the horse through the remaining throngs at the waterfront.

For a moment, there is only the sound of the horses' hooves clomping steadily on stone. It soothes Maude's rattled nerves.

She lifts a hand and tucks a loose strand of hair behind her ear. She probably looks a fright. Edward will be…no, she mustn't think of him yet.

Neil turns down another pier and pulls up next to an empty warehouse. Maude can see the tension in his shoulders. Then he shakes it off and looks her straight in the eye.

"Mrs. Hepworth, your husband has been running a prostitution ring from the asylum where he works."

Maude blinks. "Excuse me?" But the truth of the words sinks in.

Neil continues, voice even, as he explains that Edward, her husband, arranged for the women under his care to be lent out at night to the gentlemen's club they had rescued Lucy from. When the women resisted—or tried to report it—they were drugged or bound or isolated. After all, the doctor could call all of it treatment.

Maude puts a hand to her head and squeezes her eyes shut. Had she known something, somehow? How could she have been so wrong about him?

Beneath the scratchy wool blanket, Lucy feels for Maude's

hand and holds it. "Did he have some connection to Annie's death?"

Neil gazes at Lucy's flushed face before replying. "I think so. We know Annie was also briefly incarcerated at Hepworth's asylum. I confronted him tonight. Here. On the roof. There was another murder earlier." His face hardens. "Hepworth could have been getting rid of evidence here."

Lucy shakes off the blanket and starts clambering from the carriage. "Where is he? This is outrageous! We need answers!"

Neil stops her with a strong grip on her arm. "Lucy—" He clears his throat. "Miss Rutherford. We can't." He looks at Maude with some unspoken communication. "I shot him."

Maude's whole body jerks, as if out of her own control. "Is he...?" She can't say it.

"Dead." Neil nods, solemnly. "I saw him fall off the roof. I'll collect the body now. I wanted to warn you."

"Then we'll have no answers," Lucy cries out.

With another silent look, the policeman jumps down and rounds the corner of the building, toward the waterfront. The two women wait in the carriage.

Lucy turns to Maude, who feels frozen in place. "Oh Maude, I'm so sorry. I mustn't carry on in front of you, as if you haven't just suffered a grievous loss. My poor, poor dear!" She wraps her arms around Maude.

"I can't pretend to be sorry," she says in a low voice. She feels a new feeling rising and she thinks she could name it— relief. "He put me away, Lucy." Her eyes lift to meet her friend's.

"He said I was mad and sent me to his asylum. Mrs. Cavendish helped me escape. And Miss Cobbe's women. We came after you. Oh, there is a lot to tell you." She feels tears on her face and Lucy's fingers wiping them away as her voice gives out.

Lucy looks grim. "Yes, we both have stories to tell. But—"

She breaks off at the sight of Neil rushing back to the carriage, looking stunned. "What is it?" she asks briskly.

"He's not there." The three of them look at one another in silence. "The body, I mean. It's gone." With a fierce look, Neil climbs back into the carriage. "He'll float downstream with the tide. We'll dredge the river if we have to." With a jerk of the reins they start in motion.

"Are you sure he's dead?" Maude asks quietly.

"I shot him at twenty feet. He fell from three stories. His body must have been swept away. We'll have to send officers to scour the area. If he was injured, he can't get far. We'll find him. I swear it!" His voice escalates as if making a vow to the whole street.

The two women huddle together and say nothing.

### THE TIMES (LONDON)
November 13, 1888

The HOME SECRETARY announced yesterday, in the House of Commons, that SIR CHARLES WARREN tendered his resignation on Thursday last, and that it has been accepted by the Government. It has been tolerably well known for some time that the relations between SIR CHARLES WARREN and his official chief have not been of an entirely pleasant or harmonious nature.

Chelsea, November 13

Frances Cobbe lays down the newspaper and frowns. Warren was a decent fellow. He should never have trusted Lord

Rutherford though. She taps her fingers on her desk and takes a sip of tea. She stares out the window of the back parlor of her modest townhouse, calculating.

A solitary leafless tree shivers in the autumn air. She has gained valuable insights in this latest campaign, she thinks, and now she can maneuver the lord to her own advantage. Mr. Smith's articles have put him in a tight corner. Yes, an idea is forming. Her women detectives need space to train and funds for equipment. She has the heavy expenses of greasing wheels… And who has resources to spare? She nods with satisfaction and scratches a note on some stationery.

She returns to the newspaper, reading carefully, as always. Between her literary labors and her reading habits, her fingers are permanently ink-stained. A small black-bordered box jumps out at her:

*It is with the deepest sorrow that the City News Agency reports the loss of one of their finest reporters. Mr. Jonathan Hinton passed away unexpectedly last week of a sudden hemorrhage of the heart. His colleagues send their thoughts and prayers to his grieving mother and sisters as Mr. Hinton goes to his eternal rest. May God rest his soul. He will be much missed.*

Cobbe shakes her head sadly and turns another page. There are mysteries that surpass our understanding, she thinks, and worlds beyond our own.

Mayfair, November 23, midnight

Lucy Rutherford is wide awake. She has had no more nocturnal wanderings, and there is no need for Sally to sleep next to her mistress to prevent her from leaving her bedroom.

But what Sally does not realize is that there is no longer a need for Lucy to leave her father's house by the front door.

She has other ways of going out into the night should she wish to.

A lone dog howls in the distance. Lucy stands by the window and releases the sash. She feels strangely alive and powerful. The night calls out to her, a siren song that has no words, only shapes and feelings. She shudders, and closes the window to resist the temptation. Twice she has been able to crawl down from her bedroom window and stand in the darkness, letting the thick night air fill her lungs. She was not frightened. But she went no further than the iron railing circling her father's property.

Lucy has not told Maude about this. It is her secret for now. She thinks suddenly of Constable Neil and his strong arms around her as he pulled her from the Thames. She has longed to see him again, but has had no recourse to. Yet thinking about the constable helps Lucy return to herself, the self that she takes to bed, though she is not tired in the least. She will rest during the day tomorrow.

# Epilogue

**EAST LONDON ADVERTISER**
Saturday, November 24, 1888

## THE WHITECHAPEL ATROCITIES
## FUNERAL OF THE LAST VICTIM

The remains of the unfortunate woman, Marie
Jeanette Kelly, who was murdered on November 9th,
in Miller's Court, Dorset Street, Spitalfields, were
carried on Monday from the Shoreditch mortuary to
the Roman Catholic Cemetery at Leytonstone, for
interment, amidst a scene of turbulent excitement.

The coffin was carried in an open car drawn by two
horses, and two coaches followed. An enormous crowd
of people assembled at an early hour, completely
blocking the thoroughfare, and a large number of
police were engaged in keeping order. The bell of St.
Leonard's began tolling at noon, and the signal
appeared to draw all the residents in the neighbourhood together.

There was an enormous preponderance of women in the crowd, and scarcely any had any covering to their heads. The wreaths upon the coffin bore cards inscribed with remembrances from friends using certain public-houses in common with the murdered woman.

As the coffin appeared, borne on the shoulders of four men, at the principal gate of the church, the crowd appeared to be greatly affected. Round the open car in which it was to be placed men and women struggled desperately to get to touch the coffin. Women with faces streaming with tears cried out "God forgive her!" and every man's head was bared in token of sympathy.

WHITECHAPEL, DECEMBER 19

The streets of Whitechapel are shrouded in fog. Thick as pea soup, it clings to the rough cobblestones. It attaches itself to the dilapidated lodging houses, where the poorest men and women sleep several to a bed. It even sticks to threadbare clothing and skin, freezing the inhabitants caught in its icy breath.

The thick fog muffles some sounds—horses' clopping—and amplifies others—the sound of men and women arguing, the cries of young children who sleep with nothing but the night sky for a blanket. The fog conceals couples fornicating in doorways or in dark, damp alleyways. It wraps its shroud around this section of East London, refusing to let go. Even in daylight, the air is thick with haze, almost viscous to the touch.

And then there's the smell, which Amelia Cavendish finds worst of all. Breathing in the yellow fog hurts her lungs, as she makes her way down the warren of cramped, dirty streets, being careful not to step in excrement—whether human or animal, she does not know or care to find out.

The air is thick with the industrial smell of coal from chimneys and factories. It's mingled with the musty, damp smell of mildew and mixed with rotting garbage piled on the streets and fecal matter wafting from open sewers. Amelia raises her scarf to her nose as she steps carefully, taking pains not to slip on the wet cobblestones.

She is in a hurry. But it is not because she fears for her life, as she might have done if she were traversing these streets just several weeks ago. The Ripper is long gone. No new murders have been committed since Mary Jane Kelly was brutally killed in her bed. No one knows where the murderer went or who he was. The newspapers have several theories: the Ripper was an escapee from an insane asylum and then recommitted. He was an immigrant who returned to his country. Or he committed suicide. She laughs at all of these theories. Preposterous.

Amelia has a good idea of the murderer's identity, but she is not one to tell journalists. She is only pleased that the women who call Whitechapel home have no reason to fear the butcher who stalked these streets hunting for easy prey. She and her sisterhood have seen to that. They have their own female detectives—secretly, not publicly, of course, but they are not in it for the publicity.

When she arrives at 19 Whitbourne Street, formerly a gentlemen's club, but now a gentlewomen's club, she is greeted by a sea of friendly faces. And many others she doesn't recognize. New recruits to the cause of the New Woman, she thinks, chuckling slightly to herself at the pun.

Acquiring the club was an unforeseen boon. With a scandal pending, Rutherford needed to salvage his name by divesting his interest in the club. Miss Cobbe agreed to say nothing about his business dealings in exchange for the lease.

Amelia spots Lucy Rutherford near the front of the crowded room, her shiny red hair visible from the doorway. Lucy turns as if sensing Amelia's presence, and gives her a wide smile, revealing her white teeth. Maude Hepworth is wearing all black and sits next to her. Though Edward's body was never found, Maude wears the color of mourning. Not for her husband but for the women who have died at the hands of the Ripper and those whom the doctor had tortured and sold. The two women have recuperated from their ordeals, she notes with satisfaction. There is no medicine like an occupation.

Lucy turns and motions for Amelia to join them. She has saved a seat next to Emily and Sally.

And then the familiar voice of Frances Power Cobbe brings them to order, "Ladies, let us begin."

# Historical Note

In writing this work of fiction, we drew on our own academic training as Ph.D.'s with specializations in Victorian literature, culture, and gender studies, as well as a wide range of historical sources, some of which are listed below. Many of the characters—from Sir Charles Warren to Frances Power Cobbe—are real historical figures we have used in fictional ways. The newspaper clippings we intersperse throughout the text (with the exception of two that are entirely fictional) are all taken from actual accounts of the time, though we trim them down and occasionally adjust a date. The entry of the "Mysterious Miasma" from the *North London Standard* was entirely invented, as was the account of the mine collapse from *The Colonial Englishman*. We also moved Cobbe's article on Female Detectives from its original date of October 20 to September 2 to suit our plot. All of the Victorian articles we excerpt can be found online at the website Casebook: Jack the Ripper.

We focused our novel on the five "canonical" victims of Jack the Ripper, murdered in that terrifying autumn of 1888 when the police had no success in finding or preventing the scourge against working-class women. For details about the lives of Nichols, Chapman, Stride, Eddowes, and Kelly, we relied on Hallie Rubenhold's impressively researched re-evaluation of the Whitechapel murders, *The Five*. We followed the known facts of the crimes as much as possible but changed the discovery of Mary Kelly's murder to earlier in the morning of November 9th in order to fit our plot.

The map we included in the prologue is based on Charles Booth's London Poverty Map (1886-1903), a rich source of data about demographics in London.

*Endnotes*

## CHAPTER TWO

*East London Observer,* September 8, 1888.
https://www.casebook.org/press_reports/east_london_ob
server/elo880908.html
great fire at docks *East London Advertiser,* September 1, 1888.
https://www.casebook.org/press_reports/east_london_ad
vertiser/ela880901.html
*Morning Advertiser (London),* September 1, 1888.
https://www.casebook.org/press_reports/morning_adver
tiser/18880901.html

## CHAPTER FIVE

no blood *East London Observer,* September 8, 1888.
https://www.casebook.org/press_reports/east_london_ob
server/elo880908.html and
https://www.jack-the-ripper.org/mary-nichols-newspaper-
reports.htm
*Daily News (London),* September 1, 1888 (changed to
September 2).

https://www.casebook.org/press_reports/daily_news/
18880901.html

## CHAPTER NINE

*Illustrated Police News*, October 20, 1888 (changed in to
September 2).
　　https://www.casebook.org/press_reports/illustrated_po
lice_news/il881020.html

## CHAPTER TWELVE

Neil's testimony *Daily News (London)*, September 3, 1888.
　　https://www.casebook.org/press_reports/daily_news/
18880903.html
　　*Times (London)* September 24, 1888.
　　https://www.casebook.org/press_reports/times/
18880924.html
　　Purkiss, Green, etc. *St. James Gazette*, September 18, 1888.
　　https://www.casebook.org/press_reports/st.
_james_gazette/880918.html
　　Mrs. Purkiss and Mrs. Green mentioned in *Daily News*
September 4, 1888.
　　https://www.casebook.org/press_reports/daily_news/
18880904.html
　　Widow Bessie comes from Widow Annie in "Who is
Leather Apron" in *Lloyds Weekly Newspaper*, September 9, 1888.
　　https://www.casebook.org/press_reports/lloyds_week
ly_news/18880909.html

## CHAPTER FIFTEEN

Annie Chapman's inquest September 10, 1888.
　　https://www.casebook.org/official_documents/inquests/
inquest_chapman.html

Annie Chapman's dialogue *The Daily Telegraph*, September 11, 1888.

https://www.casebook.org/press_reports/daily_tele graph/dt880911.html

*East London Observer*, September 15, 1888.

https://www.casebook.org/press_reports/east_london_ob server/elo880915.html

*Morning Advertiser*, September 10, 1888.

https://www.casebook.org/press_reports/morning_adver tiser/18880910.html

## CHAPTER SEVENTEEN

bloodhounds in detection *Daily News (London)*, October 10, 1888 (changed to September 11).

https://www.casebook.org/press_reports/daily_news/ 18881010.html

## CHAPTER EIGHTEEN

*Evening Standard (London)*, September 11, 1888.

https://www.casebook.org/press_reports/evening_stan dard/18880911.html

## CHAPTER NINETEEN

*Evening News (London)*, September 11, 1888.

https://www.casebook.org/press_reports/evening_news/ 18880911.html

## CHAPTER TWENTY

Piser infirmity and knives *Evening Standard* (London), September 12, 1888.

https://www.casebook.org/press_reports/evening_stan

dard/18880912.html

Piser description/portrait *The Star*, September 11, 1888.
https://www.casebook.org/press_reports/star/
s880911.html

*Daily Telegraph*, September 11, 1888.
https://www.casebook.org/press_reports/daily_tele
graph/dt880912.html

## CHAPTER TWENTY-THREE

Inspector Thicke's testimony from inquest, with name
changed from Joseph Chandler, Inspector H Division
Metropolitan Police. *Daily Telegraph*, September 14, 1888.

Annie Chapman's inquest. Day 3 September 13, 1888.
https://www.casebook.org/official_documents/inquests/
inquest_chapman.html
https://www.casebook.org/press_reports/daily_tele
graph/dt880914.html

*Munster News* and *Limerick and Clare Advocate*, September 15,
1888.
https://www.casebook.org/press_reports/munster_news/
880915.html

## CHAPTER TWENTY-FIVE

*East and West Ham Gazette*, September 15, 1888. (Date changed
to September 19)
https://www.casebook.org/press_reports/east_and_west
_ham_gazette/880915.html

## CHAPTER TWENTY-SIX

first Ripper letter, received at Central News Agency
September 27, 1888.
https://www.casebook.org/ripper_letters/

Letter published in *Evening Standard (London)*, October 1, 1888, among others.

https://www.casebook.org/press_reports/evening_stan dard/18881001.html

*Evening Standard,* October 1, 1888 (date changed to September 29).

https://www.casebook.org/press_reports/evening_stan dard/18881001.html

## CHAPTER TWENTY-EIGHT

Ballad "I've Been Roaming" published in Lilian of the Vale (1826), pseudonym George Darly

https://www.gutenberg.org/files/26715/26715-h/26715-h.htm#page56

Kate's conversation at jail

https://www.casebook.org/press_reports/east_london_ad vertiser/ela881013.html

## CHAPTER TWENTY-NINE

*East London Advertiser,* October 6, 1888 (date changed to Octo-ber 1).

https://www.casebook.org/press_reports/east london_ad vertiser/ela881006.html

second Dear Boss postcard *Evening News (London)*, October 1, 1888.

https://www.casebook.org/press_reports/evening_news/18881001.html

## CHAPTER THIRTY-TWO

vigilante group conversation and Jonathan's article "Ama-teur Detectives at Work," *East London Advertiser*, October 13, 1888.

https://www.casebook.org/press_reports/east_london_ad
vertiser/ela881013.html

Jonathan's article excerpt from *Evening Standard (London)*
October 1,1888.

https://www.casebook.org/press_reports/evening_stan
dard/18881001.html

## CHAPTER THIRTY-FOUR

"supernatural element"

https://www.jack-the-ripper.org/jack-the-ripper-and-the-
supernatural.htm

Anderson's proclamation re prostitutes from Robert
Anderson, *The Lighter Side of My Official Life*, pp.134-137, and
Hallie Rubenhold, *The Five*, p. 291.

Phantoms letter October 23, 1888.

*Kurier Codzienny (Poland)* Friday, 27 October 1888.

https://www.casebook.org/press_reports/kurier_codzi
enny/kc881027.html

## CHAPTER THIRTY-SIX

Rutherford's newspaper reading *Evening News* November 12,
1888.

https://www.casebook.org/press_reports/evening_news/
18881112.html

## CHAPTER FORTY-ONE

Mary Kelly's conversations and backstory adapted from *The
Five*, pp.266-269 (trunk getting stolen; made enemies in
France); p.277 wearing no bonnet, p.281 broken pane of glass,
stuffed full of rags, p.283 friend Lizzie, p.285).

*The Daily Telegraph*, November 10, 1888.

https://www.casebook.org/press_reports/daily_tele
graph/dt881110.html
    testimony in Kelly inquest *Evening News (London)*,
November 12, 1888.
    https://www.casebook.org/press_reports/evening_news/
18881112.html

## CHAPTER FORTY-THREE

"Men must work and women must weep!" Song lyric from
Charles Kingsley's "The Three Fishers" (1851).
    https://allpoetry.com/The-Three-Fishers

## CHAPTER FORTY-NINE

Mary Kelly murder scene from the press reports and *The Five*,
p.280.
    *Morning Advertiser (London)*, November 10, 1888.
    https://www.casebook.org/press_reports/morning_adver
tiser/18881110.html
    *The Daily Telegraph*, November 10, 1888.
    https://www.casebook.org/press_reports/daily_tele
graph/dt881110.html
    *Pall Mall Gazette*, November 10, 1888. (Number of victims
changed from 9 to 5 and date changed to November 9).
    https://www.casebook.org/press_reports/pall_mal
l_gazette/18881110.html

## CHAPTER FIFTY

Rutherford's reading excerpts November 9, 1888 are both
from *Evening News (London)* November 12, 1888.
    https://www.casebook.org/press_reports/evening_news/
18881112.html

## CHAPTER FIFTY-SIX

Warren's resignation *The Times (London),* November 13, 1888.
   https://www.casebook.org/press_reports/times/
18881113.html

## EPILOGUE

funeral description *East London Advertiser,* November 28, 1888.
   https://www.casebook.org/press_reports/east_london_ad
vertiser/ela881124.html

# Selected Resources

Anderson, Robert. *The Lighter Side of My Official Life* (1910).

Belloc-Lowndes, Mrs. "The Lodger." *McClure's Magazine* (January 1911). A short story based on the mystery of Ripper's identity.

Casebook: Jack the Ripper. A useful compendium of online sources for information about the Ripper murders and investigation, including digitized press clippings.

Cobbe, Frances Power. *The Life of Frances Power Cobbe as told by herself* (1894).

Jack the Ripper 1888. Another online source for history and theories about the murder.

LeFanu, Sheridan. *Carmilla* (1872). An early short story predating Stoker's *Dracula* about a female vampire.

Mitchell, Sally. *Frances Power Cobbe: Victorian Feminist, Journalist, Reformer* (University Press of Virginia, 2004). The only full-length biography of Cobbe.

Polidori, John William. *The Vampyre* (1819). A short story written during the same evening of writers trading ghost stories that produced Mary Shelley's *Frankenstein*.

Rubenhold, Hallie. *The Five: The Untold Lives of the Women Killed by Jack the Ripper* (London: Transworld, 2019 and NY:

Mariner Books, 2020). Invaluable source on the lives of the five "canonical" victims of Jack the Ripper.

Rymer, James Malcolm, Thomas Preskett Prest, and Finn J.D. John, Editor. *Varney the Vampire; or; The Feast of Blood—In Two Volumes* (1845-1847).

Stoker, Bram. *Dracula* (1897). The original novel, constructed from invented diaries, letters, and documentary evidence.

# Acknowledgments

Christina and Victoria were Victorianists first, then became close friends and co-authors later. We met at The Dickens Project when we were each writing dissertations on Victorian women. With Laura Mann, Lisa Nakamura, Christina Olsen, and Susie Wise, we formed a Reading Group to support each other's writing. Thirty years later, we no longer read together but are still deeply interconnected. This book first of all owes its life to those precious long-standing friendships.

The Dickens Project also connected us to our first academic reader, Dagni Bredesen, whose expertise in Victorian mystery-writing was a godsend for our project. We are greatly indebted to her suggestions and corrections, though we are solely responsible for all opinions and fact-checking. We also got an important early and careful reading from our editor, Kristen Tate. As we neared production, we were very grateful to Scott Peterson and A.J. Seiden for their expertise with visual and design elements. Our Author Nation cohort made our Kickstarter campaign possible and successful beyond our expectations as newbies: many thanks to Destini Beckham, Danielle Blum, Lily Cahill, Jamie Davis, Jan Foster, Theresa Goodrich, John Kiss, Isabella Lisak, Bernadette Malcolm, Cody Sisco, and Richard S. Thomas.

Finally, and importantly, we truly appreciate the early support and enthusiasm of our Kickstarter backers: Stacey Andrews, Abigail Asher, Author Ventures LLC, Ariane Beauparlant, Oren Bloedow, Danielle Blum, Jonathan Buchanan,

Lily Cahill, Yanne Cantin, Eve Capkanis, Mary Capkanis, Dennis K. Crosby, Serafina Culhane, Jamie Davis, Eileen, Ethan Espie, Zack Fissel, Jan Foster, Sonia Glab, Elliott Goldkind, Theresa L. Goodrich, Jane Hammons, Natasha Hill, Khadija Hussain, Beth Johnson, John Kiss, Tania O'Connor Kleckner, Jodi Koenig, Kristen, Robert Kotowich, Corey LaBranche, John N. Lefler, K MacLeod, maileguy, Jill Malter, Laura Mann, Deb Manzari, Heidi Markee, Viviana McKenney, Melody, Meredith, Cynthia Morris, Amanda Murray, Stephanie and Rob Nelson, Hillary Newton, Nicole J., Christina Olsen, Margrit Olsen, Jen Olson, Kathleen M Pape, Amy Pease, Scott Peterson, phoenix_17, Ravyn M., John A. Rigopoulos, Sara Seiden, Daniel Seltzer, Susannah Sheffer, AJ Shinall, Janet Simpson, Cody Sisco, Trisha Slay, Vanessa Spencer, , Rachel Strehlow, Kate Stuppy, Richard S. Thomas, Ryan Todd, ValerieAnne, Clyde Watson, Lindsey Watson, Ronald L Weston, Michelle White, and Susie Wise. We couldn't have done this without all of you!

From Christina:

I've wanted to partner with Vicky again ever since she proposed we co-edit a collection of essays when we were newly minted PhDs. Decades later, I'm thrilled and grateful to have the chance. Vicky is the best co-writer and friend a person could ask for. I've never had so much fun writing a novel. A big thanks to Colleen Paretty who first led me to Rubenhold's *The Five*. And to Jane Hammons, my dear friend, who shares the ups and downs of the writing life and is always a thoughtful and perceptive reader. Thanks to Stephanie Nelson, who's read and supported my work since fifth grade. And to my home team, Scott and Gus, and the four-legged ones, Henry and BB, who fill my life with love, laughter, and adventure.

From Victoria:

My biggest debt by far is to Christina, who came up with the idea of returning to our Victorian roots and pitched writing a mystery to me as a lark. It turned into a wonderful adventure, and it's been a pleasure to work so closely with such a smart, funny writer and dear friend. I also want to shout-out Josh, Naomi, A.J., Tina, Margrit, and my mother Roberta, who support and delight me every day.

# About the Authors

**Christina Boufis** is the author of a jail mystery series: *Burial of the Dead*, *We Die Soon*, and *Killing Time*. A former academic with a PhD in Victorian literature and Women's Studies, Christina spent nearly eight years teaching women in the San Francisco County Jail. As C.B. Peterson, she's also the author of a domestic thriller, *I Want Him Dead*. Her nonfiction includes *The Complete Idiot's Guide to Writing Nonfiction*, as well as a collection of essays, *On the Market*, co-edited with Victoria Olsen. Christina's short stories have appeared most recently in *Pulphouse Fiction Magazine*, *Kings River Life Magazine*, *Larceny and Last Chances* anthology, and *Rock and a Hard Place*.

She lives in Alameda, California with her family.

**Victoria Olsen** is a freelance writer and author of the biography *From Life: Julia Margaret Cameron and Victorian Photography*. She has a PhD in English literature and taught expository writing at New York University for eleven years. Her articles have appeared in *Smithsonian Magazine*, *the Chronicle of Higher Education*, and *Salon*, as well as other publications.

Victoria has also published *Word-Blind*, a middle-grade novel set in Victorian England, and *On the Market*, a collection of essays co-edited with Christina Boufis. She is also working on a memoir about her father's art career, *Daddy-O: Art, Family, and Secrets in Midcentury America*. She writes the Substack newsletter From Life with Victoria Olsen and lives in Brooklyn, New York with her family.

For updates about new releases and behind-the-scenes accounts of our research and writing process, sign up for our newsletter on www.somedarkforce.com. Follow us on Instagram at @victoria_c_olsen and @christina_boufis. You can find us on TikTok at @pennydreadfulmedia

*Excerpt from Dark Circles*

---

---

## PROLOGUE

The figure stands motionless, eyes staring into space. Inside, though, thoughts whirl in a chaotic jumble before settling into a clear plan. This is how it works, from disorder to order, all through the funnel of the controlling presence. The presence is there, solid, reliable – and rapacious. A hungry mouth wanting more– more adulation, more money, more followers.

It is time!! The steps are as clear as the marks on the floor of a stage, ready to follow. The figure checks a hidden pocket, confirming again that the vial is in place. Yes, the stage is set. Tonight someone would die.

## CHAPTER ONE

The foyer of the Egyptian Hall is abuzz with excitement when Sybil steps into the Piccadilly theater. Suddenly, she's transported from dark, rainy London to the arid and dramatic landscape of ancient Egypt.

Mysterious hieroglyphs decorate the rich red walls of the lobby. Images of enormous pyramids rise out of the vast desert and peer down at her, guarding their secrets. Gas-lit sconces like torches shed pools of amber light and throw the rest of the entryway into dark shadows.

Sybil takes a step and is hit by the sweet cloud of ladies' expensive perfume, heavy notes of rose and lavender and a slight lanolin smell from damp clothing. There's a palpable air of excitement among the well-dressed men and women standing in groups in the entranceway, their voices echoing off the marble floors.

Sybil too is vibrating with energy, though of a slightly different sort. They are all here to see the married clairvoyants: the great Leto and his wife, Madame Leta.

Looking around at the theater patrons, the women in their jewel-colored gowns, rich burgundy and emerald green, Sybil is keenly aware that her own black muslin dress is plain and free of adornment. She's also aware that she lacks a warm, fur-trimmed cloak and a husband to check it for her. Nevertheless she is here. And she has saved almost a week's worth of wages, nearly three shillings, to enter the Egyptian Home of Mystery she has heard so much about.

Sybil moves towards the glass display cases with Egyptian artifacts that line one wall. As she does so, she catches her reflection in one of the enormous golden-framed mirrors that grace the foyer. Her face looks even paler and thinner than normal. Deep purple shadows under her eyes tell of sleepless nights. She hopes she doesn't appear as nervous to others as her reflection indicates. But no one pays even the slightest attention to her.

The lights of the torches flicker, indicating the performance is about to start.

Sybil follows the red velvet ropes toward the auditorium. The attendant takes her ticket and points her towards the staircase and the cheap gallery seats located at the very back of the theater. The upper-class women rustle by her on their way to box seats, trailing yards of taffeta and silk behind them, unaware of her existence.

Sybil takes her seat on the hard wooden bench in the upper gallery and peers towards the stage. Her view is slightly blocked by a large portico. No matter. She has eyes and can see where others cannot.

Ethereal music rises from the orchestra pit, setting the stage for what is to come. Sybil finds the violin tunes a bit melodramatic for her tastes but understands the performative aspect of the show she's about to witness. After all, she has come to watch and to learn. Some gifts can be taught. Most cannot. But she is here to learn from the best – or at least the most popular of the spiritualists who draw hundreds of patrons twice a day to this packed theater.

Underneath the melancholy notes of the stringed instruments, Sybil hears a whisper. At first, she believes it is coming from one of her neighbors on either side of the hard wooden bench, both working class women like herself by the looks of them. But no. It is an internal voice, one she recognizes well.

Not now, she tells it. Please. Not now.

But the voice is insistent. Warning her to be careful and take action. Again and again. With the voice comes an image, blurry but ominous. She doesn't want to look any closer.

From the first moment she saw the broadsheet advertising the famous Leto and Madame Leta, the voice has come unbidden. Sybil knows it wants her to stop what is about to occur. But how can she? She only hopes the voice – and her vision – are wrong. What can she do?

Suddenly, the gas lamps flicker and dim. The theater is plunged into shadow and silence.

Sybil's neighbor gasps as the wall of red velvet curtains begins to part.

From behind the opening of the curtains the great Leto himself steps out onto the stage. He is of modest height with jet black hair and a closely-trimmed beard and mustache. Yet his very presence commands attention. He strides out onto the middle of the stage, his shiny black boots beating a staccato on the wooden stage floor with each sharp step.

Leto is dressed in a black evening suit with a dark cape on his shoulders. With a sweep on one hand, he dramatically tosses one side of the cape over a shoulder, revealing a waistcoat of the deepest midnight blue. The same color is echoed in the lining of this cape which shimmers as it catches the light like water rippling in an oasis in the desert.

The clairvoyant suddenly stops and stares out into the audience from left to right, as if peering into the souls of every patron in the theater.

"Ladies and gentlemen, good evening," he says. Leto's voice is rich and thick like treacle. Despite her tension, Sybil finds herself relaxing under the commanding tone of the spiritualist.

"I am Master Leto who brings you messages from the great beyond." Leto pauses. Then he looks up toward the ceiling of the theater and spreads his arms wide so that the cape fans out. Sybil watches as heads turn in the direction of the ceiling. She can see nothing but the tops of the curtains.

"What you are about to witness tonight is as unknown to me at this moment as it is to you. We will see if the spirits will honor us with their presence and divine insight. To assist me in this quest is my wife, the lovely Madame Leta." Leto turns towards the curtains and raises his hand.

The orchestra bursts into a rumbling dramatic tune. Fog rises from the stage. The red curtains part further to reveal the tall, silhouetted figure of a woman. Sybil can see at once that Madame Leta is very tall, taller than her husband.

Madame Leta is as still as a statue. When the fog dissipates, Sybil sees next to Madame Leta a small table covered in a dark purple cloth. On the table is a large, milky crystal ball. Sybil herself has never found much divination in such an object and she's curious to see how the couple will use it. Two ornately gilded chairs are positioned in front of the table facing the audience with one plain wooden chair between them.

Master Leto advances to one of the ornate chairs and pulls it out for his wife.

The theater is silent and hushed as Madame Leta walks towards the chair. Before taking her seat, she bows slightly towards her husband and the audience. All eyes are on this impressive figure of a woman.

Sybil too is entranced. Madame Leta's thick, dark hair is coiled on top of her head. A velvet band with tiny gems adorns her forehead. Her gown is the deepest purple, interlaced with metallic threads that catches fire when the light hits it just right. An enormous opal brooch is pinned to the front of her gown.

Madame Leta takes her seat without saying a word.

Sybil closes her eyes as an unwelcome image comes unbidden. Through closed eyelids she sees the stage. And she sees what will happen.

The great Leto asks for a volunteer from the audience to have her fortune read.

"No!" Sybil is unaware that she has stood and that the protest has come from her lips. She feels a hand reaching for her dress to pull her back into her seat, but she resists.

A woman climbs the stairs at the side of the stage. She is dressed in the latest fashion, a plum-colored dress with a plunging neckline and tight bodice that highlights her hourglass figure. A small bustle trails behind her as she makes her way across the stage.

Sybil too is up and moving. She is heading for the exit. She doesn't apologize to the patrons on the bench who hiss at her as she inconveniences them. She only knows she must get to that stage. She must stop what she knows will happen to this poor woman.

To get to the stage, Sybil must go through the lobby. She

hurries down the stairs into the entranceway. She turns right and then left until she spots a doorway that leads to the front-row seats.

A hand reaches out and stops her as she tries to enter.

"Ticket, Miss?" the uniformed attendant asks her. He knows she doesn't have a ticket for the orchestra seats.

"Please. You must let me in. Something terrible is about to happen." Sybil tries to shake him off. Her voice rises and she sees some patrons turn their heads to glare at her.

"No ticket. No entrance," he says.

"I must. You don't understand." She is almost sobbing.

Someone in the audience shushes her. Others ooh and ah at the palm reading that is underway.

"Miss, if you don't …"

Sybil pushes past him and races down the empty aisle. The stage has a single spotlight on the table, with its three seated figures. Madame Leta bends over the fashionable lady's palm and speaks in a low, carrying voice. The audience is enrapt. And the Great Leto is looking directly at Sybil as she approaches, desperate to stop the scene she sees in her mind's eye.

Then, the lady jerks as if pulled by a marionette string. Sybil screams and both Letos turn to stare at her.

Sybil is too late.

She knows, even before a doctor from the audience is summoned, that the lady on stage is dead.

Above the gasps and cries from the audience, rises a single voice from Professor Leto. He raises a long finger and points at Sybil, "What have you done?" His eyes bore into hers. "Detain her!" he shouts.

Sybil turns away from the stage. She feels the eyes of others on her. She tries to lose herself in the tide of the patrons fleeing the theater. She cannot help the woman now. She must try to save herself.

## CHAPTER TWO

The meeting room is already full by the time Lucy Rutherford arrives. She rises onto her tiptoes to peer over the sea of hats for an empty seat. Neat felt cloches and beribboned bonnets, mob caps and a few kerchiefs tied under chins. Someone waves an arm wildly in the air. Lucy smiles and pushes through the crowd toward the waving hand. She plops her reticule onto the empty folding chair and begins unpinning the half-veil from her auburn hair.

"Finally. I saved it at great trouble, Lucy!" The seated woman is small and pale, dressed in mourning gray. Her light brown hair is neatly parted down the middle and combed back into a chignon. Lucy gives her a hug as she settles into her seat.

"I know, darling. I'm late again. I can't seem to help it." She shrugs. "Luckily Miss Cobbe is often later than I am." She glances again around the room, noting the crowd and nodding at a few acquaintances. Light filters through the heavy red curtains, left over from when the building was a gentlemen's club. The room now occupied by women was once a gambling hall and it was still filled with small round tables and chairs of plush velvet upholstery. A gilded mirror spans the long side of the rectangular room and a raised dais in the front had once been a long bar serving drinks. Over the past few months Miss Cobbe's army of female detectives had converted the establishment for their own use. She and her women met here weekly in the afternoon, when maids and nannies were best able to sneak off in the middle of errands, and ladies could claim to be on "morning" calls. A few of the women are holding babies on their laps or rocking prams with one foot while they wait for Miss Cobbe. A huge mahogany desk now sits on the dais, its legs carved with scrolls and leaves. A gray-haired matron stands at its side, like a sentry. Lucy and her companion both wave at her and receive a small smile in return.

"I told Mrs. Cavendish again that we were ready for more responsibility, that we had little to do now that the Count and my husband are gone. I told her that I am bored silly with tea visits from Edward's former patients, fishing for information about his disappearance."

"He is dead, Maude. He must be. He was shot and has never reappeared in all these months. You are free." Lucy speaks gently, taking Maude's cold hand into her own. "But I agree that we need more excitement in our lives! Oh, here is Miss Cobbe." She presses Maude's hand once more and sits up straighter in her chair.

A short, squat woman advances into the room and scrapes a heavy chair back from the desk, seating herself and resting her elbows on its surface to face the audience. For a moment there is no sound in the room as she looks over the assembled women.

"My mateys. My fine soldiers. My fierce comrades! How do you fare this morn? Are you prepared to claw and scrabble for every right that should be yours by natural law and God's great benevolence?" Her voice grows louder as she speaks until it booms through the room like a wave crashing.

She is a force of nature, Lucy thinks, not for the first time. She remembers how Miss Cobbe had raced into one of the rooms above her head now, ready to rescue Lucy from the vicious vampire who had drawn her to this club. The creature had planned to abduct her to wreak vengeance on her father, Lord Rutherford, for unearthing him from a diamond mine in South Africa. She had only survived because of her own resistance and the combined efforts of Miss Cobbe, her right-hand woman Mrs. Cavendish, the sympathetic Constable Neil, earnest young journalist Jonathan Hinton, and her friend Maude Hepworth. The vampire, Count Vloeden, had disappeared into the Thames during their final confrontation. Both the Count and Maude's husband, Edward, were implicated in the disappearance of impoverished young women from Whitechapel. Lucy is sure both men are dead but she knows Maude harbors fears that her husband could return.

The memory of that last night, when the vampire held her captive, still gives Lucy nightmares, though she no longer sleepwalks. Jonathan fought to save her from the vampire's clutches, but he was no match for that dark immortal force. Maude confided in Lucy that Jonathan had disappeared before her eyes that night, never to be seen again. Now, Lucy senses her own blood pumping strongly through her veins— it is a sign that she is still alive and a reminder of her own transformation.

The women in the room erupt into cheers and whistles, pounding their boots on the carpeted floor. Lucy feels the vibrations in her bones. They are safe now. They are safe here.

"Some of you have been a-moaning and be-wriggling for more clandestine operations." Cobbe pushes her wire-rimmed spectacles up her nose and squints at the room again. She sighs. "As if we are a mere agency." She spits out the word. "An office of beat-walkers and thief-catchers, hired to find bracelets and catch adulterers!" Her gray curls bounce about her head as she nods emphatically. "No! We are a righteous army pledged to reforming society! We do not take commissions or direction! The small job is beneath our talents and our ambitions! We do not seek glory or recognition but toil earnestly in the shadows until women receive the justice and standing they deserve!"

Miss Cobbe pauses to take a deep breath. Her voice softens. "And we will prevail. We will win this long war, battle by battle." The room goes quiet. No one moves. For a loaded moment, the muted sounds of horseshoes on the cobblestones outside are the only sound.

Then the door in the back of the hall crashes open and a young woman staggers into the room, out of breath and looking behind her in terror. The room jolts with energy as women speak over each other in confusion. One woman jumps up to catch the stranger before she collapses on the floor. "Whatever…? Who…? Goodness…!" Murmurs rise up from the seated crowd and Lucy cranes her neck to see the disruption.

"Quiet!" Miss Cobbe shouts. She has risen from her seat and stalks toward the intruder. "Who are you?"

"I … I am being followed…! I…" The stranger clutches her chest, still heaving. She is covered in a wool coat that hides her completely, with a hat pulled low over her face. Lucy gets a glimpse of dark eyes and hair.

"Who are you?" Miss Cobbe repeats, more gently.

"I heard you protect women.' The woman's voice is still halting. "I heard you…" Her voice fades and her legs seem to crumple as other women rush to support her. "I saw something. In my mind. I saw someone die. Now they… help me!" Her eyes flicker, then she slumps to the floor.

It takes several moments and some concerted efforts to revive the woman, but gradually Lucy can see the color return to her face as she is led to a chair in the front of the room and plied with tea.

Miss Cobbe returns to her desk and faces the newcomer, now composed but still trembling. "This is a right muddle, but we'll square it. So I ask you again, my dear. And no wobbles. Who are you?"

"Sybil Montello, ma'am. I apologize…"

"No need." Miss Cobbe waves a hand in the air. "Are you in danger?"

Miss Montello glances around uneasily. "I believe so. I believe I was followed here."

"We take precautions for that. You are safe here with us. We are friends." She waves another hand out toward the listening audience. Lucy feels the supportive presence of the women around her and is grateful again for this community.

"Tell us," Miss Cobbe says simply.

Miss Montello inhales deeply. "Have you heard of the spiritualists at Egyptian Hall?"

Miss Cobbe exchanges a sharp look with Mrs. Cavendish, who is standing at her side. "Indeed, go on."

"I see you know already." Miss Montello sips her tea. "I was there. I saw it."

Miss Cobbe lets out a heavy sigh and leans forward to pat Miss Montello's hand. "Well!" She nods to Mrs. Cavendish. "You explain."

Looking grave, Mrs. Cavendish addresses the assembled women. "You may have heard of a recent death at a Theatrical Seance last week. Daphne Moreland died on stage in a tragic accident as Professor Leto and his wife Madame Leta were reading her fortune on her palm. Doctors say her heart overheated under the excitement. The hosts from the Society for Spiritual Enlightenment proclaim it was a surge of psychic energy that struck her very soul." Her voice is level but Lucy thinks she hears Mrs. Cavendish's Scottish skepticism in her tone. "The matter would not concern us, except for a conversation Miss Cobbe overheard." She nods and Miss Cobbe takes over.

"At Lady Sinclair's table Wednesday last, I learned that the deceased was her sister. We all sympathized with her tragic loss, but I heard her whisper to a guest that her sister had recently made a new will and left her entire estate to the Society." She paused until the murmurs of the audience faded. "Exactly. This smells manky. The Sinclairs are in a right state. I said nothing at the time but now here is Miss Montello who can tell us more, I hope. Please—"

"I saw her die on stage. I'll never forget the desperation on her face as she tried to draw breath. But I had seen it before." Miss Montello pauses for effect. "In a vision!"

The room bursts into conversation and exclamations again, until Miss Cobbe shushes them.

"I know," Miss Montello wrings a handkerchief in her hands. "You don't believe me. But I am plagued by these visions. They are never wrong." She looks up. "And now I am being followed. I am sure of it!"

Miss Cobbe frowns. "How do you know? Describe this miscreant."

"He is like a shadow behind me, never quite visible! I see just the rim of a brown fedora on the omnibus, or the same pair of galoshes behind me. When I turn, he's gone!"

Lucy can see Miss Cobbe choosing her words.

"Are you sure you are not beset by the death you saw on stage? Perhaps you…"

"I know it!" Miss Montello sounds clear and commanding suddenly. Lucy revises her opinion of the poor woman.

"Just so. Then we must investigate. These seances are becoming more and more popular with women especially. We need ladies to attend these meetings, maids to rummage through homes, secretaries to take dictation… Who will volunteer?"

Hands shoot up across the room. Lucy and Maude look at each other and grin, arms in the air.

"Hmmph. I approve of your enthusiasm. Have you memorized our codes for communication? Have you been practicing with your pistols, my fair ones? This may become dangerous. A lady has perhaps been boldly and devilishly murdered."

The room quiets at this, then a voice calls out, accented from Eastern Europe. "How do we approach Lady Sinclair? Whom did she speak to?"

"Excellent question, Miss Stansky. I have an idea." Miss Cobbe's hawk-like gaze lands on Lucy. "Lady Sinclair confided in Lord Rutherford. Miss Rutherford, see me after this meeting. Mrs. Cavendish, please see Miss Montello home safely. We will want more details from her." Without waiting for acknowledgement, she begins sorting through papers, calling names and waving people up to her massive desk.

Lucy sits very still, her blood racing. Her father had fallen from power during Jack the Ripper's rampage last fall. He had been Home Secretary and his Chief of Police, Sir Charles Warren, had been unable to nab the killer. Both men had lost their jobs. The killings had stopped, but no one was sure why. Maude believed the Ripper had been the Count all along, draining blood from his working-class victims. But Lucy knows she had been with the Count, racing through the streets of London, when the last victim was murdered. She believes the Ripper could have been Maude's husband, Dr. Hepworth.

"I guess our prayers have been answered," she says quietly to Maude.

"Be careful what you ask for," Maude whispers back.

### Keep reading!
**For updates about new releases and behind-the-scenes accounts of our research and writing process, sign up for our newsletter at www. somedarkforce.com. Follow us on Instagram at @victoria_c_olsen and @christina_boufis. You can find us on TikTok at @pennydreadfulmedia.**